# BACKFIRE

## BROTHERS OF SHADOW & DEATH

# SYDNEY'S REBIRTH

### - BOOK ONE -

# AUTHOR NOTE

**While this is a PNR, dystopian world things will come across as very contemporary. Sydney doesn't know about anything like magic or cults, the world to her is as normal as it is to us. The PNR aspect of this world is a slow build and will be much more prevalent in future books.**

# WARNINGS

**This is a dark romance and is intended for a mature audience. Reader discretion advised. This book contains but is not limited to, violence, profanity, references to abuse, references to mental illness, nonconsensual and dubious consensual sexual scenes.**

"Don't Play" By Halsey
"Sharks" By Imagine Dragons
"Therefore I Am" By Billie Eilish
"Time Of The Seasons" By The Ben Taylor Band
"I Found" By Amber Run
"What's Up" By 4 Non Blondes
"I Put A Spell On You" By Annie Lennox
"Skin" By Rihanna
"Body" By SYML
"One Right Now" By Post Malone
"Shivers" By Ed Sheeran
"Unstoppable" By Sia
"Showed Me" By Madison Beer
"I Ain't Worried" By One Republic
"Barracuda" By Heart
"Let's Go" By Trick Daddy

# WORDS AND PHRASES

Appreozo -Spell to make something invisible

Ass Over Tea Kettle - To flip over backward in a somersault fashion

Aye or Ya - Yes

Bassalsinn- type of demon

Canne -Long wooden weapon that resembles a thick stick. Can have metal or carvings along the wood.

Cannie - Cannot

Da - Dad or Father

Daft -To be slow to understand

Dat - That

Den - Then

Dem -Them

Dere -There

Dey - They

Din't - Don't

Dinnie - Don't or Doesn't

Dis -This

District -City within a Faction

Donkey - To act in a senseless manner

Faction - The divisions created across the world that are controlled by those with magic

Feck -Slang for Fuck

Fir -For

Flitter - Person without magic

I'ma - I am

I'za or I'z -I am

Levetatio -Spell to make someone float

Ma - Mom, Mum or Mother

Naw -No

Pairing Ritual -Where the number one and two males in triad are chosen by the spirits of ancestors long passed.

Petrobile -Spell to freeze someone in place for a short time

Samhach -Spell to make someone mute for short time

Shouldna -Should not

Ta -The or Thee or To

Triad - Three people of magic coming together in union to create a power structure to support the needs of a Faction

Whaddya - What do you

Whatta -What are

Wit -With

Ya - Yes or You

Yer - You are

Go dtuga na spioraid rochtain agus cosaint do magus mé ag taisteal ina réimeas - May the spirits grant access and protect me as I travel in their realm

Lig do na spioraid mé a threorú agus na cinntí a dhéanaim a chumhachtú - Let the spirits guide me and empower the decisions I make

Coinnigh mo lámh agus lig dom taisteal abhaile le scian I mo lámh agus faic I mo dhroim. Is é seo a iarraim - Hold my hand and let me travel home with a knife in my hand and nothing in my back. This is what I ask.

Demon a beheith imithe - Demon be gone

Éiríonn triúr ar cheann -Three becomes one

# NAME PRONUNCIATION

**Alexander Kelly:**

Al-ex-an-d-er – Son of Norris (Deceased) Kelly – Brother to Olivia Kelly

**Ashlin McKinnon:**

Ash-lin – Daughter of Wallace McKinnon – Sister of Owen McKinnon

**Angus Adair:**

An-guss – Head of the Adair Family - Father of Rook, Devlin, Magnus and Wyatt Adair – Brother to Gregory Adair

**Avril McKinnon:**

Ah-v-ril – Daughter of Kingsley McKinnon – Sister to Falcon and Rylan McKinnon

**Barry:**

Bar-ee – Red Squirrel

**Belle Adair:**

B-ell - Daughter of Gregory Adair – Sister to Mari Adair

**Blaine McGregor:**

Bl-ay-ne - Son of Rayland McGregor – Brother to Ronan and Riegan McGregor

**Caleb McCabe:**

Kay-lub – Son of Sullivan McCabe – Brother to Leon McCabe

**Camryn McKinnon:**

Cam-ryn – Son of Keith McKinnon – Brother to Kayayn McKinnon

**Charmine Ricci:**

Sh-ar-main – Mother of Sydney Ricci

**Cora:**

Cor-a – No Last Name – History Unknown

**Crispin Kelly:**

Krisp-in – Son of Nigel Kelly

**Devlin Adair:**

Dev-lyn - Son of Angus Adair

**Elewyen:**

Ell-ew-wen – No Last Name – History Unknown in Book 1

**Fabian Kelly:**

Fay-b-in – Son of Nigel Kelly – Twin brother to Flynn Kelly and brother to Crispin Kelly

**Falcon McKinnon:**

Fal-con – Son of Wallace McKinnon – Brother of Rylan and Avril McKinnon

**Fiona McGregor:**

Fee-o-na – Daughter of Rian McGregor – Sister of Rhys McGregor

**Flynn Kelly:**

F-lynn – Son of Nigel Kelly – Twin brother to Fabian Kelly and brother to Crispin Kelly

**Gregory Adair:**

Greg-or-ee – Father to Mari and Belle Adair – Brother to Angus Adair

**Haylee:**

Hay-lee – No Last Name – History Unknown

**Kayayn McKinnon:**

Kay-anne – Daughter of Keith McKinnon – Sister of Camryn McKinnon

**Keeva:**

Kee-va – No Last Name - Non Blooded Sister to Elewyen – History Unknown

**Keith McKinnon:**

Kee-th – Father of Kayayn McKinnon – Brother of Kingsley McKinnon

**Kingsley McKinnon:**

King-s-lay – Head of the Mckinnon Family – Father to Falcon and Kayla McKinnon

– Brother to Wallace McKinnon

**Leon McCabe:**

Lee-on - Son of Sullivan McCabe – Brother to Caleb McCabe

**Lochlin Kelly:**

Lock-lyn – Son of Niall Kelly – Brother of Reese Kelly

**Magnus Adair:**

Mag-nus – Son of Angus Adair – Brother to Rook, Devlin and Wyatt

**Mari McGregor:**

Ma-ree – Daughter of Gregory Adair – Sister to Belle Adair

**Niall Kelly:**

Nee-all – Father of Lochlin and Reese Kelly – Brother to Nigel and Norris (Deceased) - Kelly

**Nigel Kelly:**

Ni-gel – Head of the Kelly Family – Father of Crispin, Flynn and Fabian Kelly – Brother to Niall and Norris (Deceased) Kelly

**Norris Kelly:**

Nor-iss – Deceased – Father of Olivia and Alexander Kelly – Brother of Niall and Nigel Kelly

**Olivia Kelly:**

Oh-liv-i-a – Daughter of Norris (Deceased) Kelly – Sister to Alexander Kelly

**Owen McKinnon:**

Oh-win – Son of Wallace McKinnon – Brother of Ashlin McKinnon

**Pascello Ricci:**

Pass-cell-o – Uncle to Sydney Ricci

**Reese Kelly:**

Ree-ce – Son of Niall Kelly – Brother to Lochlin Kelly

**Rian McGregor:**

Ri-an – Deceased – Father of Rhys and Fiona McGregor – Brother to Rayland and Riddick McGregor

**Riddick McGregor:**

Rid-dick – Exiled - Father of Unknown – Brother of Rian and Rayland McGregor

**Riegan McGregor:**

Ree-gan – Daughter of Rayland McGregor – Sister to Ronan and Blaine McGregor

**Ronan McGregor:**

Ro-nan – Son of Rayland McGregor – Brother to Riegan and Blaine McGregor

**Rook Adair:**

Ro-ok – Son of Angus Adair – Brother to Devlin, Magnus and Wyatt Adair

**Rhys McGregor:**

Ri-ze – Next Head of the McGregor Family – Son of Rian McGregor – Brother to Fiona McGregor

**Rylan McKinnon:**

Ry-lyn – Son of Kinsley McKinnon – Brother of Falcon and Avril McKinnon

**Rayland McGregor:**

Ray-land – Temporary Head of the McGregor Family – Father of Ronan, Riegan and Blaine McGregor

**Shyla McCabe:**

Shy-la – Exiled - Sister of Sullivan McCabe

**Sullivan McCabe:**

Sull-i-van - Head of the McCabe Family – Father of Leon and Caleb McCabe Brother to Shyla McCabe

**Sydney Ricci:**

Syd-nee – Daughter of Rossco Ricci

**Wallace McKinnon:**

Wall-ass – Father to Owen and Ashlin McKinnon – Brother to Kingsley McKinnon

**Wyatt Adair:**

Why-att – Son of Angus Adair – Brother of Rook, Devlin and Magnus Adair

**Wynter:**

Win-ter – No Last Name – History Unknown

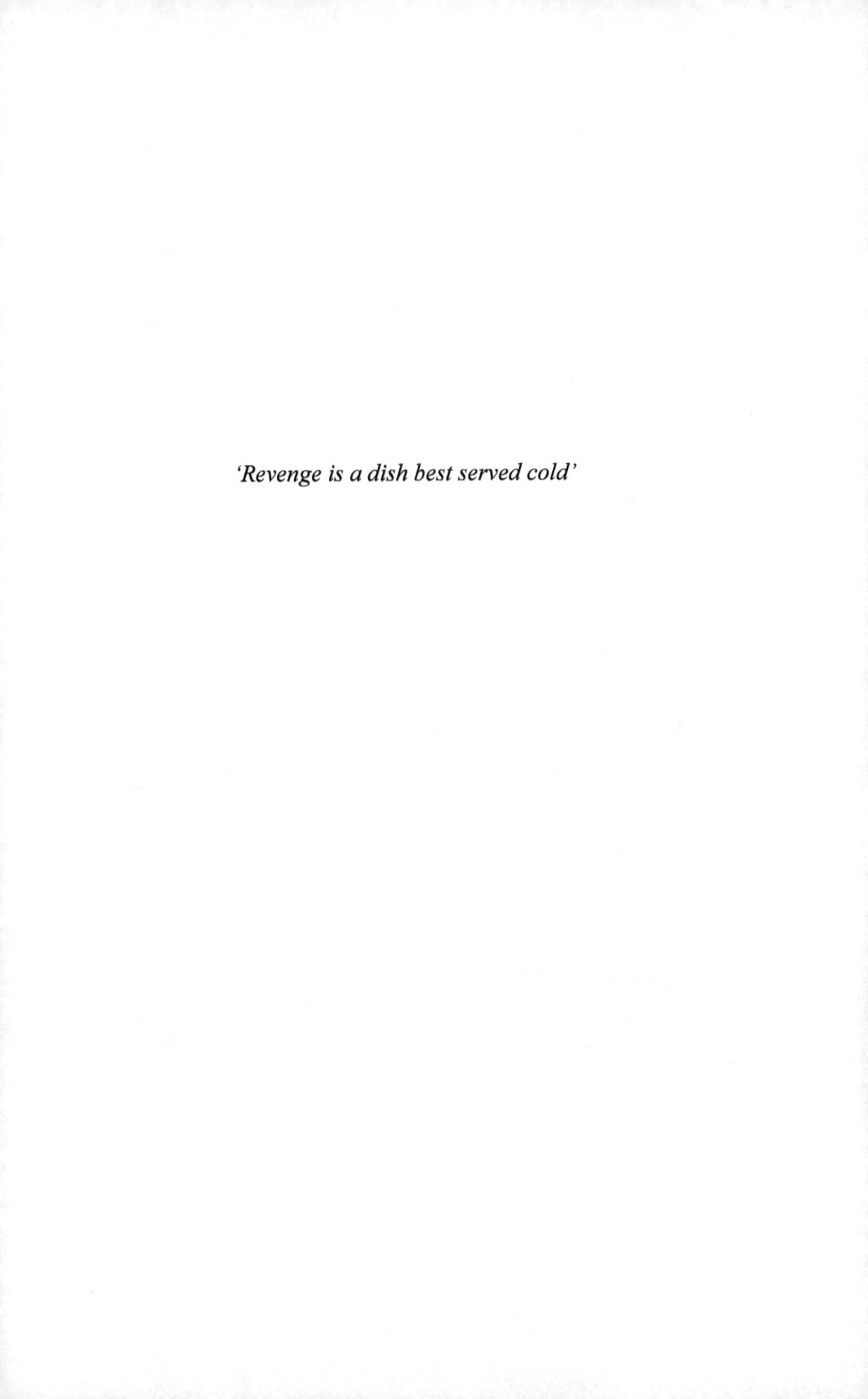

*'Revenge is a dish best served cold'*

# Forward

Centuries ago, our world descended into chaos as war erupted amid the masses. Those with magical abilities fought against those without, leaving the weaker of the two desperate to remain free. In the battle, we lost many, flooding our streets and waterways with the blood of the innocent.

After decades of war across the globe, peace settled amongst the people. Most forgot the years of death and destruction, though others spoke about it as nothing more than myths to be passed on to younger generations.

Factions became the new world order, run by those with magic. They outlawed guns, closed prisons, and disbanded armies. Yet crime rates were the lowest they had ever been. These mystical groups took control of the world's leading industries, from food production to machinery and technology.

However, most of these factions wanted to remain untouched by a more modern society. They chose to bypass technological advancements, allowing only the most prestigious of families to own simple machines such as cars.

Those without magical abilities became known as Flitters. And to them, nothing had changed. But to those with powers, the world would never be the same. That was a secret they kept, day in and day out.

Like any world order, the Factions understood jealousy could still bring them down. They banded together to create stronger alliances.

The most powerful of those groups became a united front, controlling what they called Faction Three—The Brothers of Shadow and Death. The Adair, Kelly, McCabe, McGregor, and McKinnon families have grown to be an immensely powerful alliance. They now have dangerous targets on their backs, for the other envious families crave their power and prosperity.

Lurking within the shadows, there is yet another group that emerged from this war. The Hunters are a rebellious sect that comes from a long line of Flitters who remember those battle-stricken days and strive to annihilate the Factions at all costs. Their mandate is to set free the Flitters from their perceived oppression.

As each ritual moon draws near, and a new triad union is announced, the Hunters become more active. Their goal is simple: Eliminate the triads.

Welcome to Faction Three… Where you will meet the strongest and most desirable we have to offer.

Book one in the same world by Brooklyn Cross: Anywhere

# Chapter 1



WHY DID PEOPLE HAVE THIS PRECONCEIVED NOTION THAT IT WAS important to preserve the innocence of children? I mean, I got it. It was so much nicer to think that the garden was full of fairies instead of worm-filled dirt. But the world was a dark and dirty place.

All lying about that did was cover the grime up in an illusion that would eventually shatter. Then what? What did you say to your kid when they found out there were no fairies in the bushes?

*Sorry, kid, but it's really the rotten scraps from the compost bin that make the flowers grow.*

Talk about a letdown.

"We're almost there, Sydney." My latest foster mother's enthusiasm was way too over-the-top for this endeavor.

Not that I was surprised by her chipper tone. Stacy was one of those people who needed kids to believe in magic. It didn't matter how she sugar-coated things, she couldn't hide the truth forever. No matter how much she wanted to.

Even when you wrapped crap up in a pretty bow with sparkles and gems, it still smelled like crap. Just like referring to my mother as "ill" didn't change the fact that she was batshit crazy.

"Look at this place. It's so pretty. Imagine the people you'll meet here." Stacy leaned over and gave me a playful nudge. "Maybe a boy or two?"

Oh boy, there was something to be excited about. The last boy I'd met had been Stephan Myers. He was so obsessed with fire that I'd spent most of our date wondering if I was going to be doused in gasoline by the end of the night.

I eyed the sign that read, 'Welcome to Northridge,' and flopped my head back on the seat. The mountainous terrain full of lush trees was pretty. I'd give Stacy that, but this was just another example of making something sound better than it was.

We weren't going to Disneyland. I was moving yet again. Supposedly, for the last time. I lost count of how many times I'd been told that lie.

Stacy rolled down the window, allowing the fresh mountain air to pour into the car.

"I'm so happy for you."

At least one of us was.

I was already starting to miss the stink of smog in the city. This place was too clean, and I didn't just mean the air. The town looked like it was plucked straight out of the fifties.

All the buildings appered shiny and new but still had that old architecture feel that one might find in an artsy town, and there wasn't a single piece of trash on the ground.

"You'll fit right in."

That statement made my brow rise. "Yeah, I'll be playing varsity volleyball in no time."

Stacy and I had vastly different definitions of fitting in. If the black floral tattoos taking up most of my left arm weren't enough to grant me outcast status, then the tongue and upper cheek piercings definitely were.

"You can hide behind your sarcasm all you want, Sydney." Her eyes rolled my way. "But I know what a beautiful soul you are."

"I've only lived with you for two months."

Don't get me wrong, I had nothing against her. As far as fake parents went, she wasn't that bad. At least her husband didn't try to sneak into my room at night. Had a couple of those. Nothing a loud scream or swift kick to the nuts couldn't solve.

"It doesn't take that long to get to know someone. Besides…" She steered the car around a corner and up a hill covered in pine trees. "You're going to be reunited with your mom. You must be happy about that."

I shrugged. "I guess."

Happy wasn't the word I'd use. My childhood was spent watching Charmaine's descent into insanity. It started with little things. Locking the door twice and constantly checking over her shoulder.

That escalated into tin foil on the windows and booby traps. She even went so far as to dig through any food we'd ordered at a restaurant.

When I was little, it was kind of fun. Like a game we were playing a secret game. As I got older, I realized that normal people didn't do these things. CPS got involved when I was eight because she'd locked me in a closet, claiming *they* were coming. Charmaine was taken away, and I began my nine-year trek through the foster care system.

A few months ago, she was deemed no longer a danger to herself or others. Since CPS was all about family reunification, I was being sent to live with her again. Wasn't sure how I felt about that. I supposed it was better than visiting her in that state-run nuthouse.

Ever been to one of those places?

That shit in horror movies was the plaza in comparison. There were people muttering to themselves, throwing things, and having tantrums in the corner. Some of them weren't even dressed. And don't get me started on the smell. I'd never get rid of that stench, or the nightmares it evoked.

No child wants to see their parent in a place like that. Every time I saw that glazed look on Charmaine's face, my heart broke a little. Just because she needed to be there, didn't mean I had to like it. She was still my mother.

As far as I was concerned, CPS had lost their minds. I saw Charmaine a week before some doctor declared her cured, and she was still muttering about the infamous *they.*

*"They found us, Sydney. You have to be astute – they play tricks with your mind."*

Didn't sound very sane if you asked me.

"I talked to your stepdad today. He seems like a nice man."

Oh, and there was that.

"Whatever you say," I muttered.

What kind of person married someone fresh off the crazy train? Not sure about Stacy, but that definitely raised red flags for me. He could be the nicest person in the world, even Mike Brady had a screw loose.

No one was that happy all the time. And what about when Charmaine inevitably fell off the wagon? What happened to me then? Would they throw me back in the system, or leave me in the care of some guy who clearly had issues?

I really should've taken time to study custody cases. Guess it was too late now. Not that it would've changed anything. According to the law, I didn't have the right to decide things for myself. At least not for another year and two weeks. Apparently, people weren't legally in charge of themselves until they were nineteen.

So, I was at the mercy of the courts. Who, in my opinion, had no idea what they were doing. For now, I was stuck in this midwestern town with a strange man in a house that quite possibly might have tin foil on the windows.

Welcome home, Sydney.

Never thought I'd miss Stacy's quaint little three-bedroom house, with the white picket fence and roses out front. I never thought I'd miss her, either.

"Thank you for bringing me." I gave Stacy a little smile. "You didn't have to."

Normally, it was my social worker, Perry, who did drop offs. Not this time, for some reason.

"Of course, I did." Stacy smiled back. "We're going to miss you around the house."

That was a lie. Then again, that's all the system was. One big, giant lie. When I first showed up at a new home, everyone would pretend to be nice. Welcoming me with open arms as if they were happy that I was there. When in reality, all I was to them was a paycheck. I'd seen so many fake smiles over the years, I forgot what real ones looked like.

"Here we are."

"Great," I grumbled while gearing myself up for the uncomfortable introductions.

I hated this routine. Everyone expected me to smile and make friends, but what was the point? Eventually, I'd have to leave them behind, so why bother with attachments?

When we crested the top of the hill, I couldn't help but cock a brow. Most of the time, we pulled up next to some middle-class home or apartment. There was even one place that was over a pizzeria. The house we were approaching now was bigger than the asylum Charmaine was locked up in.

I eyed the marble pillars framing a large deck.

*This has to be some kind of mistake.*

"I think you took a wrong turn."

"Nope," Stacy insisted. "This is the place."

They told me that my stepdad was well off. I thought maybe a plumber or some other blue-collar trade. Not this. What the hell did he do? Run Vegas?

"I'm sure you'll be very happy here."

Gawking up at the vines framing the brick building, I whispered, "Whatever you say."

I was more likely to end up buried in the backyard or shipped off to a boarding school. Anyone who lived in a house this well put together didn't want a stepdaughter roaming around. Even the large black doors and matching window shutters were perfect.

I couldn't see a single scuff or dusty spot anywhere. To the right was the rocky side of a mountain where I swear I could hear the distant sounds of water trickling.

My gaze shifted to the left, where there was a courtyard with an arched iron gate. It was the perfect place to hide something. Like, say, a body? I'd been here less than a minute and already dubbed the owners as killers. But come on. Who in their right mind would live in a place like this and marry Charmaine? Was I moving into Frankenstein's castle?

Did the yard end at the forest, or was the forest more of the yard?

"He came out to meet us. Isn't that nice?"

"Who?" I asked, "Igor?"

"Very funny." Stacy tipped her chin and added, "Your stepdad."

My brow rose at the man standing in the driveway. He was dressed in a clean navy suit with his broad shoulders rolled back.

*That was my stepdad?*

Don't get me wrong, Charmaine was pretty, in a classic sort of way. I could see her ending up with a slightly buff mechanic. Not this guy. If there was a Daddy version of GQ magazine, he'd not only be on the cover, he'd be the whole reason that spin off started.

"Are you selling me into the sex trade?"

"What?" Stacy shrieked. "Why would you say that?"

"He looks like a sex trafficker."

"And how would you know what a sex trafficker looks like?"

She may have a point. Technically, I'd never met one. Not that I knew about, anyway. But… "I watch movies."

My suspicion rose when Daddy GQ tipped his head and smiled in at us through the windshield. The emptiness in his turquoise gaze was disturbing. Even fake smiles included a little twinkle in the eyes.

Stacy laid her hand on my jean-covered leg and gave a reassuring squeeze. "You'll be fine."

*Easy for you to say.*

It wasn't like I had a choice, but shouldn't Charmaine be out here? I glanced around, trying to spot my mother's honey hair. The only thing I saw was Mr. GQ with his perfect smile and oversized mansion.

Stacy must've picked up on my thoughts because the first thing she said when we got out of the car was, "where's her mother?"

"She's resting," my supposed stepdad explained, while walking over to hold his hand out to me. "I'm Angus."

*Angus?*

Huh? Didn't see that one coming. Sir Stephan the Third, maybe? Or Michael William Wainwright. He seemed like the kind of guy who would have three names. Like that pompous prick I had to put up with in my last group home. Henry Alexander Mitchell. Not Hank or Henry, but all three. All the time. Guess which kid got beat up the most in that place.

"It's a pleasure to meet you, Sydney." That stern tone definitely fit the aura of authority he had going on. "Your mother talks about you all the time."

If that were true, then where was she?

I took in his dark hair and straight shoulders before tentatively placing my palm in his. What the hell was this guy doing with Charmaine?

"You look nothing like your father."

That statement took me by surprise. While he was right–I had Charmaine's light hair and fair complexion–my father died before I was born. The only thing I had was a picture, which I'd neatly packed in one of the three boxes Stacy was already pulling out of the car.

"You knew my dad?"

Sometimes I'd stare into the dark eyes of that picture and wonder who I got my silver orbs from? Was it someone in his family? What were they like? What was my father like?

Angus's smile widened. "We went to college together."

My dad went to college? I knew Charmaine had, but I didn't recall her mentioning Angus. Though it did explain how someone like Angus knew her in the first place.

"Well, that's it." Stacy placed the last box on the ground next to us and brushed her hands off on her skirt. "I guess I should get going?"

If I didn't know any better, I'd say she looked hesitant to leave. Stacy had a big heart. Leaving me here with a strange man probably wasn't sitting right with her.

Her lips pressed together as she glanced around. "I'd feel more comfortable if I could speak to her mother."

"Of course." Angus nodded. "I can wake her if you like. She's had a long day, and given her recent issues…"

'Issues' was a nice way of putting it. Apparently, Mr. GQ liked to sugar coat things as well.

"I didn't want to overwhelm her."

The concern fell off Stacy's face faster than a fart traveling in a windstorm.

"Oh, that's not necessary."

*Yes, it is.*

"Are you sure?" He arched a brow. "It's really not a problem, and I'd hate for you to leave feeling uncomfortable."

*I'm uncomfortable.*

"No, no." Stacy waved her hand through the air and walked back to the driver's door of her sedan. "It's fine."

There was something off about this whole thing. Charmaine wasn't the best mother, but not once, in all the years we'd been separated, had she ever missed a visit. When I was late—even if it was only five minutes—she'd flood my social worker with calls. There was no way she'd miss my arrival for a nap.

When I opened my mouth to say something, Angus cut me off. He threw his arm over my shoulders and pulled me into his side in the stiffest mock hug I'd ever experienced.

"Smile, Sydney," he whispered while giving Stacy a wave. "We don't want your foster mother worrying."

*Why did that feel like a threat?*

I told myself to stop overreacting and did what he said, giving Stacy a smile as she pulled away. I trusted this guy about as far as I could throw him, which wasn't very far. I was only five-feet tall, and he had to be over six. But that didn't mean my instincts were right.

When one had no idea what kind of place they'd be living in or who the people were around them, mistrust was natural. So were anxiety, discomfort, and nervousness. None of which were valid reason to worry Stacy.

*Still...*

Once the sedan was out of sight, I dropped the ruse and pushed Daddy GQ's arm off me. "Where's Charmaine?"

"Do you always call your mother by first name?"

"Do you always answer a question with a question?" My gaze zeroed in on the slight tic in his jaw. "Is there something wrong with wanting to see my mother?"

"Of course not." He gave me another empty smile. "But as I said, she's resting."

I crossed my arms. "So?"

"Why don't we get you settled before we bother your mother?" He spun around and walked towards the house, waving at me to follow. "Come. I'll introduce you to my sons."

*He had sons? Great.*

Teenage boys were one of two things. Dweebs or dicks. If their father was anything to go by, then I was guessing I wouldn't be finding any pocket protectors tucked into their shirts.

Angus pushed open the front door and gestured for me to enter.

"Welcome home, Sydney."

*Ominous much?*

Brushing the thought away, I huffed out a breath. It was just my imagination. Wouldn't be the first time I looked for problems where there were none. I was convinced my second foster home was run by vampires. In my defense, the adults in that house didn't get out of bed until the sunset.

I sighed and bent down to scoop a box off the ground.

"Don't worry about those." Angus stopped me. "I'll have someone bring them in."

My eyes tipped down to my tiny pile at my feet. It wasn't much, but every single possession I owned was in those boxes. I didn't like leaving them unattended.

*Stop being paranoid, Syd.*

I suppose I should give him a chance before I condemned him. Angus hadn't been rude or unwelcoming at all. Maybe this time, when

I walked through those doors, I'd find an actual family. How terrifying was that?

Those first few steps were some of the hardest I'd ever taken. Every time I lifted my foot, I felt the heaviness of doubt weighing me down. I paused before crossing that barrier and looked up at Angus.

He smiled and nodded for me to go inside.

*Maybe he wasn't so bad?*

With one last steadying breath, I stepped over the threshold. For a few seconds, I thought I was back in a group home, minus the marble flooring and fancy furniture, of course.

In the corner, next to a large staircase, were the tangled limbs of two teenage boys. One had the other in a headlock, though it was kind of hard to tell if they were two people or one wrestling some weird bendable mirror. They were literal carbon copies of each other. Well, at least their blonde hair was. I couldn't really see their faces.

"Stop it," one yelled while swatting at the other as he stuck a finger in his ear.

"You gonna do it?"

I'd seen 'the make him do it' game before. It was a favorite amongst the boys at the group homes. Guess boys were idiots no matter where you went.

"Fine," one growled and gave the other a shove. "I'll show the bitch around."

*Did I say idiots? I meant dicks.*

Angus cleared his throat. They froze and turned their heads in our direction.

The first thing I noticed was how the sparkling blue color of their eyes matched Angus's. The second was how quickly they snapped to attention.

"Sydney, these are my sons." Angus sighed and waved at them. "Wyatt and Magnus."

I could spot differences now. One had a couple of tattoos on his left arm and a grumpy expression.

"I'm Wyatt, the better looking one," the other one said, while shooting me a playful wink.

Magnus groaned and rolled his eyes at his brother's comment.

Wyatt's better-looking comment made me snort. Though it wasn't entirely wrong. Wyatt had a sparkle in his eyes, and the curl on the corner of his mouth that promised a lot of bad things in the best way possible. While Magnus had the brooding tattooed asshole thing going on. Combine that with their angular jawlines, broad shoulders, and aura of arrogance, and most girls would be screwed.

Except for me. I'd dealt with enough cocky pricks in my life.

Angus's next words caused me to arch a brow. "Where's Devlin?"

*There's another one?*

"He left right after Rook did." Wyatt said.

Was I in the testosterone manor of Midwestern USA? How many boys lived in this place?

Apparently, Angus didn't like Wyatt's answer.

"I told Devlin to be here," he stated while pointing at the ground, as if he could magically make his missing son appear. "He knew how important this was. Has he no respect for his mother?"

Both boys shrugged in response.

*His mother?* "Aren't you married to Charmaine?"

Angus's eyes snapped to mine. "That's who I was referring to. She is his mother now."

I supposed that made sense, but if he expected me to call him dad, he had another think coming.

"Tell Devlin to come and see me when he comes home," Angus grumbled and walked away. "And show Sydney to her room."

I stood there staring at the twins, who did not look very impressed that I was here. At least we had that in common.

Deciding to break the ice, I gave them a small wave. "Hi."

Other than a snort from Magnus, I didn't get a response.

Scratch that. Unimpressed wasn't the right word. Magnus was downright pissed. His brother, on the other hand...

Wyatt's eyes were glimmering with something that made me way more uncomfortable than I was in the driveway.

*Well, this is awkward.*

I could try to find my own way around. Anything was better than standing here and getting scrutinized by the dumbass duo.

Magnus's eyes narrowed in on me. "So, what's your deal?"

We stood there for god knows how long, not saying a thing, and now he decided to speak? And it wasn't a greeting or something else to make me feel welcomed. It was *what's your deal*. Did he just decide I was broken like Charmaine?

"What's your deal?" I shot back.

"Excuse my brother." Wyatt gave Magnus a small shove.

*Him, I might be okay with.*

"What he meant to say was, which one of us are you going to fuck first?"

I was wrong. Wyatt could bite my ass, too. Not that I'd say that to him, because he might actually bite my ass.

"Come on, Foster Care." A smirk pulled at the corner of Wyatt's mouth. "You can't tell me you haven't been around. I'm sure you had a daddy or two who wanted a little extra love."

*Ah, so this was the game we were playing. All right.*

I smacked my lips together and crossed my arms. If they wanted to try to intimidate me, good luck. I had fourteen different foster brothers and six sisters. All of whom had a chip on their shoulder.

"What's wrong, sis? Cat got your tongue?"

Sis sounded way too dirty on his lips. "Don't call me that."

"Why not? That's what you are, isn't it?"

He may have a point, but that didn't mean I was going to take part in any of this. "You know what else I am?"

He arched an intrigued brow.

"Leaving," I said and walked away. I'd find my own damn room.

Magnus had other ideas.

When I made for the stairs, he stepped in front of me, blocking my path.

"Do you mind?"

His response was to lean back and silently size me up.

*Whatever.*

One of the benefits of being short was that I could squeeze through small spaces. Like, say, under the arm of an asshole.

With a quick roll of my eyes, I slipped past him and stormed up the steps.

"Watch your back, Faster Care," Magnus called after me.

"I think you should be more worried about your back." I paused to glance over my shoulder. "Your brother looks like an ass man."

*Go fuck yourself, Magnus, and take your dipshit brother with you.*

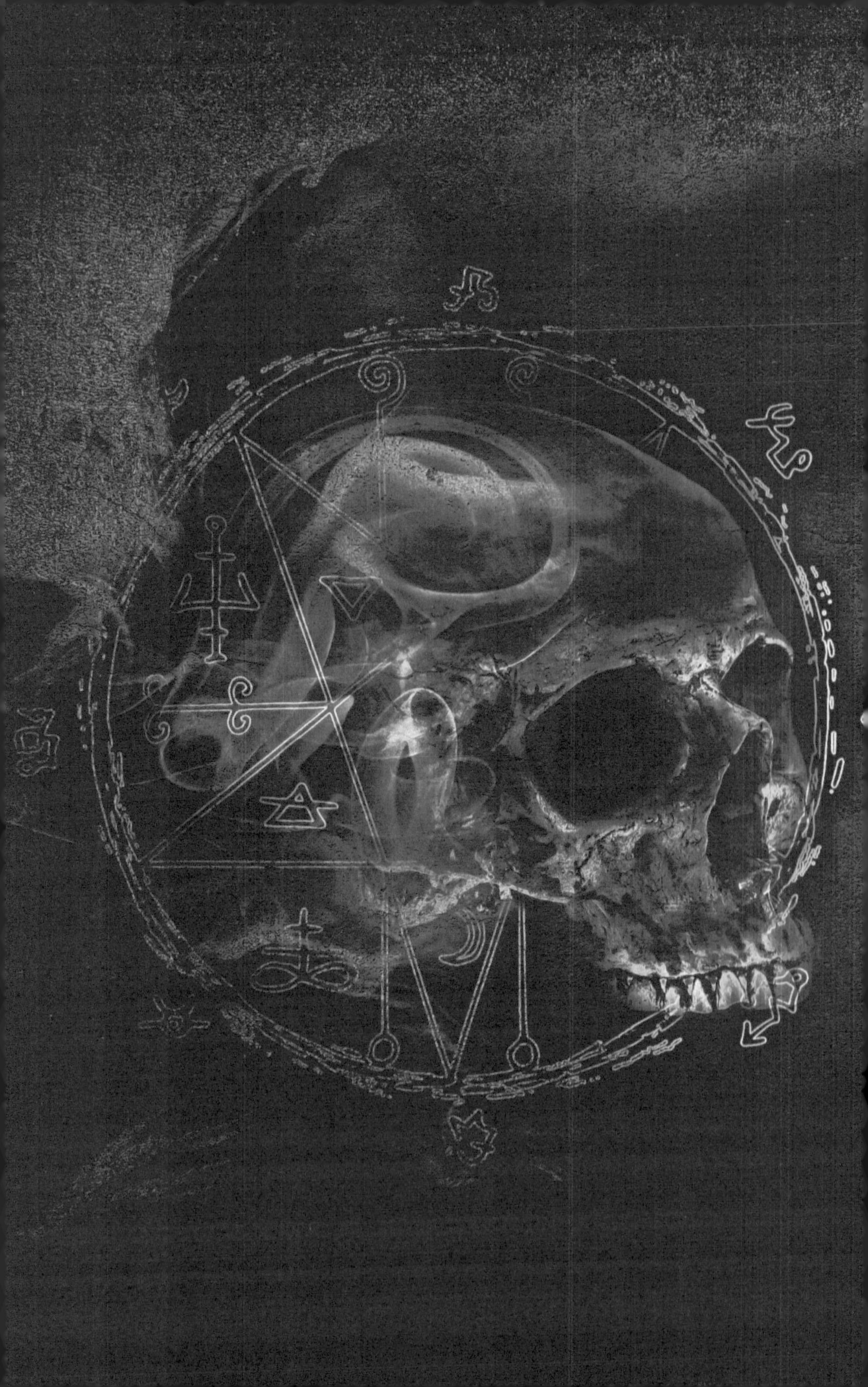

# Chapter 2

One would think that finding a bedroom wouldn't be that hard. Yet here I was, lost in a mansion for what felt like hours, and I still had no clue where my room was. Mind you, I could've found it already and not known. So far, I'd counted around twelve bedrooms. On top of the various offices, sitting rooms, and other rooms.

It was seriously ominous how huge this place was. At one point, I could've sworn I'd stepped through a time portal and was wandering around Dracula's castle. Ever been in a hallway lined with suits of armor? It was creepy as fuck.

I kept glancing over my shoulder to make sure one of those metal men wasn't following me. Then I went around a corner and was suddenly face-to-face with a pair of empty eyes. I damn near kicked it.

One thing was for sure: I was never going down that hallway again.

All I wanted to do was find my room. Was that too much to ask? Hell, at this point, I'd settle for one of those unreadable maps the zoo had, or a big neon sign with a flickering arrow.

Every room I went into with the intention of finding my clothes.

Stacy shipped most of them up here last week. So I assumed whichever room was mine would house my wardrobe of jeans and t-shirts.

Shouldn't be too hard to find in a place like that, right?

Wrong.

The only closet I came across that didn't house brand name clothing was full of brooms and mops. Not nearly enough, in my opinion, for the square footage that had to be cleaned.

I did find a few interesting things. An old journal written in another language, a closet full of mismatched socks—don't know what that was about—and a theater room. That was one room I might use one day. There was nothing like watching a movie all alone with a tub full of popcorn.

Magnus's and Wyatt's bedrooms were the next ones I found. I knew they were theirs because Wyatt's was full of pictures of himself. With a shirt on, with a shirt off, posing somewhere, and of course there was the naked album, which I quickly threw across the room.

The first thing I learned about my stepbrother shouldn't be that his nipples weren't the only thing pierced.

Magnus's room was right beside Wyatt's and nowhere near as vain. In fact, it was kind of plain. It had a white and tan color scheme, with a few electronics, and was very neat. Everything seemed to be in its place. Including the open laptop on his desk with an essay or something he was currently working on.

Curious, I peeked down at the screen, but couldn't understand the language it was written in. Maybe Magnus was taking Latin or something? Whatever. I liked his room better. Wyatt's was a pigsty. He had clothes all over the floor. All of which I carefully stepped around, given the album I came across.

I stepped out and carefully closed the door before looking over at the two rooms across the hall. It would make sense if one of those were mine, but which one? Neither door stood out. They both had the same clean wooden appearance, with a brass doorknob.

*Guess there's only one way to find out.*

I marched over to the one directly across from me and threw it open. My jaw dropped, though I wasn't sure if it was out of awe or fear?

The bed was one of the biggest I'd ever seen. I definitely could've done without the headboard. It was made of metal that had the same dull, almost black, appearance as cast iron. Two large snakes slithered around thorny roses and twisted their heads up to meet in the middle. A shiver ran up spine as I stood on the gray slate-like carpet staring at the onyx gemstone eyes.

Some people didn't like spiders. Others weren't a fan of heights. I didn't like snakes. Their long bodies and beady eyes scared the hell out of me. And in this room, they were everywhere.

There were three holding up the glass tops of two bedside tables. Another one wound around the gray stone of a fireplace set in the opposite wall of the bed. And finally, there were the two climbing a tree painted in the corner of the room.

I followed the thick black trunk up to dark leafy branches that spanned across the roof. This place was my literal nightmare. It wasn't just because of the snakes. In one corner of the room sat what looked like an old electric chair.

Beside that was a navy and gray mosaic that said *Mors Vincit Omnia*. Not sure what that meant, but given the ambiance of the place, I doubted it was something motivational like *hang in there* or *keep your chin up*.

Adding to the creep factor was a curvy bench at the foot of the bed. It was upholstered in a navy hued leather that matched the bedspread. My gaze locked on to two handles, one at the head of the bench and one at the foot.

Big metal loops glinted in the sunlight pouring through the windows. They were closer in appearance to the loops in a dungeon than to the handles of a drawer. Binds that were meant to tie someone down. Given the shape of the bench, they'd be bound in a rather revealing position.

I shrugged off a shiver and glanced over at an accent wall of mirrors behind the headboard. Each piece of reflective glass was dulled at the edges by a fog of black. The only normal thing in this place was a polar bear rug sitting next to the fireplace, and that thing still had its claws and head.

This was one room I was not going to search. I didn't give a shit if it was mine or not. I'd rather sleep outside.

"I am so out of here, Snowball." I spun away from the bear's judgmental gaze and moved to leave.

That's when the doorknob jiggled, and a masculine voice wafted in.

"I can't come tonight."

*Shit!*

My heart stopped as a freezing spike shot up my spine. Whoever slept in this place was not someone I was in a hurry to meet.

The door creaked open, and I panicked, diving for the first place I could think to hide. Under the bed. In hindsight, it probably wasn't my best idea—I'd seen enough movies to know that—but in that moment, that dark space under the mattress of torture seemed like my best option.

When a pair of booted feet came into view, I sucked in and held my breath. Each press of those feet into the carpet moved through my chest in cold vibrating spikes.

"You can't flake out."

That voice was different from the first and had the slightly distorted tinge of speakers. Whoever came in must've been on the phone.

"You had a party yesterday, Reese."

Gotta say, the tone in that guy's voice definitely matched this room.

A deep, gravely sound that vibrated through my entire body. Then again, it was highly possible that I was just psyching myself out. I was huddled under a bed in the den of serpents, after all.

"So?" Reese said. "You weren't complaining when Lexi was sucking your dick. How was she, by the way?"

"Eh."

*Ugh, typical.*

I could practically picture the jerk teetering his hand in a so, so manner.

"Come on, Devlin," Reese whined. "You have to come."

So, not only was I hiding out in a possible serial killer's room, but said killer was my missing stepbrother. *Fantastic*. Guess it was time to stop holding out hope that one of them was a decent human being. Even if he was a good guy, I wasn't exactly set up to make a great first impression.

*Hi, I'm Sydney. Why was I hiding under your bed? Oh, I'm pretty sure you're a serial killer. Nice to meet you.*

I watched the black soles of Devlin's boots strut across the room and looked over at the only other thing I could see from under here, the glittering stare of a dead polar bear.

*Don't judge me.*

"I can't," Devlin grumbled and walked over to a black dresser next to the bed, making me shift farther into the shadows. "The Sergeant's insisting on family time."

My gaze narrowed on the bear. Did he always have that curve in his mouth, or was he mocking me? I stared at the glass eye glittering in the sunlight. He was definitely mocking me.

*Great, even the rug's an asshole.*

"Oh, that's right. Your sister arrives today. What's her name again?"

"I don't know," Devlin grumbled out a dissatisfied groan. "Cindy or something."

Guess I could cut him out of the welcome party.

"You seen her yet?" Reese asked. "She hot?"

Seriously? Did boys think about anything else, or did their mind automatically go to pussy? Girls didn't do that. Sure, we thought guys were cute, but we didn't immediately focus on what was hanging between their legs. Well, most girls... I had a few foster sisters who talked way too much about dick.

"No, I haven't seen her."

I got it. None of us wanted to be thrown together, but did Devlin have to sound so sour about meeting me?

Apparently, Reese agreed with me, because he sang, "Look on the bright side. You might enjoy playing with her."

Playing with me? Really? Guess I could cut Reese out of the welcome party too.

"I doubt it," Devlin grumbled. "Her mother's plain as fuck."

"Well, fuck you too." I quickly slapped my hand over my mouth. *Shit. Did he hear me?*

I couldn't tell. The only thing I could hear was my blood whooshing through my ears. I held my breath and remained as still as I could. Every muscle in my body tensed. I didn't even let my eyelids flutter. Not until I saw his feet move towards the door.

"I better go check in with my dad," Devlin said and left.

When the door clicked closed, I let out a long breath, closed my eyes, and dropped my head on the floor.

Thank God, that crisis was adverted. I can't imagine that meeting would've went well. Though it wouldn't have been too bad compared to the other greetings I'd gotten in this place. I was really starting to miss Stacy and her apple pie smile.

Her house was kind of nice, and her husband wasn't that bad. He didn't really pay attention to me. Now here I was, torn from the comfort of Stacy's baking and brought to the house of testosterone and horn dogs.

I snorted. "Welcome home, Sydney."

"Why are you under my bed?"

I jumped, smacking the back of my head on the bottom of the bed. Let me just say, the frame was just had hard as it looked. That shit hurt. Pain radiated through my skull, making me almost forget about the other person in the room. Until he spoke.

"I asked you a question."

*Shit.*

My eyes shot open. My powers of observation were seriously lacking. How could I not notice that Devlin was still here?

*Maybe if you hadn't closed your eyes like a dumbass…*

"Hello?" Devlin's deep tone rumbled through the room.

Rather than responding, I chose to stare down at the fibers of the carpet my face was smashed into. Up close, they were kind of pretty. Gray and white threads twisted together to form a thicker, plusher strand.

My brows knit at one of the white swirls. There were two blue threads in those strands. Was that on purpose? If that part of the carpet was supposed to be white, why would they put another color in there? Maybe it made the white stand out more?

"I know you're there."

I begged to differ. He had absolutely no proof that I was here. Other than the fact that I said something, that was. But people heard crap all the time. Like Charmaine, for example. The infamous *they* were always waiting around every corner.

"You have two choices." Devlin let out an annoyed sigh. "You can come out. Or I can drag you out."

*He could try.*

I rolled my head along the floor and stared at the toes of two boots pointing right at me. This bed was pretty big, and he was all the way on the other side. Judging by the size of his feet, I doubted that he'd have an easy time getting under here. I would have to get out of here eventually, though.

*Or would I?*

It wasn't so bad. At least there weren't any snakes. It might get a little cold at night without a blanket, but I could warm myself with fuzzy thoughts of not dying.

"All right. Have it your way."

When the bed shifted above me, my heart lurched in my chest. Did he just move the bed? Jesus, how big was this guy?

"Okay, fine," I yelled when the bed moved again. "I'm coming out."

Crawling on my belly like an animal was not how I envisioned this meeting going. If I was being honest, I didn't want to meet him at all. The only person I did want to see was Charmaine. As far as I was concerned, the rest of them could disappear into the darkness.

It took a lot of self-pep talking to pull myself away from that safe place and stand up, and when I did, I immediately wanted to scuttle back under there.

The man glaring down at me was huge. There was only one other person I had to lift my chin up so far to look in the eyes. One of my foster father's was six foot six, and Devlin had at least a couple inches on him.

It probably didn't help that he was right there, less than a foot away. I really needed to work on my situational awareness.

I kind of expected him to say something. Like scold me or give me shit for snooping. But he didn't. He just stood there with his arms folded over his broad chest.

"Um… Hi?"

Still nothing.

All right, so stepbrother three was an asshole. Though I did have to admit, he was nice to look at. There was a slight curl in his neatly cropped dark hair. I could see it at the tips of the longer strands, which framed his face, making the angular lines of his jaw stand out.

Not one single freckle or dot marked Devlin's tanned skin. Even his mouth was perfect. Thick, full lips that still appeared soft when pressed in a scowl.

He was studying me too. Curiosity glittered in the green flecks of his brown eyes. At least, I think it was curiosity?

The more his gaze raked over my body, the darker it got. Was it wrong that I was staring at him? I mean, he did just find me hiding in his room. I should've left, but my feet wouldn't move. I just stood there, gawking.

*Way to look like a creep, Syd.*

It wasn't until Devlin shifted to take a step closer that I could move. Not much, mind you, but I did manage to jump back.

He huffed out a snort. "You don't look like your mother."

I was too busy resisting the urge to wrap my arms around my waist to respond. In this situation, I was not the predator. My eyes dropped to the black tribal lines dancing along his forearm as his muscle flexed. I didn't want to be the prey either.

I got the distinct feeling that Devlin got off on that kind of thing.

He clapped his hands together, making me jump again. "Can you speak?"

"Yes." *I just don't want to talk to you.*

The corner of his mouth lifted in a smirk that had my stomach flipping. It was seriously wrong how tempting that crooked smile was on him.

My forehead furrowed. Why was I staring at him? This asshole wasn't the first hot guy I'd seen. One thing foster care had a lot of was bad boys. Which was pretty much what Devlin was, standing there with his arms crossed and chest puffed out. They were big, firm arms but no different from any of the other assholes I'd met.

"You're a timid little thing, aren't you?"

My eyes snapped up to his. "Think what you want."

I'd happily show him otherwise. There was enough fight in me to take on Devlin and both his brothers. I just thought it was a waste of time to engage people like that. Besides, it tended to piss them off more when you ignored them.

This time, when he took a menacing step forward, I managed to stand my ground.

"Care to tell me why you were hiding under my bed?"

*Not really.*

"I was looking for my room." I couldn't help but notice how his chest pressed against the white fabric of his shirt, giving me a glimpse of the hard ridges underneath. This guy was stacked. There was no way I'd win a test of strength against him. Might have to go for the balls with this one.

"It's next door." He lifted his chin, tipping it at the wall behind me.

*Oh, well, that solved that problem.*

Wait… My room was next to his? Oh, I didn't like that.

"So… my room is right…" I glanced over my shoulder and came face to face with the eyes of a cast iron snake.

Screeching, I sprang back and smacked right into Devlin. After which, I jumped away again and slammed against the wall.

*Great, Sydney, just great. Cue the slow clap.*

This was literally the world's worst first impression. Not only was I hiding in his room, but now I was jumping around like a kangaroo trapped on a trampoline while on steroids.

Devlin took full advantage of my nervousness.

"What's wrong, Doll?" He braced his palms on the wall behind me and leaned in. "Afraid I'll come creeping into your room at night?"

"No."

*Kind of.*

"Or is it the snakes that have you all skittish?"

"Pfft. Snakes are just animals." And by animals, I meant creepy, slithering minions of the underworld.

This time when Devlin dragged his eyes down the length of me, I couldn't stop myself from hugging my waist. There was something about the way he was staring at me. I couldn't tell if he wanted to rip me apart or swallow me whole.

He shook his head and headed over to his dresser. "Get the fuck out of my room."

That, I didn't have a problem with. I skipped over to the door as fast as I could without being obvious. I was almost out when he spoke.

"See you at dinner."

I paused to peek over at him fiddling with something on his dresser.

"I'm not hungry."

"No one asked if you were hungry."

The testosterone in this place was really starting to overwhelm me. "I'll eat when I want to eat."

"Is that what you think?"

"No." My eyes narrowed. "That's what I know."

Devlin's shoulders shook with a quiet chuckle. It pissed me off even more. The least he could do was look at me.

"Good luck with that." He sighed. "Now get the fuck out before I decide to have a little fun before I eat."

Intent on standing my ground, I crossed my arms and huffed. "You won't be having any fun with me."

I wasn't the pushover he thought I was.

He turned his head and locked his dark glare on mine. "Care to test that theory?"

It was the promise glittering in his eyes that made me slowly back out into the hall.

# Chapter 3

My bedroom wasn't as decorative or ominous as the others, which was fine with me. I didn't need fancy decorations. I was happy with my two paintings. One of a lotus flower, floating in the water, and the other of a fluffy orange kitten sleeping on a blanket.

To people like the Adairs, those pictures were probably pretty generic, but to me they were beautiful. Hell, this entire room, with its bland off-white color scheme, was the plaza compared to some of the places I'd stayed.

I could stretch out on the bed and still not touch either end of it. Plus, there wouldn't be any mysterious smells here. I buried my nose in the fluffy cream-colored bedspread and inhaled the sweet scent of jasmine. Maybe it was honeysuckle? Who cared? It was way better than the lemon fresh fabric softener Stacy used.

One place I stayed, had this weird sourness everywhere. I searched for the source for weeks. No one wanted to know the crap I found stuffed in the corners of that house. Looking back, I suppose I shouldn't have been surprised. The father in that family smoked two packs a day and drank whiskey like it was water.

He was also the first grown man that tried to sneak in my room. Hence the short stay. Perry might be an uptight prick, but he didn't put up with shit. All he had to do was see the way I looked at the man, and I was rehoused. My social worker was the one department I lucked out in.

Most kids in the system were thrown away and forgotten. Perry wasn't burnt out yet. He made all scheduled visits, as well as many surprise visits.

He was the closest thing I had to a father. Even though he didn't do the drop off this time, he'd called twice. Something he didn't have to do, considering that, technically, I wasn't in the system anymore.

I think he even called Angus, because ten minutes after I complained that I hadn't seen Charmaine, my stepfather was knocking on my door with her in tow. She didn't say long, but I was comforted by her smile. I was starting to think these people had her buried in the backyard or something.

We talked for a bit while Charmaine played with my hair. She was always twisting her fingers in my straight locks. I chalked it up to the fact that hers was curly. People tended to want what they didn't have. The tall wanted to be short, people with freckles wanted a clear completion, while others wanted the spots, and so on.

Personally, I thought people should embrace their flaws instead of complaining. It was those subtle differences that made people unique. I had a rose-colored, star-shaped birthmark on my inner right thigh, and you didn't hear me whining about it. No, I wore it proudly. I mean, who else could say they were born with their own star?

I carefully rested my dad's picture against the lamp on my oak bedside table and smiled. Before Charmaine left, she said we'd go shopping for some things to spruce up the place.

This photo was the only thing I needed. Saying goodnight to his brightly lit face was a ritual of mine. I couldn't sleep without doing it. Sometimes it felt like he was the only thing keeping the monsters at bay.

Satisfied that my dad was in his rightful place, I headed back over to dig through my boxes for some pjs.

Most of these cardboard squares were filled with various jeans, t-shirts, and hoodies. I had a few nice items, like the black silk dress one of my foster sisters gave me, and a pair of strappy heels. But my favorite thing was a worn out, flimsy white nightgown decorated with three tiny red flowers. It was Charmaine's before it was mine, and the last thing my dad gave her. So, in a way, it was kind of like it came from him.

I pulled the nightgown out and quickly changed. It fit me a lot better now than it did when I was ten. It was a tad tight. I was curvier than Charmaine was, and the cotton was so old it didn't really have much give left. So the hemline sat just below my ass. Didn't matter. It wasn't like anyone was going to see me in it.

I thought back to my interaction with Devlin and snorted.

So much for his care to test that theory comment. Did I go down to dinner? No. And did anyone come and tell me I had to? Also no.

I was seventeen, not five. More than capable of deciding when I did or didn't want to eat. Right now, the only thing I wanted to do was go to sleep. Stacy was ushering me out the door at the crack of dawn.

Yawning, I padded over to my bed and was just about to slide under the covers when the door flew open, banging against the wall.

I looked over as Wyatt sauntered in, clicking his tongue off the roof of his mouth. "Bad move, Foster Care. You should've listened to my…"

He stopped mid-stride and cocked a brow.

It took me a second to realize what he was staring at. I quickly snatched the blanket off my bed and wrapped it around myself. Just in time, too, because Wyatt wasn't alone. Magnus and Devlin were right behind him.

"Too late, baby cakes." Wyatt chuckled. "I already saw the goodies."

He probably got quite the eyeful. My breasts were practically spilling out of the flimsy fabric.

"What the fuck do you mean, you saw the goodies?" Devlin's voice boomed through the air. "Are you walking around here naked?"

"So what if I was?" I returned his scowl with one of my own. "This is *my* room."

I was tempted to take a step back when Devlin's cold glare locked on me. But I didn't, because this was my room, and they had no right to barge in.

Magnus leaned his shoulder against the wall while eyeing me up. "She doesn't have any goodies to show."

I shouldn't be insulted by that, but I was.

"Get out!" I ordered, and pointed at the door.

Not one of them responded or acted like they heard me at all. It was official. I hated my stepbrothers.

Magnus glared at Wyatt when he slapped him on the chest, then smiled at Devlin. I was assuming Devlin was the eldest of the three. He was certainly the biggest.

"You should see what she's got on under there."

*This mother…*

I tried again. This time glaring directly at Wyatt's smug grin. "Get out of my room!"

Magnus shook his head. "Leave it to you to walk in on some girl wearing lingerie."

"Oh no, it wasn't lingerie. It was this white thing with tiny little straps." Wyatt pinched his fingers together and ran them over his shoulders, drawing imaginary lines. "Dude, it's so thin you can see her nipples."

Devlin's brow rose along with Magnus's.

Did that mean they acknowledged my existence? Of course not. I mean, why would they do that? It wasn't like they had barged into *my* personal space.

"How'd they look?" Magnus asked with a straight face.

*Seriously?*

"Nice and pink with pert little tips," Wyatt explained, then added, "tasty," with a lick of his lips.

*Oh my god.*

"Helloooo," I called out.

Devlin charged forward and shoved Wyatt back. "We didn't come up here to stare at her fucking tits."

*Were they deaf, or had I been granted the powers of invisibility?*

"It's not my fault she decided to wear the most revealing pyjamas ever made."

*I was gonna go with invisibility.*

"Bullshit. Look at her." Devlin waved his hand in my direction. "I doubt she owns a half decent dress."

*If I were invisible, then Wyatt wouldn't be able to give such a vivid description of my nipples. Maybe I was given the power of silence?*

Wyatt shrugged. "Tell her to drop the blanket and you'll see what I mean."

*Should I use my powers for good or evil?*

"I gotta admit"—Magnus tipped his head in a small nod—"I'm kind of curious what she's got on. The last time Wyatt was this worked up was when Jackie Thomas showed up in that string bikini."

Devlin cocked a brow, as if he were considering it.

*All right, that's enough of that.*

I picked up a little China dog sitting on the bedside table and chucked it at them. It whizzed through the air, narrowly missing Devlin's nose, and smashed against the wall. Finally, they turned to look at me.

Well, except for Wyatt. He stared down at the broken pieces and whined, "I picked that out for you."

"Well, now you can shove it up your ass on your way out of my room."

None of them seemed to like that very much. Well, too bad for them. I didn't give a crap if they were pissed. Let them stare at me with clenched jaws. I wasn't scared. Though I did have to push back a shiver when Devlin's eyes darkened.

*Maybe I was a little scared of him.*

Devlin uncrossed his arms and took a step forward. "You didn't come down to dinner."

"I told you I wasn't hungry."

"And I told you…" When he took another step, I had to remind myself to stand my ground. "No one asked if you were hungry."

Apparently, Mr. High and Mighty had a superiority complex. *Shocking.*

"Hmm?" While tapping my finger on my chin, "What was it you said to me? Oh, yeah…" I glared directly at him. "Get the fuck out of my room."

The tick in Devlin's jaw was all the reaction I needed. "You think you're pretty smart?"

"I have my moments."

Sure, I could tell him off. Throw a few snarky comments and call Devlin on his bullshit, but what would that accomplish? Nothing. Other than giving him the satisfaction of my reaction.

Magnus tipped his head at Devlin. "How long do you think she'll be able to keep that act up?"

Wyatt muttered something about feisty girls being more fun, while Devlin simply crossed his arms and stared me down.

"Not long."

*We'll see about that.*

I returned his stare down with one of my own.

The only difference between the jerkoffs I grew up with and Devlin was that he was better dressed. And better looking. Oh, and he was bigger and totally had that *'I'm gonna kill you'* glare down pat.

Okay, so there were a lot of differences. That didn't mean I was gonna back down. I'd been taking care of myself for as long as I could remember. I was just as capable as he was. A fact that I was bound and determined to prove.

When Devlin let out a huff, I let out a huff, and when he arched a brow, I arched one right back at him. Because fuck him, and fuck his brothers too.

Two words. That's all it took for my bravado to bleed into the ground.

Devlin tipped his head back and said, "Grab her."

A stare down was one thing, but getting physical… Yeah, that I was not about to do. Unfortunately, I was stupid.

My first mistake was trying to run in a blanket ten times my size. The second was choosing to sprint across the bed. Instead of making a grand escape—which is how I pictured it in my head.

I ended up tripping on yards of fabric and fell face first onto the mattress. There was no awesome superhero landing for me. Just the imagined face palm I gave myself as I got an up-close view of the white sheets.

Magnus and Wyatt were on me in a flash. Each one grabbed an arm and stretched it out above my head, while Devlin tore the blanket off my body. Cool air kissed the back of my thighs, sending a wave of mortification flowing down my cheeks and into my chest.

Next thing I knew, Devlin's heavy hand was landing on my ass, making me cry out.

"Would you look at that?" He growled and did it again.

"Told ya," Wyatt sang.

I gritted my teeth and used the sting radiating across my flesh to fuel my rage, kicking my feet out. The only hope I had was if I hit a soft spot, then I could claw the other two idiot's eyes out. But Devlin didn't have any soft spots. A fact I learned when my heel crashed into his thigh.

I winced as a sharp stab shot up my leg.

*Was he made of stone?*

"Let me go!" I snarled at the other two.

Magnus shoved my face back into the mattress and snapped, "Shut the fuck up."

I still clung onto hope that I'd get away. Until I felt the heavy weight of Devlin crawling over me. This was the part where the prey realized what they were… Fucked.

I stopped fighting. The only thing it was doing at this point was depleting precious energy.

"What do you want?"

I was expecting the usual responses. I'm the head honcho here, you'll do what I say, yada, yada, yada. What I got was so much worse.

"What do I want?" Devlin folded his body over mine and grazed the tip of his nose up my neck to my ear. "I want to hurt you."

His words caused my entire body to tense. It suddenly seemed as if there wasn't enough air in the room. I fought to take in a breath while my pulse fluttered along so fast that I couldn't tell if it was still beating or had stopped all together. I'd had my fair share of pain, but something told me that Devlin's idea of hurt and mine were very different.

That thought alone terrified me so much that all I could do was softly breathe out, "Why?"

"Why would I need a reason?" Devlin ran his fingers through my hair, grabbed a fistful, and yanked my head off the mattress. "Maybe I just like breaking things."

I could see that. My so-called stepbrothers seemed like the type who liked fucking with people, but this…

My eyes swung from the glimmer on Wyatt's face to Magnus's lips pressed in a tight scowl. Devlin was another story. I could not only feel the rage coming off him, but I could taste it. The bitter flavor lingered with each breath he took, warming my skin with pure, unadulterated hatred.

These boys didn't just hate me. They loathed my very existence.

There was only one reason I could think for that. "I know Charmaine's a handful…"

Wyatt cut me off with a loud laugh. "She thinks this is about her mother."

"No one said she was smart." Magnus cocked his head, aiming his glare down at me. "You think we give a shit about that bitch?"

"Then why are you doing this?"

"Because we can." Devlin exhaled and laved his tongue up the side of my neck.

I tried to shrink away, but he just tightened his grip in my hair, twisting his fist until my scalp was screaming for relief.

"Let me go!"

Devlin's brow rose. "Why would we do that?"

I twisted my head as much as I could and firmed the glare on my face. "I'll scream."

"Yeah?" His lips curled just a bit. The next thing I knew, he had his fingers shoved in my mouth. "Scream now," he growled, while digging his thumb into the bottom of my chin. "And don't even think about biting me. If you do… I'll knock your fucking teeth out."

What could I do but placate him? I wanted to bite him, every fiber of my being told me too, but I also really liked my teeth, and I fully believed his threat. So, I went still and prayed that if I played the docile kitten, they'd get bored and leave me alone.

That didn't happen.

I did get a reprieve from the fingers gagging me, though. Once Devlin was satisfied that I wouldn't fight him, he removed his hand from my mouth. I thought they might knock me around a bit or call me names. Typical bully stuff.

I was so wrong.

Devlin lifted one of his fingers, glistening with my saliva, and pulled on my hair to force me to watch him push it through his lips.

Seeing him suck on the finger he just shoved down my throat should not be as hot as it was. Even if he wasn't holding me, I wouldn't have been able to look away. All I could do as his eyes rolled in the back of his head was drop my jaw and gawk.

"You taste pretty sweet, *Bréagán*."

A part of me hummed at how his voice flowed smoothly over that word. I hadn't noticed his slight accent before, but it was there. Hidden just under his deep tone.

Was it wrong that it made him more appealing? The first thing I was going to do—after killing these guys, of course—was look up what *Bréagán* meant.

"I wonder…" Devlin leaned in and licked the side of my face. "Do you taste as sweet in other places?"

*What?*

My heart dropped. He couldn't mean what I thought he meant.

His fist loosened in my hair, letting my scalp sigh. That small relief was gone the instant his hand inched down my side to my hip.

*Oh my God!*

My eyes went wide, and I started kicking while screaming out my objections. I didn't care if he hurt me or knocked out my teeth anymore. The only thing I could focus on was getting his heavy weight off me.

I tried, fought with everything I had. But there were three of them and only one of me. I was easily contained.

Magus took my arm from Wyatt while he shuffled forward to lift my head and clamp a hand over my mouth. When Devlin climbed off me and forced my thighs open, there was nothing I could do but let tears drip from the corner of my eyes.

Then it all stopped.

The room went so still and silent that I even stopped trying to scream from behind Wyatt's hand. Whatever was happening, the three of them seemed just as shocked as I was.

*Did their dad come in?*

"Fuck me," Devlin grumbled and brushed his thumb over a spot on my inner right thigh. "Are you seeing this?"

*Seeing what?*

Wyatt rose to his knees and glanced over my back. "Yeah, I'm seeing it."

*What the hell were they seeing?*

"You know what that means?" Magnus added.

*Know what, what means?*

Somebody needed to tell me what was going on. Not that any of them would. Assholes just held onto me and ignored my muffled murmurs, which was more frustrating than when they were accosting me.

"You think he knows?"

"No." Magnus shook his head at Wyatt. "If he did, Reese would be here."

Devlin's attention snapped back to his brother. "Why the fuck would Reese be here?"

"Because our mark showed up on our hip," Wyatt answered. "Where's yours, Devlin?"

Okay, now I was starting to get scared. Mark? What the hell was going on? Did I have a cancerous tumor or something?

I tried to wriggle away from Magnus enough to speak, but his hold was too firm. All I could do as Devlin stared down at me was growl incoherent curses.

"Fuck!" Devlin barked out and ran his fingers through his hair. "Get off her!"

To my surprise, that's exactly what his brothers did. Wyatt and Magnus let me go and sprang off the bed. Devlin, however, kept his hand on my leg. When I looked back at him, he was staring down at my thigh while his thumb swept over my birthmark.

*Really? That's what all this was about.*

I yanked my leg out of his grip and kicked him in the chest. "Get out!"

His dark eyes locked on mine. "Careful, Sydney."

"Fuck you!" I snarled and jumped off the bed to puff my chest up against him. "You think you're funny, coming in here and picking on someone half your size."

I jabbed my finger in his chest.

"I've got claws too. And you don't want to see what I can do with them." I glared over my shoulder, shooting daggers at his brothers and added, "Any of you."

Wyatt snickered. "Sounds like a challenge to me."

"Try it," I shot back at him. "And you…" I spun back around to face Devlin. "Just because I walked into the wrong room doesn't give you the right to do this."

*Whatever this was.*

"Don't worry. You'll be seeing a lot more of my room." Devlin seized my chin and dug his fingers into my cheeks. "You're mine now, *Bréagán*. That doesn't mean I won't hurt you. Don't. Piss. Me. Off."

All my anger came out in the laugh that tore from my lips. "Oh, you haven't even begun to see pissed off."

"Trust me, little girl. You have no idea what pissed off means." I could feel the heat coming from the anger burning in his dark eyes. "If it wasn't for Reese, I'd have slit your throat already."

Normally, I'd have brushed off his threat as nothing more than empty words, but something in his tone told me that he wasn't lying. Devlin did want to kill me. That was okay. I wanted to kill him too.

I had one goal in life now. Make Devlin's existence a living hell.

And I'd drag his brothers along for the ride.

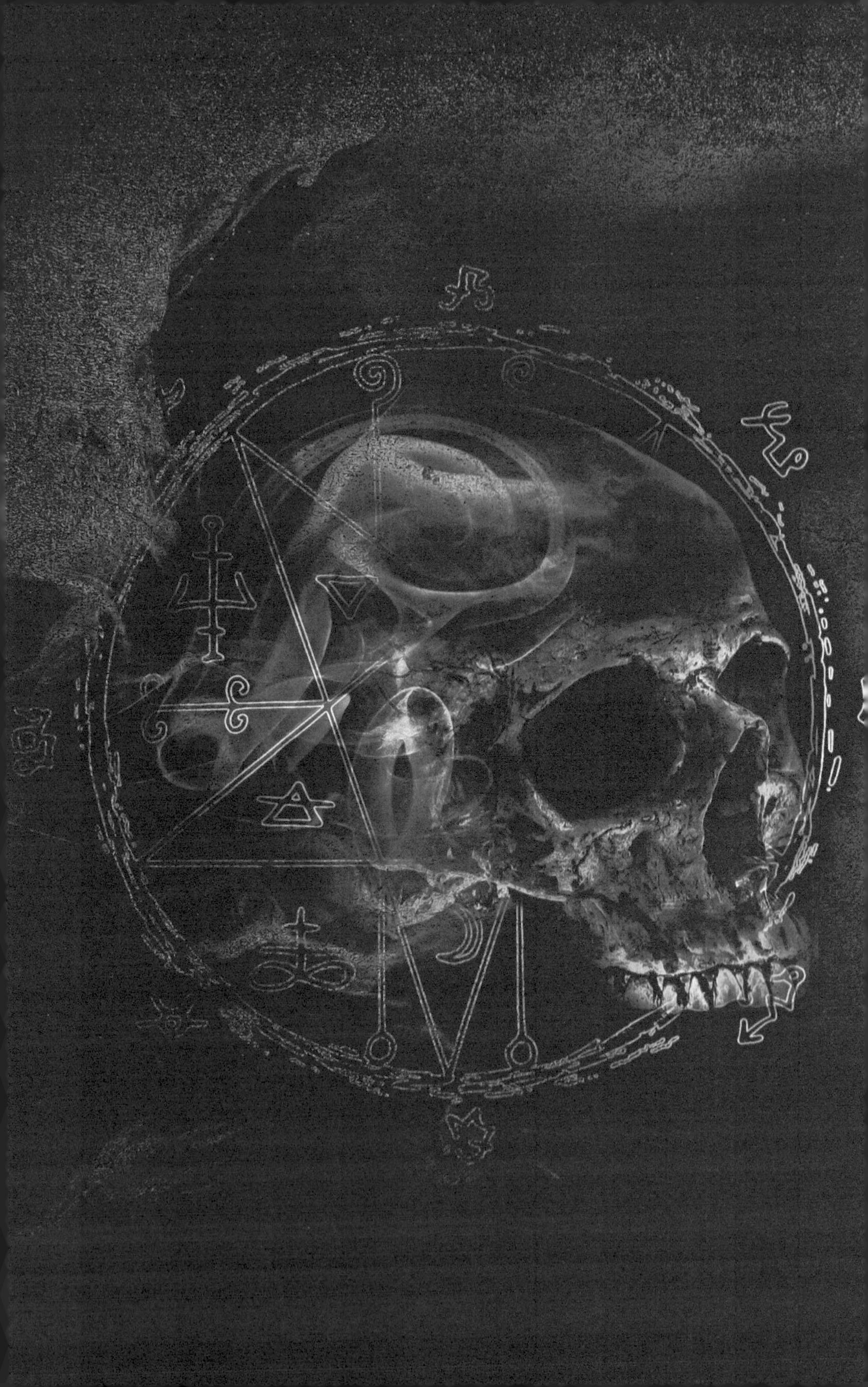

# Chapter 4

For the last seven years, my mornings were pretty much the same. Someone came barging into my room, yelling at me like the house was on fire and I had to run for my life.

Sometimes that's exactly what I'd think was happening. I'd grab a coat and run out of my room, only to find out that the emergency was simply that I might be late.

I chalked this up to the fact that CPS didn't take it too kindly when school was missed. Therefore, it was up to the foster parents to make sure the kid was up and gone in time. Who knew, maybe it wasn't like that for some? For me, heart attacks were a normal part of my morning routine.

But here, in the Adair household, things were very different.

Disturbing didn't even begin to explain what it felt like to be gently nudged awake. That feeling didn't get any better when my eyes fluttered open to see some lady was smiling down at me.

Honestly, I had no idea what to do. I just stared at her while trying to figure out if I was dreaming. It wouldn't be the first time some creepy, sweet smile haunted my subconscious.

"Good morning, miss."

*Miss?*

This girl couldn't be much older than me, and she was calling me miss?

I cocked a brow at her white and black uniform. Was she a maid? Who else would wear something like that? A stripper, maybe?

One of my foster sisters did some dancing to make a little extra money before she aged out of the system. She had something similar. Though hers was more of a booty skirt and a tiny shirt that showed a lot more cleavage.

This girl was very formal. She had her hands closed behind her back and spoke in a soft, pleasant tone. "Would you like your bed turned down?"

If she was waiting for an answer, she'd be waiting a while. I had no idea what turning down a bed meant. How did one do that? All I could picture was this small woman rolling my bed up—sleeping bag style—and storing it in the closet.

Speaking of which, I should probably check out the closet. Hadn't been in there yet. None of my clothes needed to be hung up, so I didn't really see the point. Might help if I actually unpacked them.

It just made more sense to leave them in boxes. I never knew when I was going to be moved, and there was less chance of awkward good-byes if I was ready to go.

Guess that wouldn't be happening here. Unless Charmaine had another breakdown, I was here to stay. Still wasn't sure how to take that. It felt weird to think of any place as home. Then again, it was weird to have some girl staring at me, too.

*Why was she still standing there?* "Um… Do you need something?"

"No, miss."

The longer I lay in bed watching her, the more eerie her politeness got. And I'd been around some pretty rotten people. I'd take Henry's way-too-friendly touches over this crap.

A click to the right drew my gaze to the opposite side of the room. "Did someone just go into the bathroom?"

"No." The maid smiled. "It's just you and me."

I could've sworn that door just closed. Then again, I had just woken up and my brain didn't function properly until at least my second cup of caffeine. Add in the girl staring at me…

"Would you like me to lay your clothes out for the day?"

My eyes once again darted back to the bathroom door. A shower might be nice. There wouldn't be anyone watching me in there. At least, I didn't think there would be.

I wouldn't be surprised if there were hidden cameras all over the place. Apparently, my stepbrothers lacked any sense of personal boundaries. They proved that last night with their haze-the-new-girl stunt.

*Assholes.*

As much as I wanted to hate them, I really didn't know them. Don't get me wrong, they weren't making the best impression, and I had every intention of paying them back. Especially Devlin. But the longer I thought about it, the less angry I got.

I don't suppose I'd be too happy if I were in their shoes. A foster kid coming into your house was one thing. That was a temporary situation. But when you had someone thrust into your home to permanently join your family… I could see how that would be upsetting.

"Miss? Your clothes?"

*Right, she was still there.*

"Uh… no," I said and slipped out of bed to pad over to the bathroom. "I'm good, thanks."

Uniform girl didn't say a thing when I walked by. I don't think she even looked at me. If she did sneak a peek, I didn't catch her. I did notice the snake tattooed on the bottom of her neck, though. Its beady little eyes followed me, while hers stayed fixed on some imaginary spot on the wall.

*That's not creepy at all.*

"Fucking snakes everywhere," I muttered and slipped into the bathroom while shaking off a shiver.

It could be worse. One place I stayed at had a huge Boa. That thing scared the crap out of me. Everyone insisted that he was tame and wouldn't hurt a fly, but I knew better. I saw him watching me whenever I came into the room.

At least none of the snakes here were real. That was something to be thankful for. Right about now, I'd take whatever positivity I could get.

My mouth dropped as I closed the door and spun around.

*This was my bathroom?*

I was definitely going to need a search for cameras, which would be a lot easier if there weren't so much useless space. The toilet had its own room, with a cupboard for storage, and the shower and bathtub were separate.

Although I wouldn't complain about the four-claw tub's size, or the roof of raining water in the shower. The abundance of counter space and two sinks on the other hand…

Since when did someone need more than one sink? What was I supposed to do with the other one? Wash my feet while I washed my hands? That's what the shower was for. I did like the color scheme, though. A dark jade green with black accents. I wasn't much for green, but in here it looked good.

Half the time I scoured the room for tiny lenses was spent glancing over my shoulder. Every little sound echoed off the tiles walls, making the hairs on the back of my neck rise. Even my own breath bounced back at me and vibrated through my ear. I finally understood why one of my foster sisters used to complain about the prank calls she'd gotten.

Never thought I'd miss the confinement of the closet-sized rooms I was used too, but I did. There wasn't a huge chance of finding someone hiding in a small room. Something like this, however… three people could fit in the cupboards. A thought that did nothing for the sensation causing the hairs on the back of my neck to rise.

I couldn't shake the feeling that someone was watching me. Not even after I'd searched every inch.

I pushed my jitters aside and climbed in the shower to strip. As I tossed my clothes on the floor, I paused and narrowed my eyes. I could've sworn I had white panties on. Did I even own any pink ones? I mean, I must. It wasn't like I kept track. They were just something to wear.

*Oh well.*

I shrugged it off and turned the water on.

Whatever concerns I had were washed away with the warm drops that rained down. This shower was quite possibly the best thing I'd ever felt. The spray was so relaxing, and the scent of the shampoo—cherry blossoms with an undertone of jasmine—was a treat for my nostrils.

How did I ever get by using that cheap drugstore crap?

Another bonus when I was all clean, I didn't have to leave the stall to get a towel. There was a rack that sat in a dry corner with three crisp white towels hanging off it. I was seriously considering living in these tiled walls.

Especially when I stepped out.

My heart leapt out of my chest as a pair of dark eyes zeroed in on me. I screamed and sprang back, whacking my tailbone against the corner of the stall.

"Don't hurt yourself, *Bréagán*." Devlin leaned against the counter and snickered as I rubbed my sore backside. "That's my job."

*Pause for internal groan.*

I was really starting to hate him.

"Get out," I ordered, while throwing my finger up at the door.

"No."

"What do you mean, no?"

His cold stare rolled up to mine. "I mean, no."

I wasn't quite sure how to respond to that. Invading someone's personal space was one thing, but to outright deny their privacy? How'd he even get in here? I was pretty sure I locked the door. Didn't want creepy uniformed girl to come in and offering to dry me off.

*Shit!*

I glanced down at the towel around me, then over at the pile of clothes on the floor.

When Devlin's leg stretched out, taking a long stride in my direction, it wasn't embarrassment that warmed my cheeks. I knew I had a decent body and wasn't shy normally, but the way he looked at made me feel… lesser? Judged, maybe? Like he thought I should be down on my knees, kissing the ground he walked on.

Attempting to firm my stance, I crossed my arms and said, "Why are you here?"

"I should be asking you that. This is my house."

"Yeah, well, it's mine too." I argued.

While it felt weird to call this place my home, I couldn't help but roll my shoulders back and glare at him.

*That's right, asshole. What else you got?*

Devlin stopped a few feet in front of me and curled his lip.

I curled mine back.

My childhood was spent competing in these intimidation games. I was a pro player. Or I thought I was. The longer we stood there staring at each other, the harder my heart pounded. It didn't take long before each thump slapped against my ribs and traveled down my legs.

I tried to tell myself to stand my ground. I rolled my neck and held my chin up high. But my knees were starting to weaken under his stare. This was different from what I was used to. It was intense and piercing. The kind of stare down that could be felt not only in the air, but in my bones.

My grip tightened on the towel clutched around my body. Could he see the tiny cluster of freckles on my hip? Did he know about the scar sitting under my left breast? Could Devlin feel the ghosts of healed injuries and bruises?

My eyes dipped down to the pile on the floor. Right now, my worn old pyjamas seemed like a suit of armor.

Devlin snickered and stretched his foot out, pressing his boot down on my clothes to slide them closer to him.

I couldn't stop myself from holding out my hand out and rushing forward. "Be careful with that."

That nightgown and one picture were all I had left of my father.

I realized my mistake when a smirk curled the corner of his

mouth. His foot ground into the fragile fabric. Nothing in my life had ever been harder than holding back the storm of rage brewing inside me.

Instead of tearing out his eyes like I wanted to, I cocked my hip and sighed. "Are you going to hand wash that?"

Relief poured through me as confusion knit his brows. Rule number one of new home placement. Unless you want a cherished item destroyed, never let anyone know you have an attachment to it.

"Why would I do that?"

"Well…" I rolled my eyes up to his. "It was clean."

"Uh huh." He folded his arms over his chest and kicked the nightgown towards me. "Go ahead and get dressed, then."

I glanced down and tried not to linger on the panties splayed next to his foot. "Thanks, I'm good."

Devlin's brow pulled up in a judgmental arch. "We'll see about that."

I stood there, listening to drops glide across my skin and gently drip on the floor. The soft tick, tick, tick reminded me of how exposed I was. I couldn't stop my muscles from tensing.

The way that red polo shirt was hugging Devlin's broad chest wasn't helping any. The guy was an insufferable ass, but goddamn, did he make a pair of jeans look good. I couldn't help but pull my eyes over the tribal lines crawling up the left side of his neck.

They were just as intricate and flawless as the ones inked into his arms. I didn't remember seeing those before. Then again, I was more concerned with getting away from the three assholes accosting me than I was with inspecting them.

*Was that one big tattoo, or a bunch of separate designs?*

"Are you a virgin, Sydney?"

My wide eyes snapped back to his. "What?"

"It's not a hard question." Devlin took a menacing step towards me. "Are you a virgin?"

"You can't just ask someone that."

Technically, I was. I'd done some stuff with one guy, though it never got as far as actual sex. We didn't make it past the foreplay stage.

Twelve seconds in my mouth, and he was done. Awkward wasn't a strong enough word to describe that encounter.

"Answer the question, *Bréagán.*"

"Why?" I shot him a sweet smile. "Are you going to be a good brother and give me the birds and bees talk?"

"No," he stated flatly. "I want to know if I'm going to have to waste my time teaching you how to suck cock."

My jaw dropped.

"So I'll ask you one last time. Are. You. A virgin?"

*All right. I've had enough of this.*

"If you're done playing creep…" I crossed my arms and gave him a firm huff. "I'd like to get dressed."

For a second, I thought Devlin was going to argue. Instead, he leaned back and fixed a serious expression on his face.

"Breakfast is in ten minutes."

"And I care why?"

"You didn't eat last night."

What was it with this guy? None of my foster parents cared when I ate. In fact, the less I ate, the happier they were. Food costs money, and they liked to spend as little as possible. One place even had a lock on the fridge.

"Did you poison my food or something?" It wouldn't surprise me.

Not a single spark of emotion flashed across his face. "You think I'd let you off that easy?"

*Well, that's comforting.*

"I'll give you fifteen minutes," Devlin said and strode toward the door.

It wasn't that I wasn't hungry—my stomach growled at the thought of food—it was the principal of the matter that made me argue. "Or what?"

He stopped with his hand on the door. "I take it you remember what happened last night?"

I swallowed down the lump in my throat. Wouldn't be forgetting that any time soon.

"Are you going to bring your brothers this time, too, or do you think you can handle me on your own?"

The only response I got was a quiet snicker as he left, slamming the door behind him.

*Leave it to Charmaine to marry into the asshole family.*

I took my time getting dressed, carefully going through every article of clothing I owned before settling on a light pink shirt and pair of jeans. An outfit I'd already picked out in my mind, but… Well, fuck Devlin.

I even did my makeup and curled my hair a bit. Then I threw it in a ponytail, because, again, fuck Devlin. After that, I pondered over what socks to wear. Black, white, or blue?

Black was the obvious choice. They kind of went with everything, but there was something to be said about blue. Then again, barefoot was always an option, too.

Did I mention fuck Devlin?

By the time I actually left my room, I was well past the fifteen-minute timeline he gave me. I kind of expected to find him in the hall-way, tapping his foot impatiently. He seemed like the toe-tapping type. Honestly, I'd prefer squaring off with him then embarking on another adventure of 'find that room.'

Thankfully, it didn't take too long to locate the kitchen. Mainly because Wyatt's stupid laugh rang through the house, leading me right there. I thought about avoiding my stepbrothers all together, but I'd never been one to let a bunch of dicks push me around.

So, I waltzed right in with my head held high, utterly intent on ignoring them.

That was easier said than done.

Devlin's gaze was the first to land on me. "You're five minutes late."

*Only five? Damn, I thought I took longer.*

Wyatt gave me a cocky smirk. "At least she smells better."

"Smell doesn't matter when she still looks like shit," Magnus muttered.

*Someone else just joined the 'Fuck Him' list.*

I lifted my chin and sauntered over to the coffeepot on the marble island. The three of them were enjoying their breakfast at a table next to a big bay window. The fact that Devlin was seated at the head made me snort. Did his brothers always fall in line like a bunch of puppies?

Magnus had his face buried in a newspaper while Wyatt was leaning back in a chair with one leg stretched out. Based on the mischievous gleam in his eye, I'd say he was the more likely of the two to disobey his brother's orders. Perhaps that was something I could use to my benefit?

"I don't know… Those jeans look pretty good on her." Wyatt lifted a mug to his lips and widened his smile. "I guess it's true what they say."

"And what's that?" Why did I ask that? He was only going to say some smartass remark.

"That you can find a half decent look in a thrift store."

Yep, I was right. "Is there something wrong with a thrift store?"

Wyatt shrugged. "That depends on who owned them before you."

"Why would that matter?"

"What if she had some horrible disease, like syphagonaherpaliase and didn't wear underwear?" His brow rose. "Do you want to be known as the next Typhoid Mary?"

"That's ridiculous."

Wyatt tipped his head. "Is it?"

I couldn't help but wonder if he had a point. Who did wear these jeans before me? And who the hell was Typhoid Mary?

"I wouldn't worry about it." He waved his hand and returned to his breakfast. "Girls have gone through worse to have an ass that looked that good."

My face dropped. Did he not realize we were in a room full of sharp objects? I wasn't much for violence, but in his case, I might make an acceptation.

"She's wearing too much make-up," Devlin grumbled.

Scratch that. If anyone was getting shanked, it was him. I'd even take the time to search the stainless steel appliances and pretty white cupboards to find something nice and extra painful.

"All girls wear that shit," Wyatt argued.

*Exactly.*

Besides, I didn't even have that much on. A little blush, a smidge of eyeshadow, mascara, and lip gloss. I knew girls who wore way more.

Devlin's next comment made me roll my eyes. "I don't like it."

"Oh, noooo! Devlin doesn't like my make-up." My hand flew up to my forehead in a dramatic pose. "Whatever will I do?"

He shot me a dirty look, Wyatt chuckled, and Magnus tipped his brow my way. "Okay, maybe she's not that bad."

"Well, at least one of you likes me," I muttered, then walked over to join them, choosing the farthest chair from Devlin.

"I never said I liked you," Magnus corrected.

I rolled my eyes. "My bad."

"I like you." The twinkle in Wyatt's eye had the need to put him in his place burning in the back of my mind.

Unfortunately for him, I knew when I was being baited. So, rather than engage, I chose to focus on what I wanted to eat. Food was a much more pleasant option, and everything looked more mouth-watering than boxed cereal, which I considered fine dining in most of the homes I stayed.

Wyatt wasn't going to let me get off that easily. When I reached out for a bagel, he snatched the plate away. Then did it again when I went for a scoop of scrambled eggs.

Sighing, I rolled my glare his way.

He held up the bowl of eggs. "Sorry, did you want some?"

I shot Wyatt a smile and grabbed a muffin, which was on a plate closest to me. "I'd rather have something sweet."

"Oh, yeah?" His gaze dipped down. "I bet you've got plenty of sweet things."

The prick wasn't even attempting to hide the fact that he was staring at my cleavage.

"Hey!" I snapped my fingers. "My eyes are up here."

"Don't get mad at him." Devlin popped a grape in his mouth and muttered, "You're the one who came down here looking like a slut."

I coughed, barely managing to choke down my first bite. "Excuse me?"

It wasn't like I was prancing around in a mini skirt and crop top.

He waved his hand at me and growled, "Go wash that shit off your face."

Mr. High and Mighty had his head shoved so far up his own ass that the only thing he could taste was his own shit. And he had the gall to judge me. Hell no.

"I don't take orders from you," I sang with a big smile while taking a bite of my muffin.

There was a sudden change in the air. A heaviness settled in around us so thickly that it smothered the sweetness in my mouth. The blueberries had a sudden sour tang that coursed through my veins in waves of uncomfortable tingles. It was so weird.

I rolled the food around my tongue, waiting for the taste to improve. It didn't. If I wasn't so busy glaring back at the lethal expression Devlin was giving me, I might've stopped to inspect my muffin.

The rage coming off him sent a shiver down my spine. I tried to suppress it. I managed to hold on to some composure until Magnus's chair screeched along the floor. The loud sound echoed through the cloud of doom closing in on me.

"I'm not in the mood for this shit," Magnus grumbled and left.

My mind screamed at me to follow him. I wasn't sure why I didn't. Maybe it was pride, or a lack of self-preservation. Either way, I stayed where I was, glued to my seat as Devlin braced his elbows on the table and leaned forward.

"Wash that shit off your face, or I will."

Despite the cold spike of fear setting off warning bells in my head, I couldn't back down. Guys like Devlin would take an inch and turn it into a mile.

"No."

"Last chance, *Bréagán*." His eyes darkened along with his voice. "Wash. It. Off."

The smart thing to do would've been to comply. But like Sister

Anne said at Saint Jude's Group Home for girls, That mouth is going to get you into trouble, child."

"Bite m—"

Everything on the table clattered as Devlin shot across it and seized a fistful of my hair. Next thing I knew, I was being dragged through the spilled breakfast food, kicking and screaming.

My fight ceased the instant my body flopped off the table and slammed onto the floor. A sharp stab radiated over my tailbone and up my spine, stealing my breath.

My torment didn't end there.

I was left unable to do anything but clutch at his forearm as he pulled me across the room. If the ache crawling up my back wasn't enough to remind me how useless fighting him would be, then the hard muscle flexing under my hands was.

All I could think as I was slammed down on the island's hard countertop was how Sister Anne was probably staring down at me from heaven right now, laughing her ass off.

*Screw you, you mean old bat.*

When Devlin was busy turning on the faucet, I did manage to wriggle around enough to kick him in the side. That gave me a modicum of satisfaction.

His response did not.

He wrapped his hand around my neck and squeezed. "Don't need my brothers now, do I?"

Yeah, I kind of regretted saying that.

Especially when I was gulping for air and gagging on water. The stream filled my eyes, blurring my vision. The only thing I could do when his large hand scrubbed over my face was blindly slap about.

By the time Devlin finally let me go, I was more concerned with coughing oxygen back into my lungs than anything else.

"Keep testing me, Sydney." The rough hair on his face abraded my cheek as he spoke against my ear. "I dare you."

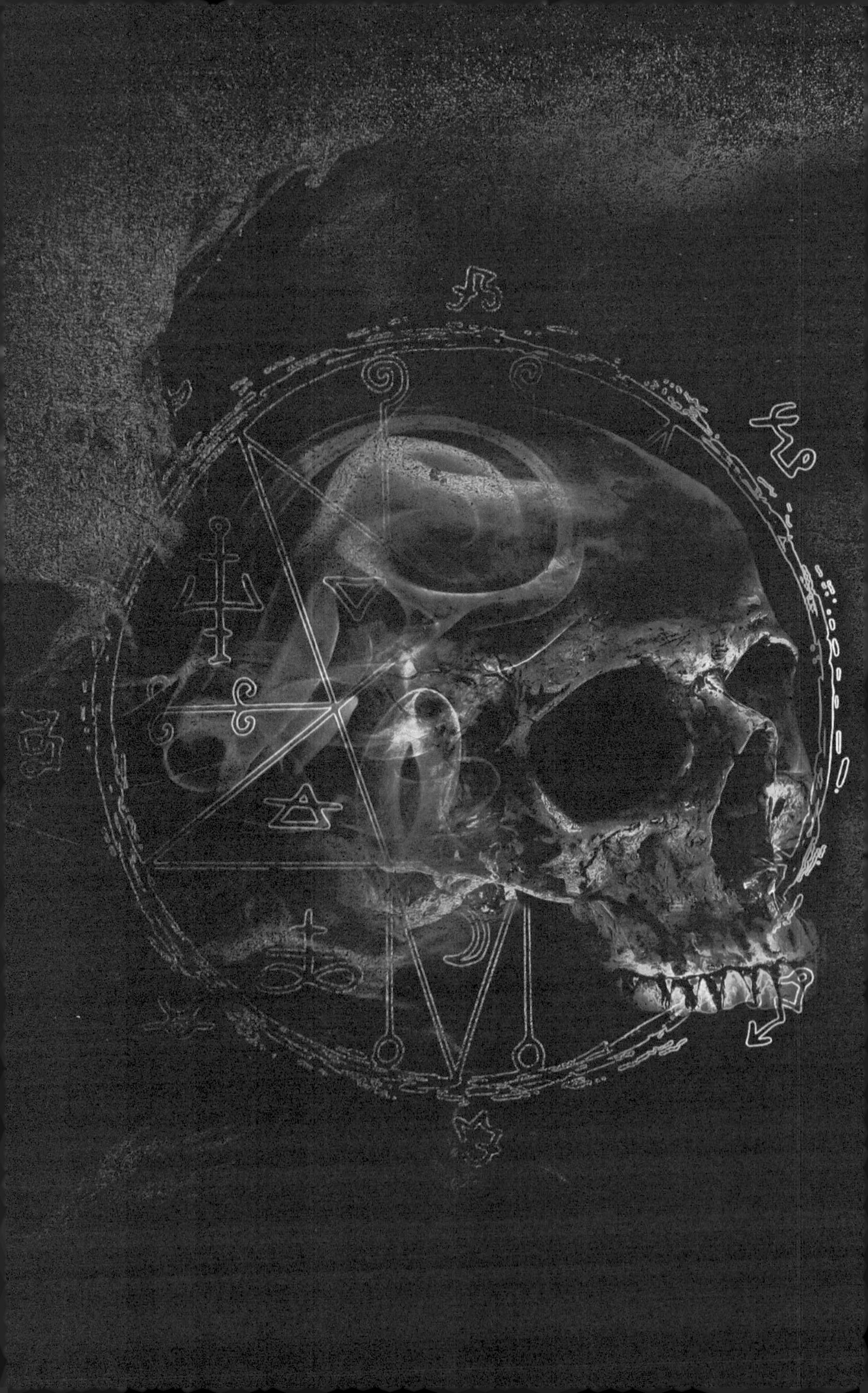

# Chapter 5



IT WAS OFFICIAL. THIS PLACE SUCKED ASS. I WANTED TO GO BACK TO Mr. Tompkins's sweaty apartment over a massage parlor. If it saved me from having to deal with the Adair boys, then I'd take his skeezy side eyes. And I meant boys, because men weren't assholes who would hold a girl's face under water.

Okay, some men were, but most of those were in jail.

Huh? Jail? There was an idea. How much time would someone get for unwanted make-up removal? In some circles, that would be considered a serious offence. And did I reapply my make-up right after? You bet your sweet ass I did. Even added some sparkles under my eyes as an extra fuck you.

Charmaine lifted her hand to touch a small flower. "Look at this. Isn't it pretty?"

"It's beautiful." I smiled down at the purple and orange petals she was gingerly smoothing her finger over.

We continued our walk down a brick path, cutting under an

archway of willow trees. I could see why Charmaine liked it in here. It took a bit for the different floral aromas to stop assailing my scenes.

It reminded me of walking into a church meeting with a bunch of older women wearing way too much perfume. Now the scent had calmed down into something soft and sweet.

I wasn't sure what a room like this would be called. Probably something pompous, like the inner sanctum of forestry. I'd go with something simpler, like the indoor greenhouse.

Though technically all greenhouses were indoors, just not smack dab in the middle of a house. Most weren't this comfortable temperature-wise, either.

Charmaine pulled me onto the small bridge and pointed down at the water below. "Look."

A smile curled my lips as a school of colorful fish swam by. Bright yellow, red, and blue scales sparkled in the light. All right, it was pretty in here. I'd give my new stepfamily that. They might have a little bit of class.

My eyes swung around the room. Okay, maybe more than a little, but that didn't cancel out the eerie factor. This entire place was made of glass that frosted when the doors shut. A private oasis in the heart of hell, with a little pond, every type of flower one could think of, and a small wooden bridge.

I'd never seen anything more misleading in my life, because the Adair household was no Garden of Eden. Yet the birds flew around singing songs as if we were in Avalon or some shit. Then again, Avalon did have man-eating dragons, so…

"It's so peaceful in here."

Charmaine wasn't wrong. All this scenery made it kind of hard to hang on to my anger and hatred. Almost as if the lush greenery sucked the negativity right out of my soul. At first, I thought it was a courtyard, but there was no sky. Just a glass view of the floor above.

Having a balcony overlooking us wasn't strange at all. I kept looking up, expecting to see someone's beady eyes staring down. Or a dark, threatening stare.

My heart nearly stopped when Charmaine jumped and clapped her hands, making the wooden planks beneath us creak. I couldn't help but glance up at the ceiling. One tiny crack in that glass dome would send a shower of shards raining down on us.

Maybe this wasn't such a peaceful room after all?

I could almost feel the scratch etching across one of the panes. Followed by tiny little clinks and screeches as the glass gave way.

"Look, Charmaine." Angus's voice cut through the haunting sounds in my ears. "Water lilies."

"Oh, my daughter would love those."

That made me cock a brow. "I'm your daughter."

Charmaine had a lot of problems, but she never once forgot who I was.

Her pupils didn't appear dilated. At least, I didn't think they did. It wasn't like I had a lot of experience in that department. I spent more time with my mother in an institution than I did at home. Would I know if she was drugged, or would sober be the abnormal Charmaine?

She stared at me, dazed for a second, and then blinked and smiled. "Of course you are. I know that."

But did she? Because I wasn't so sure. The way she was looking at me, it felt like she couldn't see me. Or she didn't think I was really here. When I was a kid, I'd hear her talking to someone. She'd say it was my dad.

I knew he was dead, but that didn't stop me from asking if I could talk to him, too. I thought she was talking to his ghost or something. When I got older, I realized that she might've actually thought he was there.

"Are you okay?" I asked, placing my palm on her arm.

"Of course, dear." She smiled and gave my hand a pat. "I'm perfectly fine."

Somehow, I didn't believe that. When was my mother ever fine? Certainly not when the infamous *they* were coming for us. It was kind of odd that she hadn't mentioned them yet. She hadn't tried to shove me in a closet either, which was a plus.

Could she really be better? Was this the blessing I'd been praying for, for years? Somehow, I couldn't see it being that easy. People like her weren't suddenly better one day. Paranoia had a way of hanging on.

My attention turned back up to the roof. The floor above had a balcony with an ornate wooden railing. I could see the tiny detailing on the ivy leaves from here. This place really was beautiful. Too bad the inhabitants were pricks. Even Angus—who was following behind us— had an aura of arrogance.

I tipped my head at him while speaking to Charmaine. "You never mentioned Angus before."

"What's that?" Her eyes widened with a little more alertness.

"He went to college with you and Dad, right?"

This time, it was Angus who cocked a brow.

"Oh… umm…"

My heart broke a little when Charmaine's face screwed up. The confused lines that crinkled her expression as she searched her memories were familiar to me.

She nodded. "Yes, I think so."

I wouldn't call that a definitive answer—not that I was expecting one—but I might've questioned her further if Angus hadn't stepped up.

"I think it's time we go have a rest, sweetheart," he said, then placed a kiss on the top of her head.

My eyes narrowed. I didn't like him infringing on our time. "She's fine."

"No, she's tired," Angus insisted.

"I am a little tired," Charmaine agreed.

Really? She wasn't helping.

I sighed. "I'll take her to lie down."

Angus's response was a firm head shake. "You know what the courts said."

Actually, I didn't. I wasn't in court when the judgment was made, but according to Perry, Charmaine wasn't allowed to be left alone with me. If they were so worried about her, then why give me back to her in the first place?

"Fine," I grumbled, knowing that there was no point in arguing.

I was the minor, legally under his control until I was nineteen.

Stupid rules. Why couldn't I live in a state where adulthood came at eighteen? Then I'd only have to wait a month.

"You should enjoy your last day of vacation," Angus said while leading *my mother* away. "Your tutor will be here tomorrow."

Tutor? "I know public schools might not be up to your standards, but that doesn't mean..."

"You're not going to school."

*What?* "Why not?"

He couldn't just pull me out of school. It was kind of a requirement.

Angus paused with his hand on the door. "Educational institutions are for the inferior. You'll be receiving private lessons from now on."

I'd met some ostentatious asses in my time, but that statement was the biggest pile of bullshit I'd ever heard. I literally didn't know what to say. Or how to act, for that matter. Agnus walked away, and I just stood there with my mouth hanging open wide enough to catch flies.

Sure, schools had their issues—some more than others—but being a teacher wasn't easy. Especially in the public system. Kids were assholes, and they were underpaid. Plus, they didn't exactly have the greatest funding.

According to one of my foster moms, secondhand textbooks and rundown classrooms didn't make for a fantastic learning environment. No wonder some teachers gave up. Maybe if the education system put more effort in...

*Wait...*

Did I just agree with Angus?

"No," I said to a bird sitting on the railing of the bridge. "I refuse to let these people influence me."

My brow knit when his little head tipped and his chest puffed out. Was this bird disagreeing with me?

"Listen here, just because I was forced to come to this place"—I wagged my finger in his direction—"doesn't mean I'm going to turn into some rich asshole."

The bright blue feathers on his tail rose as he shook his body.

"Don't give me that..." My mouth clamped shut.

*Was I seriously arguing with a bird?*

The bird let out a melodic whistle.

*Yes, yes, I was.*

"Stupid house, with its stupid people, driving me crazy," I grumbled while stomping across the bridge toward the door.

I'd be damned if I was going to let this place change me. It was nothing more than a temporary stop on my train of life. The only permanent thing here was Charmaine—who was more than willing to leave with Angus. Now that perturbed me.

She was my mother before she was his wife. Yes, she may not have been the best mother out there. I took care of her more than she did me, but she couldn't help that. Charmaine was haunted by the voices in her own mind, which was worse than being actually haunted.

At least someone could escape a ghost. There was nowhere Charmaine could go to hide from the taunts in her head.

Bet Angus didn't understand that. I wasn't even sure how long he'd known her. Had anyone bothered to do a background check on him? What if he was a serial killer? Who wanders into an asylum one day and decides to go wife shopping? It was high time I had a chat with Perry.

I pulled out my phone, prepared to dial his number, but stopped with my finger hovering over the screen. Would a call really solve anything? While Perry was a great worker, he was a stickler for the rules. Including the one about protecting minors from sensitive information.

Sighing, I slid my phone back in my pocket and continued down the hall. Guess I'd have to do my own investigation. The only question was, where to start?

Surely, someone like Angus had files or something somewhere. In my search yesterday, I'd come across a few rooms that could've been offices. They would probably be a good place to start. Well, except for one. No information was worth another trek down the suits of armor hallway.

Just thinking about that place made me shiver. Not as much as Devlin's room. I'd known him for less than twenty-four hours and wasn't at all surprised by his decorative choice. Only pure evil would sleep in a pit of snakes.

With my new quest in mind, I set out to find answers. Instead, I found confusion. All it took to get completely and utterly lost was three corner turns. My investigation quickly turned into the *'where the fuck am I'* search again.

They really needed to start handing out maps. Maybe have a kiosk in each hallway with the *you are here* symbol. Hell, I'd take crayon arrows drawn on the wall.

I spent more time trying to find something familiar than I did anything else. It wasn't all a complete loss, though. One hallway I wandered down was filled with big ornate gold-framed portraits. One of which had two familiar faces.

My parents.

I couldn't stop staring at it. There were around a dozen other people in the picture, one of whom I recognized as a younger Angus, but that wasn't what caught my attention.

Standing right beside my father was Charmaine. The clarity in her eyes stole my breath. She seemed so happy and confident. Nothing like the fragile person I grew up with.

My head tipped as I traced my finger over the smooth lines of her honey hair. How did she go from this to a someone who couldn't remember her own daughter? What happened? I couldn't help but wonder what my life would've been like if this woman raised me?

Apparently, Angus wasn't lying when he said he knew my father. I suppose that should offer me some comfort. It didn't. Because my mother wasn't always crazy.

She was a normal girl, with hopes and dreams that didn't involve paranoia. Angus had to know what changed. Or, at the very least, have some idea. And he didn't say anything. I was her daughter. There wasn't anyone else in the world more equipped to help her.

Where was he for the past seventeen years? I don't remember him helping pull her out from under the bed or forcing her to eat when all she wanted to do was hide. Where was Mr. Angus Adair when child services ripped us apart?

This man claimed to be friends with my father. Some friend.

Unless…

My eyes narrowed on the stern lines in Angus's face. Maybe he didn't want her to get better? Why else would he come back after all this time?. Charmaine was in that state-run hospital for ten years. She wouldn't have been hard to find.

"Angus, Angus," I tsked. "What are you hiding?"

"That's a loaded question."

"Jesus Christ!" I shrieked and sprang back.

A woman with deep red hair leaned against a small table down the hall, fighting back a smirk threatening to curl her lips.

"You don't have enough time to find out what Angus Adair is hiding." She leaned forward and added in an ominous whisper, "The man's soul feeds on secrets."

Does it now? *Wait a minute…*

I shook my head. "Where did you come from?"

"How impolite of me." She stepped forward with her hand held out. "I'm Fiona."

Why did people keep popping up? I'd be alone one minute, then bam, someone was there the next. The maid in my room, Devlin in the bathroom, and now this girl. Were there secret passages everywhere or something? This seemed like the kind of house that would have hidden tunnels.

Or she simply walked down a hall, and I was too focused on the picture to notice. That seemed like the more rational explanation.

I told myself to stop overreacting and accepted her handshake. "Sydney. Sorry, it's been a long day."

And by long, I meant horrible and annoying with way too many assholes and smartass birds.

"Don't worry about it." She waved her hand dismissively. "I'm sure the boys haven't made this any easier on you."

There was the understatement of the year.

"Oh, they've been a great welcoming party."

"I bet they have." Fiona snorted out a snicker. "Have they plastic wrapped your toilet yet?"

"No." Mental note, check all the toilets. "Are you their sister?"

"Oh god no. Can you imagine me related to them?"

Was I supposed to answer that?

"My father is friends with Angus, so he sent me here for school."

*How come she gets to go to school?*

"Listen, the twins are easy. Wyatt can be a little much to handle sometimes, but just compliment his hair, and you'll be fine. Their older brother, on the other hand… Have you met Devlin yet?"

Apparently, the look I gave her was the only response she needed, because the next thing I knew Fiona was hunched over, clutching her side in laughter.

"Oh, Sydney." She threw her arm around my shoulder. "I have so much to teach you."

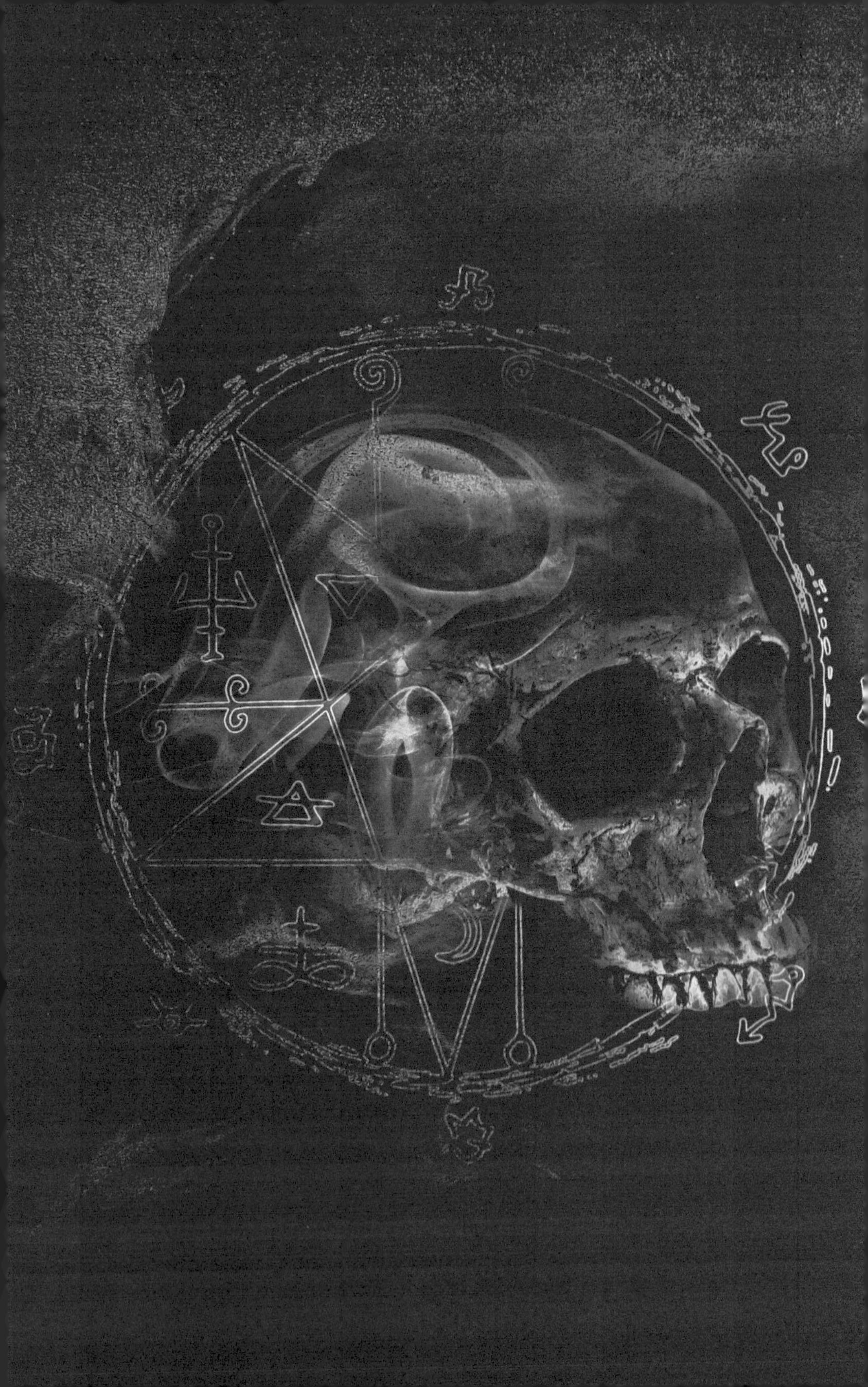

# Chapter 6

I was iffy about Fiona at first. She did just pop out of nowhere, but her philosophy that men were like boobs won me over. They were nice to look at, but no one really wanted them.

Add in the fact that Wyatt ran down the hall like a bat out of hell when he saw us coming, and Fiona was suddenly my new best friend. Anyone who could wipe the smug grin off his face was all right by me.

We spent most of the day together until she had to go. Apparently, an educational institute wasn't subpar for her. I was a little salty about that, but I looked forward to seeing her on the weekend. Wyatt may not like her, but I, however, thought she was sweet.

And she was more than forthcoming with her information about the Adair men. Magnus had a touch of OCD and couldn't stand it when something was out of place. So I stopped by his room on my way down to dinner and moved around some stuff on his dresser.

Stuffed animals creeped Wyatt out, which made me regret not keeping any of my childhood friends, and Devlin . . . Well, he was just an ass. Fiona did, however, give me a few tips on how to deal with him. One of which I was about to test out.

I stopped to readjust the top of my dress. Once I was sure my breasts were propped up nice and firm in the black cups, I pushed my way through the double doors into the dining room.

Family dinner was a formal affair, after all, and one should always dress the part. Though I doubted the tight bodice and strappy heels I wore fit the part the Adair family had in mind.

"What the fuck!?"

Well, I guess Devlin was pissed. Excellent.

If the glare on Devlin's face wasn't enough to make satisfaction fill my chest, then the sound of Wyatt choking on his drink sure was. I was going to kiss Fiona when I saw her next.

I walked right up to Devlin and pulled out an empty chair next to him.

"What the fuck do you think you're doing?"

The others may not appreciate my sex kitten look, but Wyatt did. His eyes hadn't left my cleavage. I wasn't even mad about it. If anything, I took it as a compliment, and I did have to say, I looked good.

Not only did my hair curl in perfect ringlets, but the blue flecks in my silver eyes were really glimmering. That I could contribute to the irritation openly displayed on Devlin's face.

"Oh, I'm sorry." I looked down at the plush red velvet I was about to sit on, then back up at him. "Is this someone else's spot? No one gave me the seating order."

Devlin's glare narrowed. "Do you think you're cute?"

I cocked a brow down at the breasts practically spilling out of my dress. "Cute isn't really the look I was going for."

Just when I didn't think this moment could get any better, Wyatt tipped his head. "I can almost see her nipples."

Magnus slapped the back of his head while Devlin shot him a dirty look.

Wyatt responded by flicking a forkful of potatoes at his twin. All hell broke out after that. Devlin slapped his hand down on the table and yelled at Wyatt, which spurred Magnus to come to his twin's aid and yell at Devlin that it wasn't Wyatt's fault. Meanwhile, Wyatt continued to poke both of them. It was quite possibly the greatest moment of my life.

Especially when Magnus looked at me and said, "I hope you're happy."

Yes, yes, I was.

Not that I had a chance to tell him that. They were too busy arguing to hear anything I had to say. A few fists even hit the table.

I chose to enjoy the show while I ate. Every bite was swallowed with a big smile on my face. Roast beef wasn't my favorite, but this was the best dinner I'd ever had. Then Angus had to come in and throw a wrench in my good time.

Magnus was up on the table, holding on to Devlin's arm, which was raised and ready to strike. Devlin's other fist had a firm grip on Wyatt's collar. Wyatt also had his arm ready to hit back. They all froze with one barked statement from their father.

"What's going on in here?"

I smiled up at him. "You should try the beef. It's fantastic."

His judgmental eyes fell on the cloth tightly wrapped around my chest. "I assume this is your doing?"

"Of course this is her fault," Devlin snarled. "Look at her."

"Hey." I shrugged. "I'm just here for the food."

He was the one who had a stick up his ass about meals. *Fifteen minutes until breakfast.* Asshole.

"While I respect a woman's right to dress how she wants, Devlin has a point." Angus sat down at the head of the table, spurring the boys to return to their seats. "That is not proper dinner attire."

When Devlin shot me a cocky smirk, I was tempted to slap him. Instead, I reached across the table, making sure I twisted in a way that displayed my cleavage, and snatched a biscuit.

"Sorry," I sang while taking a nice big bite. "My ballgown was at the cleaners."

Angus was obviously displeased with my attitude. Not that I cared. What was the worst thing he could do? Take away my phone and send me to my room. Good, he could have it. I didn't have any friends to text, anyway.

"I wouldn't look so smug if I were you," Magnus snarled at me. "Just because you bear the mark—"

"What mark?" Angus snapped.

The sudden silence in the room made me roll my eyes. "They're all worked up about my birthmark."

It wasn't cancerous or anything. Though I doubt they would care if it were.

"Oh, really?" Angus sat forward and eyed all three of his sons. None of whom would meet his eyes.

What the hell were they so worked up about? If I didn't know any better, I'd say they'd just got caught with their hand in the cookie jar. Except for Devlin. I could hear his teeth grinding.

"Tell me, Sydney." Angus turned his attention my way. "Is this birthmark on your right thigh?"

Why did that matter? "So what if it is?"

I don't care how proper he wanted his family to look. I wasn't getting rid of it. It was my star. Besides, Angus wasn't my dad. And even if he were, he could kiss my ass.

"I see." Angus sat back and slowly sipped on what I assumed was wine.

The only thing that could be heard after that were the clinks and clacks of dishes. It was the oddest reaction to a simple birthmark. Rich people were weird.

Whatever… They could do what they wanted. I was going to keep enjoying my food. At least that was my plan, but when I popped a forkful of the sweetest corn I'd ever had in my mouth, Angus broke the silence.

"Have you ever been raped, Sydney?"

I choked on the food in my mouth. "Pardon me?"

Where the hell did that come from?

"There are only two reasons a girl would prance around wearing something like that. They have low self-esteem. Or"—his eyes rolled up to meet mine—"they enjoy tempting fate."

I couldn't believe he'd just said that. "What I chose to wear doesn't matter."

"I beg to differ." Angus tipped his chin over my shoulder. "And I think my son would agree."

"I don't give a shit what…" All words were lost when I twisted my head and was met with the shadows darkening Devlin's expression.

Suddenly, my attire didn't seem like such a good idea. The need to cover up crawled across my skin, but I refused to give in. I didn't need permission to put on make-up or wear what I wanted.

"Maybe your son should learn how to control himself," I hissed while glaring back at Devlin.

"I couldn't agree more," Angus said.

When Devlin turned his glare onto his father, I thought the argument was shifting to them. I was wrong. Next thing I knew, my elbow was seized, and Devlin was pulling me out of the room. And what did his father do while I was being dragged away, kicking and screaming?

Absolutely nothing.

I was being manhandled by an asshole, and the only adult in the room didn't do shit other than ask someone to pass him the potatoes.

Devlin marched me out into the hall, then hauled me up over his shoulder. I fought him, of course, but just like this morning, my objections were useless.

"You can't do this," I yelled while pounding my fists on Devlin's back, which was just as hard as the rest of him. My strikes probably hurt me more than they did him.

"You did this to yourself."

"I can wear what I want." All of this because of a stupid dress. Fiona said it would piss Devlin off, but I didn't expect this.

"Like fuck you can," he barked back.

No one cared about my screams. We had to pass at least a dozen people, and not one person so much as gave us a sideways glance.

What was wrong with everyone? Did I step into the twilight zone, where everyone was a robot? Money didn't buy obedience like this. I even asked one girl for help, and she acted like she didn't hear me.

I couldn't help but think back to what Fiona had said.

*"That man's soul feeds on secrets."*

No normal father would allow this behavior. Then again, no normal man would be interested in Charmaine. Who exactly was Angus Adair?

Devlin opened a door to a dark staircase and muttered, "This would be so much easier if he'd just let me kill you."

That's when I started to get scared.

Each jarring step down into the black abyss caused my stomach to drop. I could feel the walls closing in on me. The only thing worse than the dark was snakes. I didn't like not being able to see. Anything could hide in the shadows.

"I'm sorry, okay?" I clung onto Devlin's shirt and buried my face in his back. "I won't wear the dress again."

"It's too late for that."

This wasn't a game anymore. He had to feel me shaking. "Please, Devlin."

His shoulders lifted with a sigh, and for half a second I thought he might take pity on me. But mercy wasn't in Devlin's vocabulary. He did put me down, though. I was lifted off his shoulder and placed on my feet.

The coolness of cement traveled up my toes and into my calves, which was when I realized my shoes were gone. More than likely kicked off in my fight.

Then he turned on a light, and I immediately wished for the blissful ignorance of darkness to return. This room wasn't a room. It was a dungeon, complete with a cage and manacles hooked into the stone walls.

Who the hell had child services given me to? The Manson family? What kind of person had a dungeon in their house? I needed to get out of here. I needed to get Charmaine out of here.

Devlin's shadow covered me, hiding the small touch of light I had. "Give me your hands."

Licking my lips, I looked up at the stern lines etched into his forehead. Moisture carried musty scents up my nose with every breath I took. I could taste the earth and feel coolness creep into my bones. This place was what I imagined death would feel like. Cold and alone, with nothing but dirt and stone around me.

"I don't have all day, *Bréagán*." This time Devlin held out his palms and waited for me to obey.

My gaze swung from his open hands, then up to the glint in his eyes. I didn't like the way he was staring at me. Like he wouldn't just devour me, he'd enjoy every bit of my destruction. Even that I could deal with.

This wasn't my first rodeo with an angry asshole. The hint of something darker behind all that hate, however… Now that gave me pause.

Impatience filled the air as Devlin cleared his throat. Arrogant prick really did expect me to do what he said, but I wasn't a puppy for him to order around.

"Go fuck yourself, Devlin," I snarled and moved to push my way past.

His little dungeon scare tactics weren't going to work on me. I would go where I wanted, with the clothing I picked out, any time I pleased, and there was fuck-all he could do to stop me. At least that's what I told myself.

The ball of his palm thrust against my shoulder, knocking me back into the wall. When the hard stone scraped against my back, I was suddenly thankful for the loss of my shoes. I barely managed to keep my footing as it was. There'd have been no chance with heels on.

And what did Devlin do while I was tripping over my own feet? He moved in like a predator and slapped his hand on the wall above my head.

"Last chance, Sydney." His head tipped down at me "Give me your hands."

"Why?" was the only word I could force out.

Ever had that sensation where your body was there but your mind wasn't? That's where I was. Stuck in some weird suspended state of tingles while I stared at him. His full, thick lips looked so soft and touchable that I couldn't stop staring.

Not even when he barked out, "Because I fucking said so!"

"You smell good."

Devlin arched a brow, making mine knit.

*Why did I just say that?*

Sure, he smelled good, all masculine and spicy, but that was beside the point. The last thing he needed was an ego boost.

"Compared to the mold that's probably down here, a bag of shit would smell good."

Almost instantly, the slow clap started in the back of my head.

*Good save, Syd. Why don't you say something else stupid?*

Which was exactly what I planned to do until his nostrils flared.

"Did you just smell me?"

"No," Devlin insisted, but I noticed the way his pupils flared.

"Yes, you did."

"No, I didn't," he snarled back. "Why the fuck would I smell you?"

That was a good question. Why the fuck would he smell me? The man hated me.

"Ah ha!" I exclaimed when his eyes dipped down for a fraction of a second. "You just looked at my boobs."

Devlin rolled his eyes and snorted. "Don't flatter yourself."

"Don't try to deny it," I sang. "I saw you."

The next thing I knew, I was being held back against the wall with his hand around my neck.

"You're the one that has them hanging out like a goddamn whore," he spat. "What the fuck did you think was going to happen?"

He could hate me all he wanted, but I was so done with his bullshit. "Fuck you, Devlin."

Anger pulsed through his fingers as they tightened around my throat.

"Dress like a slut, and I'll treat you like one." My pulse picked up as Devlin stepped in, pressing his body up against mine.

I couldn't help but glance over to a corner where various whips and other instruments hung. He was just messing with me, right? People didn't whip people. At least not as punishment.

The way Devlin stood there, looming over me with his shoulders rolled back, made me reconsider that thought. Other people might not do something like that, but I didn't think he'd have a problem with it. Devlin Adair wanted to hurt me.

"You don't scare me." Maybe if I stood my ground, he'd back down.

I wasn't that lucky.

"Yes, I do."

It was time for another tactic. "I guess I'll have to call child services."

There were bonuses to being a foster child. Such as the protection of someone like Perry.

"Can't call anyone if you're dead," he leaned in and growled in my ear. "And what would happen to your mother, then?"

He did not just go there.

Determination rolled through me. "Leave Charmaine alone."

A twinkle sparked in his eye as a smirk pulled on the corner of his mouth. That's when I realized if I wasn't careful, Charmaine might pay for my mistake. And I highly doubted her so-called husband would do anything about it. I was all she had, and I pretty much just laid her out on a silver platter.

I could already see the wheels turning in Devlin's head. If he treated me like this, what would he do to my mother? Charmaine couldn't handle that. She could barely handle getting out of bed. Maybe it wasn't too late. All I had to do was distract him from his current thought. That couldn't be too hard.

I don't know why I did what I did, but before I could think about it, I was up on my tiptoes, pressing my mouth to Devlin's. It was a quick kiss. Not even long enough to be considered a peck, yet it shocked him just as much as it did me.

A tingle I couldn't shake away warmed across my lips. I could still feel his mouth on mine. The fleeting touch lingered as we stood there staring at each other.

Devlin's brow knit, deepening the lines of anger in his forehead. I watched his forearm flex, jaw tick, and got ready for what was about to come. Nothing could've prepared me for what happened.

I opened my mouth but forgot what I was going to say when Devlin pushed me back against the wall and slammed his mouth down on mine. This kiss wasn't quick. Nor was it a soft touch.

It was feral and hungry and full of rage. Devlin's mouth moved against mine in a demanding manner that I couldn't resist. Despite what my mind was saying, my body gave in. I whimpered and parted my lips.

One second of his tongue on mine was all I got before the kiss was over, replaced by the tight hold constricting around my throat.

"The next time you touch me," Devlin hissed in my ear. "I'll break your fucking hand."

And then he was gone. Leaving me alone to wonder what the fuck just happened?

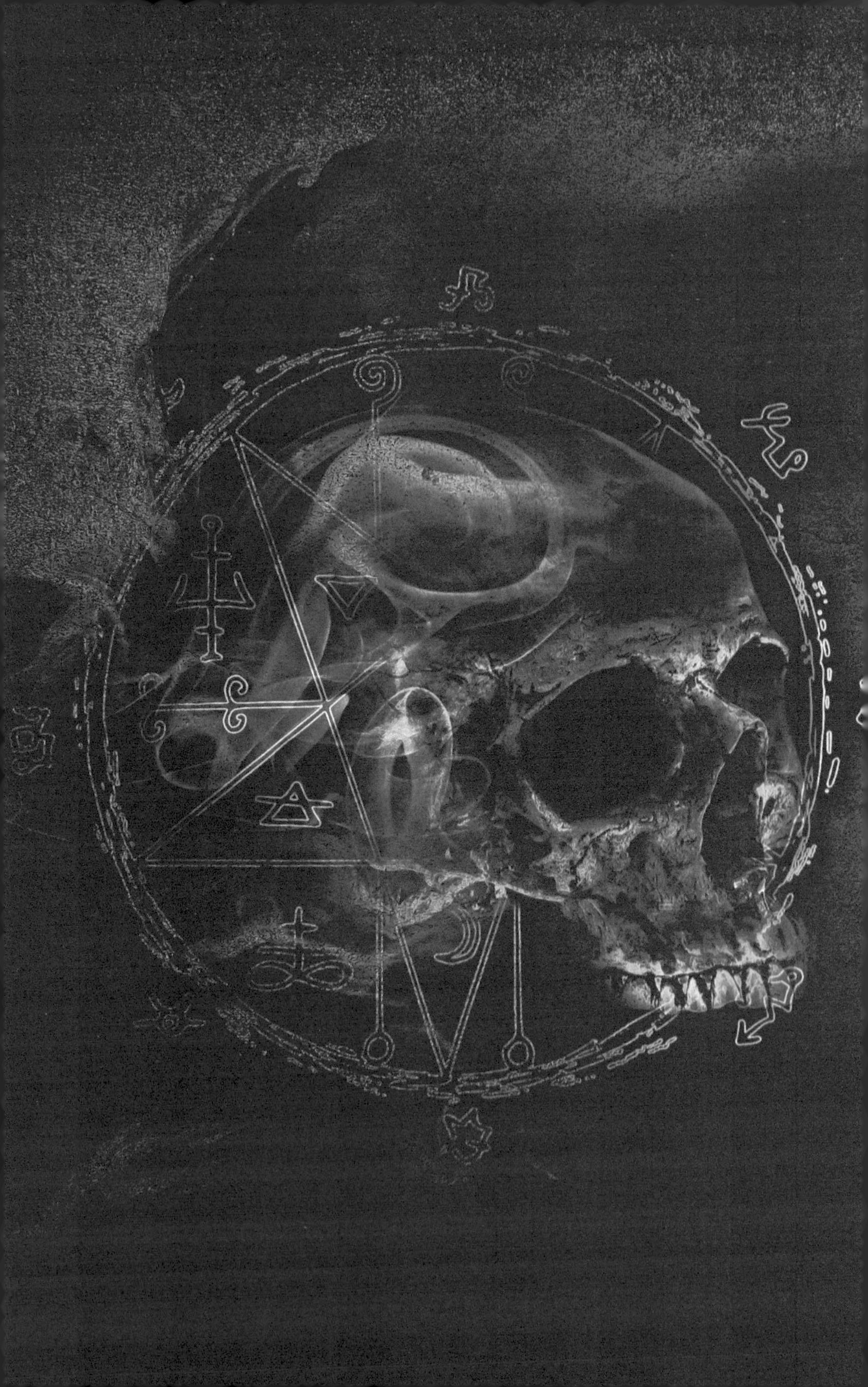

# Chapter 7



Foster care was full of all kinds of fun experiences other families didn't encounter. Like meeting new people and understanding that they didn't have your best interests in mind. Or how to pack light because you never knew when you were going to move.

But I gotta say, my favorite experience so far was being locked in a dungeon. Just when I didn't think my welcome into the Adair household could get any better, Devlin showed me what a cherry on top of a fully fermented and iced shit cake looked like.

Fortunately for me, that wasn't my first time being locked in a room. It wasn't even my fifth. There was one home where I knew every inch of my room better than I did the closet Charmaine stuck me in. Solitary confinement was just another day for me. Hell, sometimes I preferred it.

Not many ten-year-olds were given the gift of self-reflection. Besides, when else would I have had the time to teach myself how to pick a lock?

That was something I was sure Devlin didn't expect. Otherwise, he would've searched me for hidden things, like, say, a set of self-made lock picks tucked in my hair.

The Adair dungeon had a decent lock, but I still cracked that sucker in under ten minutes. I came bursting out of there, ready to kick ass, with a whip in my hand. Angus and Devlin were nowhere to be found.

I did scare the hell out of one of the maids, though.

On a side note, movies lied. Whips were not easy to handle. I think I hit myself more than I did the floor. And that shit hurt.

So, I decided to put that weapon of self-destruction away and spent the rest of the night making unanswered calls to Perry. Based on the text I was currently staring at, I'd say he got my many angry messages.

Perry: You need to calm down Sydney.

I shook my head. No wonder Perry was single. When in the history of women have the words "calm down" ever worked?

Me: I am calm.

I managed to get up, shower, get dressed, and eat breakfast without killing anyone. Considering how my night went, I'd say I was doing pretty good. Mind you, it probably helped that no one was in the kitchen when I got something to eat. Devlin might've found out what it felt like to have a spoon shoved up his ass.

Perry: You didn't sound very calm.

That was a fair point, but…

Me: Being locked in DUNGEON will do that to someone.

Perry: Stop exaggerating.

> Me: When have you ever known me to exaggerate or complain?

Most of the time, Perry had to pry information out of me.

> Perry: What do you expect me to do? You're technically not in the system anymore.

> Me: But you can still make visits…

I did my research.

> Perry: All right, I'll come by tomorrow afternoon, but I'm sure you're just overreacting.

I could practically hear the sigh with that text. Though I didn't know what he was complaining about. A visit was a much better option. After all, I was very adept at badgering someone—mainly Perry—with spam calls and texts.

> Me: See you tomorrow.

We'll see how much he thought I was overreacting when I showed him what the Adairs were hiding in their basement. In the meantime, I could waste my time in Angus's version of school, which consisted of me meeting the teacher in the library. Meaning I had to play another round of find that room.

Yay.

I could ask for directions—I heard the twins earlier in their rooms—but that wouldn't accomplish anything. Magnus might give me a grunt, and yesterday, when I asked Wyatt where Charmaine's bedroom was, he told me I should stroke his compass and unzipped his pants.

The staff in this place was just as useless. Every time I tried to talk to one of them, they just stared at me. I was seriously starting to wonder if they got docked pay when they spoke.

That was okay, because I had a plan to help with my getting lost problem. If I mapped the hallways I walked down, then I could familiarize myself with that part of the house. The next day I could work on another part and so on.

That way, if Perry didn't pull me out of here, I'd at least know my way around and maybe keep in mind a few places to avoid. Like, say, a hallway of armored men and a dungeon.

Mapping should've been an easy task. I had some skills. I could dance, was pretty decent at math, and I had an abnormally green thumb. Anyone could give me a dying plant, and I'd bring that son of a bitch back to life. Goldfish not so much.

Fred, the lightning swimmer, lasted about three days. Ignoring assholes used to be on my list of skills until I moved here. Though I would argue that Devlin jumped right over the asshole category and moved into fuckface territory. Map making, however… I was definitely lacking in that area.

By the time I found the library—which only took about an hour—I had a map that the greatest deciphers in the world wouldn't be able to decode. It looked like some kind of smashed carrot sitting on Rhode Island with a mug of beer. It was safe to say the mystery of my low grades in geography was solved.

Sighing, I crumpled up the piece of paper and looked at the closed double doors in front of me. There were large glass panes stretching from the top of each door and to the middle. I thought I'd see someone standing inside waiting for me, but I didn't.

The only thing I could see were giant shelves lined with books. They seemed endless, and when I pushed my way inside, it didn't get any better. The silence was almost as endless as the tomes surrounding me.

While this room would be a reader's paradise, for me, it was yet another maze I had to navigate. And an eerie one at that. My footsteps echoed so loudly that I half expected to round a corner and see the librarian from my old school tapping her foot.

Ms. Kitsch's tightly annoyed expression haunted my nightmares. Even if I were a reader, I would've opted for the gangs and public library over that woman. Though the more I wandered around, the more I kind of wished she were here. Or someone who knew their way around.

It was kind of like being lost in some eerie version of a forest. Except the trees were dead, skinned, and written on. Even the vast dome roof depicting a night sky full of stars loomed down on me. Mostly because I didn't recognize any of the constellations.

If it weren't for the scent of old paper rolling through the air, I might've felt like I was trapped under another world's sky. Wyatt and his compass of wonder suddenly didn't seem like a bad option.

Luckily, I didn't have to go down that road because Devlin decided to help me steer my way through the various tomes. Or his voice did. I heard his deep tone coming from the right on the other side of a row of first editions.

My so-called stepbrother wasn't high on my list of people to see, but his face was better than being trapped in the forest of tree carcasses. Besides, I was excited to find out how hard it would be to shove a book up someone's ass. School was all about learning, after all.

"I don't give a shit," Devlin growled. "This wasn't the plan."

I had no clue who pissed in his cornflakes, but someone should give them a medal.

The next voice was deeper than Devlin's, with a gravelly undertone. "The plans have changed."

*One high five coming up for gravelly undertone guy.*

"How can you be okay with this?" Devlin asked.

Gravely undertone guy chuckled. "The irony."

Why did his voice seem familiar? I was sure I heard it before, but where? Devlin wasn't talking to either of the twins or his father. It could be one of the staff, I guess. I'd seen so many people wandering around this place that I lost count an hour after arriving.

"This shit isn't funny," Devlin growled.

"It kind of is," the other guy argued, and I couldn't help but agree with him. Anything that got Devlin that upset was hilarious. "You practically threw Rook on that plane to complete his triad, and now look at you."

There was that name again. Who the hell was Rook?

"Maybe he was on to something," Devlin said.

"I never thought I'd see the day when you agreed with your brother."

Great, there was another Adair male. Fuck my life. Then again, if Devlin didn't get along with him, he might not be that bad. Wonder where I could find this Rook.

"I don't give a shit," Devlin grumbled. "I'm not doing it."

The second man responded with, "you don't have a choice."

"Yes, I do. I could get rid of the problem."

What problem had him so worked up, and could I make it worse?

"Or you could stop whining like a little bitch."

I liked this guy. He may have just replaced Fiona in the best friend category.

"I hate her." Devlin growled so deep that there was no mistaking who he was referring to.

That was okay. I hated him too. In fact, I don't think I loathed anyone as much as I did Devlin, and I used to live with triplet toddlers who survived on a diet of sugar.

"Don't worry," the other guy sang. "That won't be a problem for long."

"What did you do?"

What indeed? I was curious. Even stopped behind a shelf so I could continue eavesdropping. That is until the other guy spoke again.

"Same thing I'm going to do to her."

*And that's my cue.*

"No one is doing shit to me," I snarled and stepped around the shelf.

My intent was to put both those assholes in their place. Instead, I ended up choking on my own words as I stopped cold. There'd been plenty of times when I felt out of place. Fitting in wasn't my strong suit. It never bothered me.

Why would I want to be like everyone else? But right now, I knew exactly what people meant when they said stuck out like a sore thumb. Except, my thumb wasn't just sore, it was broken, mangled, and twisted in an unnatural way.

Despite being an asshole, Devlin had the whole hot, brooding, dangerous thing going on, and the guy standing beside him… He gave a new meaning to the term playboy. Charm oozed off him, while the twinkle in his light green eyes promised all kinds of bad things. Add in his tousled sandy hair and well-sculpted and tanned form, and any girl would be screwed.

He was the kind of guy girls knew they should stay away from but flocked to, regardless. Then probably thank him for using them. Hell, he was just looking at me, and I was ready to thank him.

I never felt more out of my league than I did in that moment. There I was, in front of two Greek gods with a beanie on my head because I barely took the time to run a brush through my hair. And don't even get me started on my clothes.

The ratty jeans I was wearing had a hole in the left knee, and my black t-shirt said "Eat me." Talk about embarrassment, which I might've had more time to dwell on if Devlin hadn't opened his mouth.

"At least you didn't paint your face like a whore today."

*Well, there goes that illusion.*

I could taste the animosity in my mouth when I smacked my lips together. "Don't worry, there's still time."

If Devlin thought my look last night was bad, just wait until I took the time to fully explore the possibilities of glitter.

"Don't be such a dick." The other guy smacked Devlin's arm, then shot me a smirk. "I think she's hot."

*Did he just call me hot?*

"Uh huh?"

My gaze narrowed. What was his game? Everyone in this house had one, and I doubted he was the exception.

He chuckled at my response. "You're a suspicious one."

"I can't imagine why," I hissed while glaring at Devlin. "Everyone's been so welcoming."

Devlin rolled his eyes. "It hasn't been that bad."

"You locked me in a dungeon!"

"You got out."

Really? That was his response. "And what if I didn't? Would you have just left me there to die?"

Of course, he would've. Bastard.

Devlin shrugged. "Probably."

That's it.

I snatched one of the tomes off a nearby shelf. It was time to find out how much force it would take to shove a book up someone's ass.

Devlin's brow rose. "And what do you think you're going to do with that?"

"I thought I'd start with a light beating,." I growled while glancing down at the hardcover in my hand.

*The Art of War* seemed pretty fitting to me.

"I like her." The other guy snickered. "She's got spunk."

He was about to find out how much spunk I had. "Don't worry, you'll get your turn."

As soon as I was done with Devlin, I'd smack that stupid sparkle right out of his eyes.

"Is that any way to talk to your teacher?"

He was kidding, right? "You're my teacher?"

This guy couldn't be what Angus deemed as higher learning.

"That's right." A smirk tugged at the corner of his mouth as he leaned back against a table behind him and crossed his ankles. "You can call me Mr. Kelly."

"What are you, twelve?"

I'd have been better off at public school. At least the teachers there didn't stare at me like they could see through my clothes. Well, most of them didn't.

"I'd be nice to him if I were you, *Bréagán*." Devlin warned. "Reese is the only thing standing between you and a dirt nap."

Oh, so this was Reese. That explained why his voice was familiar.

"I'm sorry. Please forgive my attitude." I stepped forward and held out my hand. "Devlin has told me so much about you."

Like how he was his friend who liked to evaluate women based on their oral skills. And how could I forget the *I'd slit your throat if it wasn't for Reese* comment?

Reese smiled and reached out to take my hand. The warming sensation that floated through my palm wasn't enough to detour me from my goal. My other arm swung through the air, cracking the book I held off the side of Reese's face.

I smiled at Devlin. "How's that for nice?" Then I stormed out.

Angus and I were about to have a serious talk on his choice of educator.

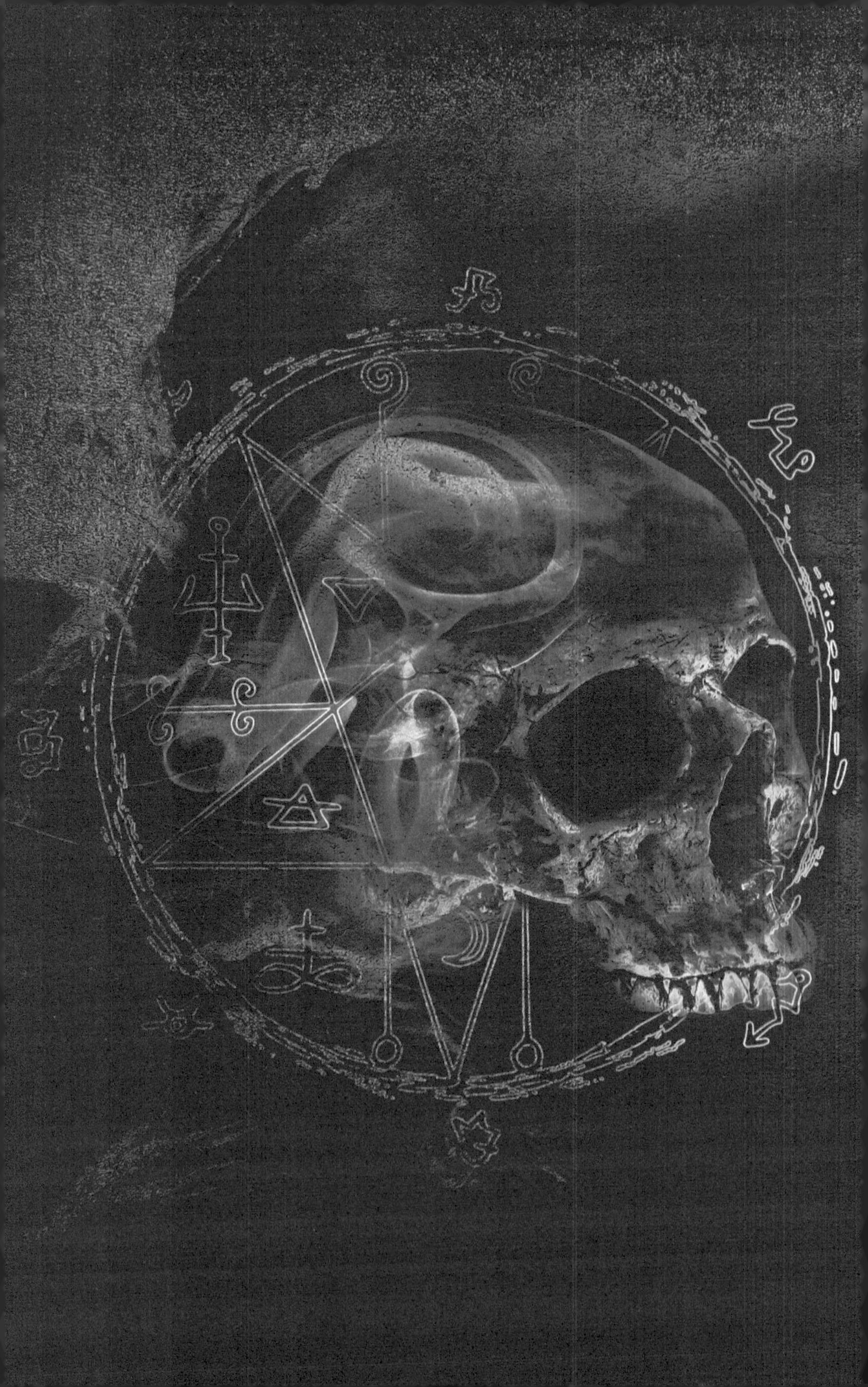

# Chapter 8

Growing up in the system taught me two things: How to survive and how to argue my point. I was pretty adept at both. Or at least that's what I thought until I barged into Angus's office.

He didn't just out-logic me, he had paperwork to back it up. Whenever I tried to argue Reese's inability, Angus would throw a file at me. Ten minutes later, and even I was willing to admit that Reese was more than qualified to handle my lessons.

The man had more degrees than I had hair clips, and that was saying a lot. I'd been collecting them since I was seven. Why I felt drawn to sparkly little trinkets, I had no idea. I never wore any of them. I just liked having them.

Instead of having tea parties with stuff animals, I had traffic jams with plastic bugs and bows. While it wasn't the most normal thing to do, I could argue that hair clips were more useful. Couldn't pick a lock with a stuffed animal.

*Speaking of picking locks...*

My gaze shifted over to a large black filing cabinet in the corner. It wasn't the small silver keyhole in the top right corner that caught my attention. It was the portrait of Angus hanging above it. Etched into the bottom of the golden frame was the same phrase Devlin had in his room. *Mors vincit omnia.*

"Is there something else I can help you with?" Angus shifted, making his leather chair creak as he tucked Reese's file back in his desk.

I shook my head. "No."

What other information did he have in that drawer? Did he have files on other people, like, say, his kids or Charmaine? The picture I found proved that Angus knew something. Charmaine had never looked at me with that much clarity. Could the answers to her condition be inside that desk?

"I trust your reservations about Reese are satisfied then?"

"I suppose."

Satisfied was a bit strong. I wouldn't hit Reese with another book, but I also wouldn't apologize for doing it the first time. He could thank his friend Devlin for that.

My eyes once again wandered back to the corner. "It's kind of tacky to have a self-portrait in your office, don't you think?"

I'd met some stuck-up people in my time, but Angus took the cake. He didn't even bother to give me a simple grunt of acknowledgment before turning his attention to the papers on his desk. Can't say I was surprised.

All it would take to see how far the stick was shoved up his ass was one look at the ebony furniture occupying his office. Which, by the way, was the one room that was easy to find in this godforsaken house.

That could have something to do with the brass nameplate on the door, but I preferred to take it as a win. For once, I didn't get lost.

How sad was that? My crowning achievement since coming here was finding a room. God forbid I ever went camping. I'd be the girl who starved to death in the middle of the forest while the search party was less than twenty feet away.

"What does that phrase mean?" I wasn't sure why I asked that. I certainly didn't expect him to answer. But he did.

"Death conquers all."

Who the hell would want that in their office? Or bedroom? As morbid as it was, the old electric chair in Devlin's room was just for decoration. He was an ass, but that didn't mean he'd actually hurt someone, right?

I looked around the room. The fancy crown molding and dark hardwood floors screamed one thing. Opulence. Which led me to a question that had been picking at the back of my mind since I arrived. What did Angus do for work? Where did the Adairs get their money? It was kind of important information to have.

Some boring corporate job was one thing, but if the source of their income was more nefarious... Well, that required a whole different skill set to work with. One of my foster fathers was a drug dealer, and not a small time one.

That was when I learned the true meaning of being seen and not heard. People who thrived in the underbelly of society didn't have a problem hurting someone. Disappearances happened all the time in their world, which, considering Devlin's threats, didn't bode well for me.

I tipped my head back to Angus. "What do you do for work?"

"I do many things."

Well, that cleared everything up. Could he possibly have come up with a vaguer answer?

"Such as?" I clarified.

"Such as paperwork, which I need to get back to." Angus cleared his throat and rolled his eyes up to me. "So, unless there's something else..."

I knew a rhetorical question when I heard one. Angus couldn't care less what I had to say. Fine with me. Anything he had to say would probably be a lie. I'd get more information on my own.

"Have a good day," I sang and walked out while glancing back at the filing cabinet.

I'd be seeing that later. In the meantime, I'd hide out in my room. Pretty school was done for the day. Assaulting the teacher wasn't a great start, but, hey, now I had time to make a plan. It wasn't like I could just walk into his office. Or could I?

I did live here, so it wasn't like I'd seem out of place. There was nothing wrong with a girl looking for her stepdad. It was a perfectly normal thing to do, which was more than I could say for my room. One step through the door, and I knew something was off.

Everything looked right, yet it didn't. Little things were off. Like the corner of my bedspread was flipped up, and my charger was unplugged. Someone had been in here, and it wasn't creepy, morning sunshine girl.

She left this place immaculate. It was disturbing how good at her job she was. My pyjamas barely had time to touch the floor before they were put in the hamper.

I scanned the area for other signs and stopped when my eyes landed on the dresser across the room. The top right drawer was pulled out. Not much, but enough that I could see the edge poking out. Why would anyone be interested in my underwear?

That question was answered when I walked over to inspect it. The drawer was empty.

My face dropped as a sigh brushed past my lips. Did someone seriously come in here and panty raid me? No, not someone.

I felt my jaw clench as I twisted my neck to look out my open door to the one across the hall. Fucking Wyatt. Let's see how funny he thought he was when the doctor was in the middle of a testicle retrieval surgery.

I charged across the hall, kicked open his door, and immediately regretted my actions.

Wyatt was on his bed, naked, with his dick in his hand.

And the asshole didn't stop. He just smiled at me and sang, "Hey, sis."

"Jesus Christ!" My hand flew up to shield my view. "Put that thing away."

What was his response? "You're the one who barged in here."

Most guys would jump up and attempt to hide what they were

doing. Not Wyatt. Based on the clapping sounds assailing my ears, he didn't even slow down. I really needed to get out of here.

"Ever heard of modesty?"

"Ever heard of knocking?"

Okay, he may have a point, but I wouldn't have had to come in here if he didn't steal all my panties.

I held out my other hand and demanded, "Give me my underwear."

Why I thought I'd be able to carry an entire drawer's contents in one hand, I had no idea. I sure as hell wasn't dropping my other arm, though. I got enough of my stepbrother's nakedness in the album I'd found.

"What kind of panties are we talking about?"

Oh my god. "It doesn't matter what kind."

"I beg to differ. Lace might look good on your ass, but they're rough on my dick. Especially when I get a really good jerk going."

I don't know if he grunted to reiterate his point or if this conversation was getting him off. Either way, I was done with his shit.

"I'm serious, Wyatt. Give them back now!"

"Sure thing. Toss them over here. I'll finish up quick." The slapping sounds picked up speed. "And hand them back."

Was he seriously playing dumb right now?

"I know you took them."

"Took what?"

*This mother...* "My underwear!"

The sounds he was making made me seriously reconsider whether or not I actually wanted them back. It might be safer to buy new ones.

"Why would I take your panties?"

"I don't know." He should be asking himself that question. "You're the genius who decided to pull a panty raid."

"Okay, first off, I'm not eleven."

That was debatable.

"And do you think I'd be using my hand right now if I had a bunch of panties?"

Eww. He did have a point, though. There was a reason I carefully stepped over all the clothes littering his floor. Let's just say that album I found wasn't just naked poses. That didn't mean he wasn't lying.

"Just give them…" I made the mistake of dropping my hand to glare at him.

I'd never get the image of his arm pumping out of my mind. And because fate really hated me, Devlin chose that moment to come waltzing out of his room.

When he stopped and crossed his arms, there were plenty of ways I could've handled the situation. Glare back at him, puff my chest out, or something along those lines. Anything would've been better than the guilty way I threw my hand back up to shield my eyes.

He arched a brow and leaned over to peek around me, igniting the slow clap in the back of my mind.

Devlin's face darkened the instant he saw what his brother was doing. "What the fuck are you doing?"

His eyes met mine, and I started questioning every decision I'd made in my life. If I had taken that piece of candy from the stranger in the park, then maybe I would be in a different place. Somewhere dark and cold, where I wouldn't have to see the rage tugging on the corner of Devlin's mouth.

"I asked you a question, *Bréagán*."

I opened my mouth to speak, then shut it before anything could come out. This wasn't an easy situation to explain away. How did one justify standing in a room while someone masturbated? No matter what I said, it would sound wrong.

*I just want my panties back?*

Something told me that wasn't going to go over very well. I could try to tell him what his brother did, and I might've if Wyatt hadn't opened his mouth.

"Don't fault her for enjoying the show."

*Yup, and there's the final nail in my coffin.*

I could literally hear the hammer banging down to seal me in the dark.

The fact that I found myself slammed back against the wall with a hand around my throat didn't scare me. I kind of expected something like that. The black look on his face, however… that did make me shiver.

"Give me one good reason why I shouldn't slap the shit out of you."

His large body blocked out the light, causing shadows to dance on the wall behind me as I lifted my chin and looked up. "I'm a girl."

It was worth a shot.

"Don't get cute with me." The shadows darkened as he leaned in to growl in my ear. "You're lucky I don't snap your neck. I just caught you watching my brother jerk off."

I wasn't watching him. I happened to walk in on him. There was a difference. That's when it occurred to me that Devlin had no right to be mad. What I did was none of his business.

I could prance around this house naked, and there wasn't a goddamn thing he could do about it. Devlin Adair didn't own me.

"Get off me," I snarled while trying to shove him away. It was, of course, useless. I couldn't even budge Devlin.

The tightening of his fingers around my throat only spurred on my anger. "Are you trying to piss me off?"

Piss him off? I wasn't the one glaring at people like I wanted to destroy them. But if he wanted me to piss him off, I could do that.

"You know what, Devlin? I have nothing to explain to you." Not that I could if I wanted to. "You don't own me. I can watch who and what I want, when I want."

"Yeah, you can!" Wyatt yelled from in the room.

"Shut the fuck up, Wyatt!" Devlin barked back at him while keeping his glare on me. "This has nothing to do with you."

"Ah, I believe it does. She left me hanging here waiting for panties."

Devlin's brow rose.

Yeah, okay, that sounded bad. "It's not what you think."

"And what do I think it is, Sydney?"

"I have no interest in your brother." Why would I? "He has a naked photo album of himself."

Apparently, this was the day for sticking my foot in my mouth. A thought that occurred to me just as Devlin's tone deepened. "How do you know he has a naked album?"

I took a second to eye Devlin up while I thought about kissing him again. That seemed to work last time. And he did smell good. Like really good. I could almost taste him on the tip of my tongue.

*No, stop it, Sydney.*

I pulled my eyes off his lips and focused on his chest, which didn't help at all. Instead of staring at the softness of his lips, I was mesmerized by the hard ridges under his shirt.

Devlin gave my neck a little shake. "Stop staring at me like that."

"I'm not staring at you." I totally was.

I couldn't stop watching his chest expand with each breath and wondering how it would feel pressed up against me.

*Wait… that wasn't right. Why was I thinking that?*

Devlin was a dick. Worse than a dick! He was an asshat. An asshat full of thick, touchable hair and firm muscles. I wanted to feel them. Even lifted my hand to do so before I stopped myself. What the hell was I doing?

"I think something's wrong with me."

"Finally, something we can agree on," Devlin rumbled while trickling his hand down my side.

The way his palm caressed my curves shouldn't have felt as good as it did. And I wasn't the only who seemed disturbed. Devlin's brows knit as his eyes watched his hand move over me. My breath hitched when his fingers dug into my hip. The way his forearm flexed, it was almost like he was trying to pull away.

My mind screamed to a stop when I sighed and leaned in a little closer to him. "Stop touching me."

"Can't." Was the only word that left his mouth.

Then, just like that, he seemed to snap out of it. Devlin's lips curled up in a snarl as he stepped away, giving me enough room to compose myself.

*What the hell was that?*

My confusion only grew when Devlin growled, "I'm going to fucking kill Reese."

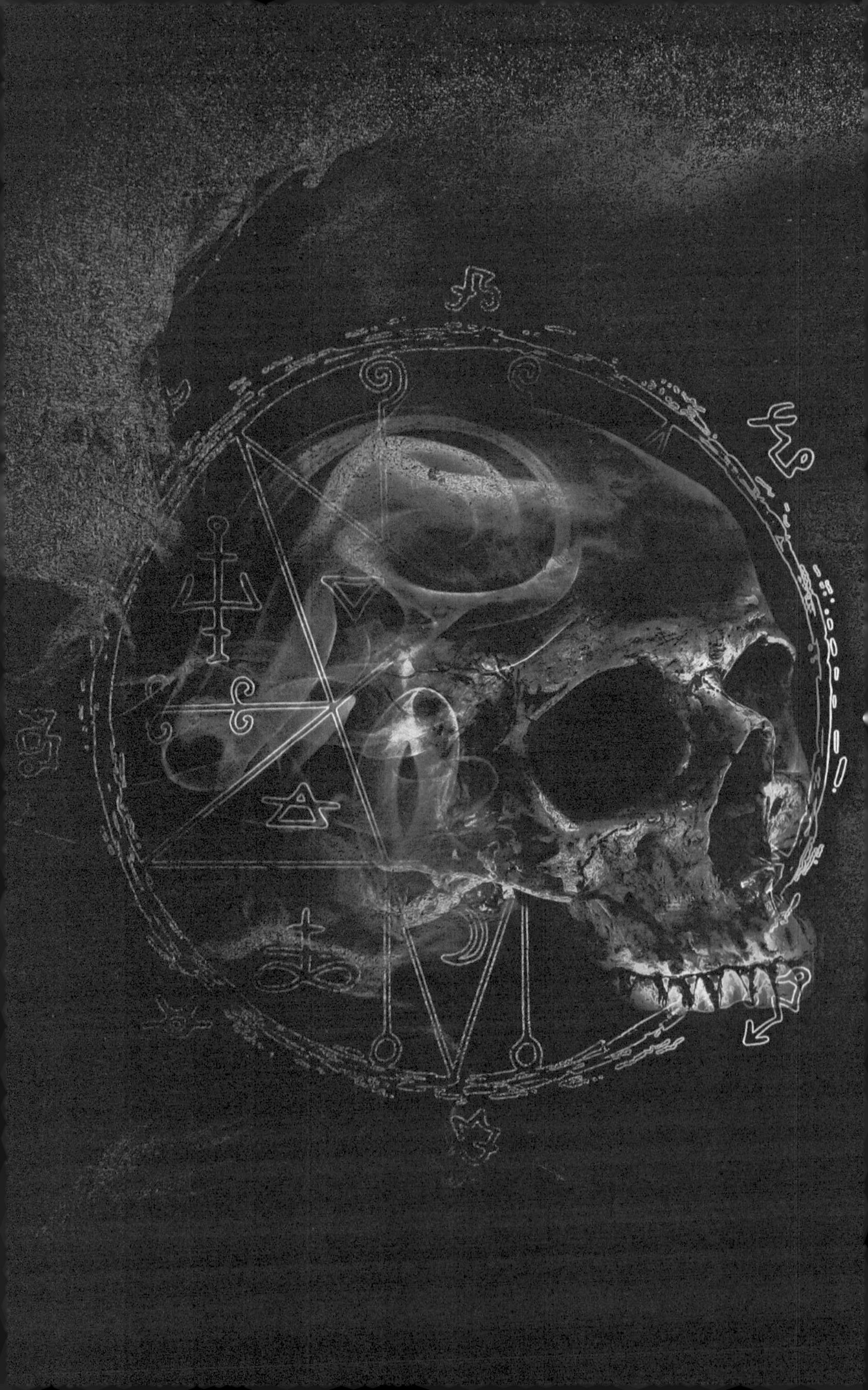

# Chapter 9



Was I floating? I must've been. Why else would I feel so weightless? Plus, I was pretty sure I was moving. It wasn't the hard jarring of steps I was used to doing, but more of a glide or drift. Like a cloud making its way slowly across the sky. It was kind of nice.

Typically, I wasn't graceful at all. Unless I counted falling up the stairs—which, as far as I was concerned, took talent to accomplish. Mind you, I could dance. Maybe I was dancing? No. Hip hop didn't make someone's arms flow through the air like this.

Coolness tickled across my skin as the scent of jasmine and something else filled my nostrils. I heard an owl call out a piercing predatory shriek as the image of brown speckled feathers flashed through my mind. I could see his neck twist while he spread his wings wide, diving to snatch an unsuspecting mouse off the ground.

Was I the owl? No, that didn't feel right. I wouldn't be moving through the air like this if I had wings. Maybe I wasn't flowing through the air at all? Maybe the air was flowing through me?

*That would explain the tingling sensation pulsing across my skin. Had I become part of the wind? How cool would that be?*

*No more assholes telling me what to do, or scheduled meetings. I wouldn't have to worry about anything other than blowing across the earth at my own pace. And nothing would be able to stop me.*

*The wind was inevitable. Not even Devlin and his stupid dungeon would be able to contain me. I'd brush right past that asshole with a smile on my face.*

*This was the best dream ever.*

*"Put her over there."*

*This was a dream, wasn't it? Because that voice sounded familiar, and not in a good way. In fact, I was pretty sure I hated that voice. Why would my subconscious put Angus in here?*

*"I know where to put her."*

*I didn't like that voice either. At least, I didn't think I did. I hit it with a book earlier.*

*"I should've desecrated the damn altar."*

*I definitely didn't like that voice. Fuck Devlin and his stupid altar. Wait...*

*What did he mean by altar? What kind of dream was this?*

*Angus's annoyed tone rumbled through the air. "Stop talking nonsense."*

*"It's not nonsense," Devlin shot back. "We can't do this stupid ritual if there's no altar."*

*My brows pulled together as I began to float down.*

*Rituals and altars? Who talked like that? I'd been placed with a couple of religious families, and some of the stuff they did seemed pretty ritualistic. Like baptisms and nightly prayers, but they never referred to them as actual rituals.*

*Leave it to pompous Angus and his asshole sons to use a word like that. Next thing, they'd be calling jeans trousers.*

*Oh, maybe I was in England?*

*"I suggest you stop whining, son, and get ready. The moon will only be up for another four hours."*

*What did the moon have to do with anything?*

*"Good," Devlin snapped. "Maybe we'll miss it."*

*"And you'll be right where you are tomorrow." Angus sighed.*

*"I don't understand why you're making me do this."*

*What was Angus making Devlin do? He sounded pretty annoyed about it. I wished I could see what was happening. I'd like to side with Angus. But I didn't think they'd be too happy about my eavesdropping. Then again... you couldn't see the wind. Meaning it couldn't hurt to get a little closer. All I had to do was gather the air around me and burst forward.*

*"Jesus Christ, Reese," Devlin growled. "Watch what you're doing."*

*Reese was here?*

*That thought was answered when another voice responded with, "I didn't do that."*

*"Bullshit. Flitters can't control their levitation."*

*Flitters? Was Devlin making up words now?*

*Angus's tone was the next to hit my ears. "She's not a flitter."*

*"What do you mean, she's not a flitter?" Devlin barked out.*

*What was a flitter?*

*"I don't know why you're surprised, son. You know who her father was."*

*Now I was really confused. When I dreamt about my dad, he was there, not being mentioned by some asshats using made-up words.*

*"Don't you think that would've been good information to have?"*

*Devlin sounded mad. Good. Asshole. I'd still like to know what they were talking about. I just assumed the "her" they were referring to was me, but maybe it wasn't. It wasn't like they knew I was here. Like I said, you can't see the wind.*

*"Devlin has a point, Angus," Reese piped in. "I might've used a different spell if I'd known."*

*Spell? Was I stuck in some weird magic place again? I hoped not. Last time I was trapped in the body of an ant. All I could do was go out and grab things to bring back for the queen, who I worshipped as a god. That was not a fun dream.*

*"I only just found out," Angus said. "Now we can continue arguing about this, or you two can get ready to call the spirit."*

*Call the spirit? That sounded like a fancy way to say prayer.*

*Oh crap.*

*Please tell me we weren't in a church. I was nowhere near dressed enough for a place like that. The only fabric I could feel on my skin were soft bands wrapping around my hips. Being naked as the wind was one thing—the wind didn't need clothes to blow—but this…*

*If the Almighty did exist, this was a good way to be struck down. I wasn't in the mood to get smited. Hmm… That didn't feel right. Smoted, maybe? What was the past tense version of smite? Smited, smote, smithers. Couldn't help but chuckle at that one.*

*Be good, my children, lest God come forth and smithers you.*

*"Umm," Reese said. "I think she just laughed."*

*Did he hear me? I should've been more careful. Just because I couldn't be seen didn't mean they wouldn't hear me. Damnit.*

*"See, this is what I was talking about." I could almost see the scowl on Devlin's face. Wait…*

*Why couldn't I see? Surely the wind needed to know where it was going. Then again, sight wasn't exactly important. It wasn't like crashing into a wall or tree would slow it down.*

*"We should call it off," Devlin suggested.*

*To which both Angus and Reese replied, "no."*

*Yeah! If Devlin didn't want to do it, then I was all for it. Fuck Devlin.*

*"I'd expect this kind of attitude from your brother," Angus said, leading me to wonder which brother he was referring to. Wyatt, Magnus, or the elusive Rook? "But not you, Devlin."*

*"Tell me, Father…" Someone was snippy. "What kind of attitude did you expect when I was given her?"*

*The arrogance made me want to roll my eyes. People weren't possessions to be given. Not that I was overly surprised that phrase came out of his mouth. Mr. I Don't Like Your Make-up So I'm Going To Wash It Off.*

*"We," Reese added in.*

*Ugh, some girl had to put up with both of them. Poor thing. I could just imagine the shit she'd have to go through. Reese would flash his charming smile while Devlin made some asshole demand like be nice or else... Hang on...*

*My thoughts fled as my body started to drop. I could feel the weight of my limbs pulling me down to the earth, which didn't make sense. Why would I be dropping? The wind didn't have weight. Unless... I wasn't the wind.*

*"I don't know what your problem is,." Reese said causing a wave of warm air to brush across my face. "Look at her. She's gorgeous."*

*My body touched down on something solid and unforgiving. A second later, coolness seeped into my bones. I grumbled and shifted to find a warm spot, but I could barely move. Why couldn't I move, and what was I lying on?*

*I could feel the texture. Whatever I was on was grainy and rough. Stone, maybe? That couldn't be right. Why would I dream about something like this? Not to mention include three of the people I hated? I'd had some strange dreams in my time. Once I was a frog, and in another, I was queen of the Underworld, but this was just weird.*

*What the hell did I watch before I went to sleep?*

*When I felt a warm palm smooth down the side of my body, my first instinct was to open my eyes. But my lids were so heavy it was almost impossible to make them move. That struggle quickly turned into a fight. I focused on my uncooperative eyes while grumbling and pushing the hand away from me.*

*I was so focused on my current task that I barely heard Devlin speak. "I thought you said you had control?"*

*"I thought I did," Reese responded.*

*A huffed-out snort vibrated through my nose. Their arrogance wasn't even watered down in my subconscious. Despite the fact that the simple task of opening my eyes continued to elude me, there was only one person who had control here. Me. This was my dream, damnit! I would do what I wanted with my body.*

*Determination rolled through me, pushing the weight off my lids, and when I finally fluttered my lashes open, I saw four eyes staring* down at me. Two green orbs twinkling with curiosity and two dark as the night sky above.

Devlin didn't appear as amused as Reese. He waved his hand over my body and barked, "Does that look like control to you?"

It was a lot easier to make my mouth move than it was to open my eyes. "Fuck you and your control."

The scowl on Devlin's face deepened, and he pressed his lips together.

Reese let out a chuckle. "I like her."

Devlin was not impressed by his friend's statement. "You like anything with a pussy."

"At least I have something useful." What good was a dick? Technically, we didn't even need it to have kids. Just a few good sperm and bam, life was created.

"You only have one use, Bréagán." Devlin snorted and rolled his eyes. "And I doubt you're even good at that."

"I've never had any complaints." Not that I had a ton of guys to reference. Just the one. And I just sucked on it a bit. But the fact that he came so quickly had to count for something.

Apparently, Devlin didn't agree. A shadow fell over his face, darkening it so much that the golden flecks in his eyes stopped twinkling. But it was the tone in Reese's voice that sent a chill up my spine.

"And who exactly would complain?"

I wanted to throw a snarky comment at him so badly that I could taste the words on the tip of my tongue. But the second my eyes met his, I forgot what I was going to say. Reese looked like he was ready to murder someone. It was such a stark contrast to the first time I met him. Instead of being flirty and charming, he was kind of scary.

Devlin's brow arched. "He asked you a question."

"Well, I'm not going to answer the question." My personal life was none of their business.

"That's okay, sweet thing, you don't need to." A mischievous curl tugged on the corner of Reese's mouth as he leaned over me and cupped my face.

If I could tear my face out of his grip, I would've. It was creepy *laying there with his palms on my cheeks while he stared into my eyes like he could see my soul. And to top it all off, Devlin shot me a smug grin.*

*I didn't know what he was so happy about. What exactly was this going to accomplish? Nothing, that's what. Reese wasn't a mind reader.*

*"Scotty Dalton."*

*What? How did he know that?*

*"Poor shmuck didn't last more than ten seconds in your pretty little mouth."*

*Okay, this was getting weird, but I guess it made sense. All that information was in my head and that's technically where we were.*

*"So dream-you can read my mind." I scoffed and slapped Reese's hands off me. "Big deal."*

*Devlin snorted. "She thinks she's sleeping."*

*Well, he wasn't going to win the award for sharpest tool in the shed. Of course, I was asleep.*

*"People don't actually fly or cast spells."*

*Dumbass.*

*Reese smiled down at me. "Of course they don't."*

*Devlin, however, rolled his eyes. "You were levitating, not flying."*

*"Heaven forbid, I misinterpret your fake magic."*

*Was it wrong that the annoyance in his expression filled me with satisfaction? Nah. Fuck Devlin. I hoped he spent the rest of his life constantly annoyed. That's what I'd call divine retribution.*

*Angus cleared his throat, drawing my attention past Devlin's scowl to a robed figure standing next to a dark brazier. I watched as he dropped something inside, causing an orange flame to flicker to life. There was a pattern etched in the metal of the brazier, but I couldn't tell what it was from my position.*

*It looked kind of like a star or maybe a series of triangles. I could make out a couple of points. Not that it mattered. I was more interested in the other robed figures moving around in the shadows. Or maybe it was three? It sounded like they were saying something.*

*"Who's over there?"*

*I strained my ears to listen, but all I could catch were a few words. Spiorad, tri, and aontas. Sounded like more made-up words to me. I guess all words were made up, but still…*

*"Don't worry about that." Reese grabbed my chin and turned my gaze back to his. "Devlin and I are the only ones that matter."*

*That was laughable. "The dirt on the bottom of my shoe matters more to me than you do."*

*That dirt could be used for a lot of things. Growing a pretty flower, messing up a clean floor, or it could be used as forensic evidence when I decided to kill them.*

*Reese slapped his hand over his heart and frowned, while Devlin muttered, "The feeling's mutual."*

*"You're so quick to judge."*

*All guys like him did the same thing, and they did it with a smile on their face. "I know enough."*

*"I happen to think I'm a very likable person," Reese argued, further proving my point.*

*"You're friends with Devlin." A trait that automatically put someone on my bad side.*

*Reese shrugged. "He's not that bad."*

*"Says you."*

*Don't get me wrong, I'd met plenty of despicable people, but none as assholish as Devlin Adair.*

*"I think once you get to know him, you might change your mind."*

*"Doubtful." Considering I'd have to actually talk to the prick to get to know him, I didn't see that happening.*

*Devlin didn't say anything in his defense, and why would he? He was perfectly happy with his title of Number One Asshole.*

*Moonlight glinted off Reese's golden hair as he tipped his head and smirked. "Would it help if I told you he has a big dick?"*

*Eww, no. Why would I care about that?*

*"Fuck sakes," Devlin grumbled.*

*"Well, you do," Reese argued. "And he knows how to use it."*

*"Can we stop talking about my dick?"*

*For once, I agreed with Devlin. Just because he smelled as good as he looked, that didn't mean I was interested in his package.*

*At least that was what I told myself while my eyes slid over to my right, where his form was looming over me. More specifically, to a particular part of his form. Based on the size of the bulge under those dark jeans, Reese wasn't lying.*

*"Stop staring at my dick, Bréagán."*

*I tore my eyes away and returned Devlin's scowl. "I wasn't staring."*

*"Yes, you were." Reese snickered.*

*There was a difference between seeing and staring. And it was kind of hard not to see something that was right there. Devlin's hips were above the stone slab I was lying on, putting his package right in my line of sight. Either he was taller than I remembered, or I was lower than I thought.*

*Speaking of which, why was I still lying down?*

*Using my elbows, I propped myself up to sit. Then froze as realization hit me. I wasn't wearing anything but a pair of white cotton panties.*

*Shit.*

*My arms quickly folded over my chest to hide my breasts. That's when I noticed the writing. It was everywhere. Over the skin on my arms, down my chest and stomach, and across my legs. At least it looked like some kind of writing. I wasn't sure what language it was, but I had seen a few of the symbols before.*

*"What is this?" I reached out to rub one of the symbols, but Devlin grabbed my wrist.*

*"Leave those alone."*

*My eyes narrowed. "Why?"*

*"Because I fucking said so."*

*Oh, well, in that case… "Go fuck yourself."*

*"I mean it, Bréagán." His fingers tightened, making me wince as a sharp ache shot up my forearm. "Touch one goddamn line, and I'll break your fucking arm."*

*Now it was a matter of pride. "Eat shit, Devlin."*

*Reese jumped in before I could do anything.*

*"You can wash them off if you want, but then what will protect you from the swamp monster?"*

*I sneered back at him. "There's no such thing."*

*"Are you sure?" His brows rose as he tipped his head. "This is a dream, after all."*

*Huh? That was a good point. I wasn't sure if I wanted to meet the swamp monster my mind made up. The thing was probably hideous with black tendrils and ooze. Or worse, it could be that evil little witch Cassie who made fun of me in second grade. Just thinking about her cackle sent a shiver up my spine.*

*"All right, I'll leave them alone," I begrudgingly agreed. "For now."*

*This was the strangest dream I'd ever had. Everything about it was weird. The air brushing across me was too vivid and crisp. So was the hint of jasmine and cinnamon floating down my throat with every breath. This wasn't right. It shouldn't be this real. I wanted to wake up now.*

*"I don't like this."*

*I especially didn't like the heat pooling in my belly every time Reese or Devlin looked at me.*

*"It's okay." Reese shushed while gently prying my arms off my chest. "You have a beautiful body. Don't be ashamed of it."*

*"I'm not," I sneered. "I just don't appreciate being on display."*

*I wasn't embarrassed or anything. I just didn't want them looking at me. It made me feel like I was caught between two predators. One of which stared at me like he wanted to choke the life out of me while he devoured my soul. And the other was hungry and almost feral.*

*Reese's charm couldn't dull the spark in his eyes. And there I was, without so much as a shirt to protect me.*

*"Well, we appreciate you being on display," Reese purred in my ear as he crawled up on the slab behind me. "Isn't that right, Devlin?"*

*"She's all right." Devlin's lip curled.*

*He could pretend to be disgusted all he wanted, but I saw his eyes slowly raking over me. And because I could, I called him on his shit. "Says the guy staring at my breasts."*

*A shiver cooled my skin when he glared into my gaze. "She'd look a lot better if she could keep her fucking mouth shut."*

*"I'm right here, asshole," I hissed back. "Or are you too much of a coward to say it to my face?"*

*It wasn't the snicker he scoffed out that made me jerk back. It was the vibrations from the force of his hands slamming down on either side of me. He bent over until his face was a breath away from mine.*

*"I'm in your face now. What are you going to do about it?"*

*Reese tried to intervene. "That's enough..."*

*But Devlin cut him off. "You're the one who signed her up for this shit."*

*I knew I didn't like Reese.*

*"I didn't sign her up for this."*

*Devlin's glare shifted to the man behind me. "You want to take it back?"*

*About that time, the figures behind Devlin moved over to the brazier. It wasn't hard to tell who they were once the light hit their hooded faces. Three faces, to be exact. Wyatt, Magnus, and Angus. They certainly wouldn't do anything to stop Devlin, and apparently neither would Reese.*

*The only word that left his mouth was a whispered, "No."*

*Even in my dreams, they were all gutless bastards.*

*"Cowards," I called out while giving a dirty look to the four men watching the confrontation happen.*

*Devlin tsked. "You're not as smart as you think you are, Bréagán."*

*"And you're not as badass as you think you are." I gave him my best fake frown and sang, "I bet little Devlin was Mommy's favorite."*

*I swear I heard everyone suck in a collective gasp, which in itself was unnerving, but I didn't start to worry until Reese wrapped his legs around me and pulled me back into him. But even that didn't break our stare down.*

*"Don't you ever talk about my mother."*

*A brief pang of guilt flowered in my chest. I knew what it was like to lose a parent. Every day, I wondered what my father was like. Would he be proud of me? Would he love me? The pain of knowing that I would never get the answers to those questions was something I wouldn't wish on anyone. Including Devlin.*

*That didn't mean I'd give in.*

*I kept my glare glued to his, throwing back just as much hate as he was giving. If looks could kill, I'd be dead right now, but so would he, and that I could live with. If the last thing I saw was Devlin Adair collapsing in agony, then I'd head into the afterlife with a big smile on my face.*

*"I should snap your neck and be done with it."*

*I was so sick of his threats.*

*"So do it." I tried to shoot forward, but Reese held me back. So instead, I tipped my chin, baring my neck. "Go on."*

*Devlin could take his holier than thou attitude and shove it right up his ass. I refused to give into his intimidation tactics. Everyone else could bow down at his feet if they wanted, but I would not budge.*

*"Calm down, sweet thing." Reese leaned in, his breath warming the shell of my ear. "You don't want to get him all worked up before the show gets started."*

*Fuck their show.*

*Despite trying to hold on to my rage, I felt the tension start to flow out of my muscles. I wanted to stay on edge and feel the anger burn through my veins, but I couldn't. My fists unclenched as my limbs relaxed and melted into the solid chest at my back.*

*Any of the hot spitefulness left in my system dissipated the instant Angus said, "Shall we?"*

*That's when Devlin reached over his shoulder to peel his shirt off. Suddenly I didn't care about being mad anymore because I was staring at a wall of muscle so chiseled that I was seriously questioning whether Devlin's abs could cut glass. And the tribal lines I'd wondered about before did indeed cover his entire torso. They wove across his tanned skin in a mesmerizing pattern I couldn't pull my attention away from.*

*I say Devlin was gorgeous because I was wrong. He was fucking hot. Or, at least, this dream version of him was.*

*Maybe I didn't want to wake up after all. This wasn't so bad. Plus, I was kind of curious about what was going to happen when Devlin spun around and waltzed over to the brazier.*

*Let me just say, I had a much more vivid imagination than I thought. The last thing I expected Devlin to do was slam his hand down on a large spike next to the fire. I hadn't noticed it before.*

*Not surprising, considering none of this was real. That didn't mean I wouldn't enjoy the way his face scrunched up in a grimace as fat crimson drops fell from the wound.*

*"Does someone have a little bloodlust?"*

*Ugh, I forgot Reese was here. "No."*

*"Oh, yeah." He chuckled and slid his hand over my thigh. "Then why are you smiling?"*

*"I'm not smiling." I totally was, but come on... How often did I have a front row seat to Devlin's pain. This shit was great.*

*Just when I thought it couldn't get any better, Devlin swung his hand over the open flame, causing the smile on my face to spread as his teeth ground together.*

*Burn, baby, burn.*

*All it took to take away my moment of enjoyment was a small movement from Reese. His had dipped down my thigh to the only part of me that was covered, and suddenly I didn't care about watching Devlin anymore.*

*My eyes snapped back to Reese's twinkling green orbs. "What are you doing?"*

*"Shh." He grazed his lips across my neck. "Just relax and enjoy it."*

*Was he crazy? "I'll never enjoy anything you do."*

*I never had anyone make me eat my words faster than he did. Reese cupped my mound, and with one flick, the insult I was getting ready to throw was sucked violently back down my throat. I choked on the bitter taste of my hatred while sparks of pleasure shot up my spine.*

*"That's it, sweet thing." Reese pressed a finger down, massaging*

*my clit through my panties, and purred in my ear, "Now let me hear your moan."*

*Fuck that. I was not going to let him know how good this felt.*

*I clenched my teeth, as a string of goosebumps traveled up my skin, and ground out, "Stop it."*

*"Why?" The hair on his chin abraded my tender skin as he dipped his head and swept his lips along the side of my neck. "You like it."*

*"No, I don't," I insisted, even though my body was screaming for more.*

*I fought against the feeling of his touch with everything I had. Tried to pull his hand away, and when that didn't work, I reached back to tug on his hair. All that got me was a tangle of soft locks around my fingers as I clung to Reese and tried not to gyrate my hips.*

*And damn him, Reese didn't miss a beat. He held me firmly and played my body like he was a master, and this was his greatest concert.*

*"Please stop," I whined.*

*I didn't want this. I didn't like how I enjoyed the feel of his hard body pressed up against me, or how his breath heated my skin. It shouldn't feel this good, but it did. Every swirl of his finger wound that coil deep inside tighter and tighter.*

*Goddamn Reese, with his charming smile and soft hair. His hand hadn't slipped inside my panties yet, and I'd never been this wound up.*

*"Please," I whined again. "Stop it." Before I couldn't stop myself.*

*"I like it when you beg." The wet trail his tongue laved up the column of my throat was enhanced by the deep growl that rumbled through his chest. "I hope you like it dirty, because I'm going to taint every pure thing you have."*

*It was hard to think past the tension building in my core, but I somehow managed to bite back, "Fuck you and your taint."*

*When the next pass of his finger flicked over my clit, I had to dig my teeth into my lip to hold back my moan.*

*"Sorry, sweet thing. Devlin has to play that game with you first before I can."*

*Oh, shit! Devlin.*

*I twisted my neck back to brazier, where I expected to find him, but*

*Devlin wasn't there. He was right in front of me, licking his lips like a feral animal. And damnit if a part of me didn't like the way he was staring at me.*

*This wasn't just a bad dream. It was a fucking nightmare.*

*Devlin tipped his gaze up to Reese. "Is she ready for me?"*

*What the hell did that mean?*

*"Oh, yeah." Reese took his hand off my pussy and tipped my chin to his heated gaze. "She's good to go."*

*No, I wasn't. I wasn't good to go anywhere, and least of all with Devlin.*

*"I'd like to wake up now."*

*"Not yet." The corner of Reese's mouth lifted. "Devlin has to make you come first."*

*Oh, hell no.*

*Devlin reached out to grab my ankle, and I swung my foot, kicking him in the chest. Next thing I knew, I was flung back on the stone slab with Devlin's hand around my neck while Reese pinned my arms.*

*I struggled to break free, but that all stopped when Devlin's hand took over the job Reese had started.*

*Except he didn't give me the curtesy of panties for protection. He swept the fabric to the side and slid a finger through my folds, making my body jerk in response. One touch was all it took for me to feel the orgasm cresting.*

*"No." I shook my head and closed my eyes.*

*This couldn't be happening. Not with him.*

*"Look at me." Devlin growled, forcing my eyes to pop open.*

*I knew I lost the second I looked into those dark orbs. The satisfaction sparkling within his eyes was as unmistakable as the ecstasy filled spasms that rocked my body.*

*The last thing I heard before darkness took me was Devlin whispering, "You're fucked now, Bréagán."*

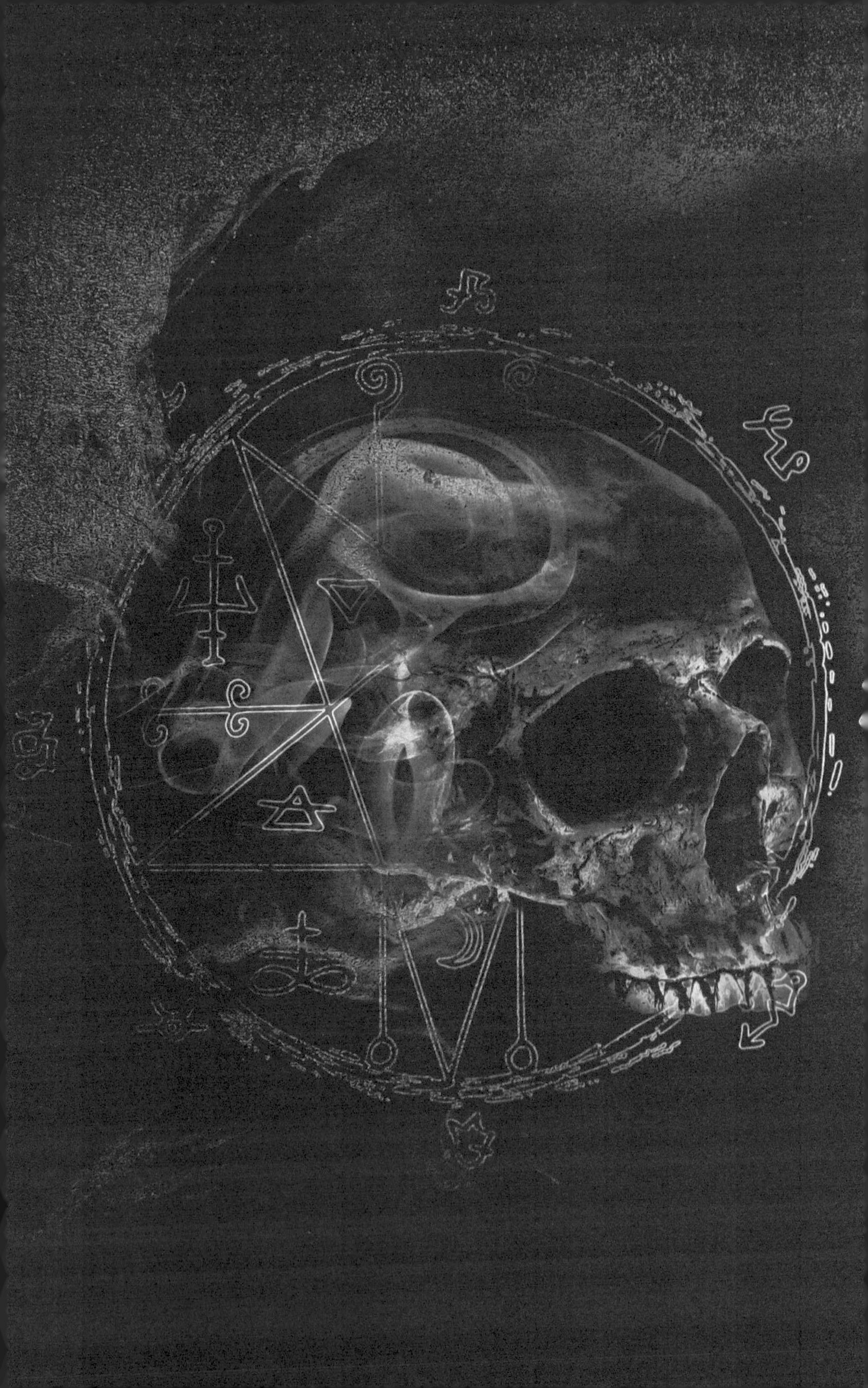

# Chapter 10

Something felt off when I woke up. At first, I chalked it up to the fucked-up dream I had. The subconscious was a tricky thing that sometimes stuck with a person long after their conscious mind had taken over.

Like when people glanced suspiciously around their room for the boogeyman, or when they were pissed at a significant other for dream cheating. It didn't matter if none of it was real, because to them, it felt real.

So when I opened my eyes that morning, I wasn't surprised that I could still feel hands on me. It was nothing more than residual dream memories, which was something that would fade with time.

I kept waiting for it to go away. In the shower, I told myself that all I could smell was the fruity scent of my shampoo, which had absolutely no hint of rosewood. Yet it was still there, tickling the back of my nose.

That was easier to ignore than the goosebumps prickling up my arms when I got dressed. It felt like I was being watched. Nothing seemed to help me shake that sensation. Not even the anger that came when I saw my empty underwear drawer.

I had every intention of giving Wyatt a piece of my mind when I joined the twins for breakfast, but all I could think about was the way their turquoise eyes looked in the firelight. It was so vivid that I could hear the flame crackling in the background. Almost as if the dream wasn't a dream at all, but a real memory.

At one point, I even opened my mouth to ask the twins about their night. Then Wyatt started talking about some girl named Poppy. Discretion was not his strong suit. Five minutes into that conversation, and I knew way more about that girl's body than I did my own.

I should've taken Magnus's cue and walked out when he did. On the upside, Wyatt's way-too-detailed account managed to take my mind off other things. However, I would never eat another banana.

My mood picked up until I walked into the library and was met with Reese's smile. Almost instantly, those strange sensations came flooding back. Though this time they were a little different. It was more like a pull than residual dream effects. As if there were an invisible force flipping in my stomach every time Reese looked at me.

Reese was a good-looking guy, so a crush could be explained away. But this shit was just fucking weird. Still, I tried to ignore it and focus on my lesson.

Let's just say I didn't learn much.

In fact, I had no idea what the hell the Reese was talking about. Now if someone asked me how many golden flecks were in his green eyes, that could answer. Eleven in the right and twelve in the left. There was also a ring of light blue around his pupil, and when the corner of his mouth tipped up, that ring darkened.

"Since English was your worst subject, I thought we'd start there."

"Uh huh."

There was a slight, gravelly timbre in Reese's deep tone that vibrated through the air. I could feel it in every word he spoke.

"What do you think?"

I think he should come a little closer so I could get a taste of the mint on his breath. Then again, I could always…

"Can I help you with something?"

*What? Oh, shit. Was I actually leaning in?*

I looked up at Reese as he arched a brow. Not only was I leaning in, but I'd moved in so close that my ass was barely on the edge of the chair.

"Do you need something?"

*Sanity, apparently.*

"Nope." I shook my head and quickly slid back into my seat. "I'm good."

And by good, I meant not at all in my right frame of mind, because a fucked-up dream apparently had my hormones going crazy. So much for missing the phase that made girls dumb around guys.

"If you're all right," Reese said. "Then we'll continue."

I swear I saw the corner of his mouth curl. Not that I was staring at his mouth or anything. He did have nice lips, though. Full, thick, soft, and way too tempting.

Did he always smell that good? Because I couldn't stop sucking in breaths. Of course he did. A guy that made a plain black t-shirt look that good, didn't smell bad. And Reese did look good in that shirt. All hard and broad with the edge of a tattoo peeking out across his collarbone.

I tipped my head to watch his chest expand.

In the right light, I could see the outline of a nipple ring pressing against the fabric. I couldn't see it now, but I knew it was on the right side. That small circular band was visible every time he twisted to the left and the sunlight hit him. Would he move over to the next table? There was more light over there.

"Now I know Shakespeare isn't for everyone."

*Oh right. I should probably pay attention.*

Straightening my shoulders, I sat back and watched Reese place a leather bond book on the table.

"Here we have all of his works…"

His hand tapped down on the cover, and I couldn't help but notice how his fingers moved. Hands like that could do a lot of things. Choke the life out of someone or hold them down. Like, say, while he did stuff with his other hand.

I gave the collar of my t-shirt a tug. The last time I felt this weighed down by heat was when I was in Florida. It'd probably help if I had underwear on. But no, some asshole decided to take them.

So now I was stuck in a pair of pink sweats that had "hot stuff" written across the ass. I handled pink about as well as I was handling the moisture gathering on my thighs. I was going to kill Wyatt.

"Is it hot in here?"

Reese slid his eyes my way and smirked as I shifted in the seat. "I'm fine."

My eyes trickled over the muscle tensing in his forearm and up to his broad shoulders.

*Yes, yes, he was.*

"Do you want to take a break and get a drink?"

*I'd like to drink you.*

"No." I shook my head. "I'm okay."

Kind of wish I didn't have so much hair. I should've cut it or at least put it up. Wasn't this supposed to be fall? Shouldn't it be cooler than this? How was Reese not hot? I mean, he was hot, but not sweating hot. How good would he look out of breath and covered in sweat? I bet he'd still smell good, too.

"I'm partial to *Hamlet* myself," Reese said, pulling me back to the lesson he was trying to teach.

*Right, school.*

I gave my head a shake and focused on the book he was tapping. That didn't help. All I could think about was how the golden letters etched in the leather glinted like the flecks in Reese's eyes.

"But I'm not opposed to doing something else."

"Sure."

His hair looked extra messy today, did he do something different with it?

"*Romeo and Juliet* is a popular one."

Who the fuck was Juliet? Was some girl waiting for him? I bet she was one of those perfect blond cheerleaders with a bubble butt and fake nails.

"Pfft, bitch."

"Okay." Reese's brow rose. "Not Romeo and Juliet."

Shit, did I say that out loud? A better question was, why did I say it at all? It wasn't like I cared what Reese did in his spare time. He could mess around with all the dumb bimbos he wanted.

Devlin probably had a line-up of women waiting for him to use. I could see the asshole walking down the row, pointing out all their flaws. *You're wearing too much make-up, go change your clothes,* and so on. Prick. He was kind of hot, though. And those tattoos…

*Wait, why was I thinking about that asshole?*

"Sydney?" Reese sang.

"Yeah."

"Are you paying attention?"

*Not in the slightest.* "Of course I am."

Doubt tugged at his expression. "So you're fine with *Hamlet*?"

Why was he talking about Shakespeare?

*Um, probably because he's your teacher.*

*Right.*

"Um, yeah. *Hamlet* is fine."

Honestly, I'd prefer to work on calculus than read, but hey, I made it through *The Catcher and The Rye,* which was like torture. I could make it through Shakespeare. I just had to stop getting distracted. That, I could blame on Reese.

He was the one that came in here in his dark jeans and t-shirt, looking like a cold drink of water on a hot day. Teachers weren't supposed to look like that. They should be wearing jackets with corduroy patches and glasses. Reese would probably rock that look. Asshole.

That's when my mind went right to how he would look sporting a tacky coat and glasses. And I was right. He would rock that look.

"Are you sure?" Reese asked. "We could start with something a little easier, like *Romeo and Juliet.*"

My disdain came through with an eye roll. "No, thanks."

If I had to read, I'd prefer to read something that didn't revolve around love-struck teens.

"What's wrong with *Romeo and Juliet*?"

"Stories like that put too much emphasis on a single kiss." It was unrealistic. When in the history of mankind had a kiss ever made someone fall in love?

Reese's brow arched. "I take you've never been kissed?"

"I'm seventeen"—I gave him a deadpan look—"not five."

Seriously, what seventeen-year—old hadn't been kissed? Hell, most kids my age had done a lot more than kiss. High schools were basically sexual meeting grounds.

"Someone trying to eat your face doesn't constitute as a kiss."

I opened my mouth to argue, but then, every kiss I'd ever had flashed through my mind. And I couldn't recall a single one where I didn't feel like the guy was trying to swallow my mouth.

Scotty Dalton was okay. At least I didn't choke on his tongue, and he didn't taste like cigarettes and beer. That was probably why he got further than anyone else.

Reese slammed his fist down on the table, making me jar back. "Scotty Dalton is an immature fuck who wouldn't know what to do with a woman if he had instructions and a map."

My brows furrowed.

I didn't remember saying Scotty's name aloud. Then again, I didn't remember half of what Reese said either.

"If you're done reminiscing..." I jerked back as Reese slammed open the book. "I'd like to get back to work."

*What the hell was up his ass?*

"Okay?"

Why was he mad? Seriously. One minute he was all smiles talking Shakespeare and the next he was glaring at the book like he could burn it with his eyes alone.

"We can do *Romeo and Juliet* if you want."

That was apparently the wrong thing to say.

Reese's entire body tensed as he slowly rolled his eyes my way. "Did Scotty Dalton like *Romeo and Juliet*?"

Was he being serious right now? Wait…

"Are you jealous?"

It was a laughable suggestion. I just met the guy. There's no way he'd care about my past relationships.

"Yes."

*Or he would?*

I opened my mouth, but nothing came out. I'd handled plenty of things before. Played mediator between foster brothers and sisters, convinced one couple to go to marriage counseling, and taught one guy what happened when he snuck into the room of a little girl who had a bat. But I had to say, this situation was a new one.

To make matters worse, Reese was staring at me like I'd betrayed him. So I tried the only thing I could think of and pointed out the obvious.

"You're my teacher."

His brow rose. "And?"

"And as my teacher, you shouldn't…" What was the rest of that statement?

You shouldn't care who I dated? No, that didn't feel right. I could go with: You shouldn't be attracted to students. That was kind of hypocritical, though, considering I'd spent all morning ogling him.

Not to mention, assuming that he liked me in that way was a big jump. For all I knew, he simply didn't enjoy hearing about people's romantic encounters. Couldn't say I blamed him.

However, he did say he was jealous.

My silence caused the arch in Reese's brow to deepen. "I shouldn't what?"

"Give me a minute." I was working on it.

A minute was not what I got. I don't think I even got a second.

Reese growled, "Fuck it." and jumped out of his chair.

Next thing I knew, I was thrown back on the table.

"What the hell do you—" was all I managed to get out before his mouth slammed down on mine.

I tried to push him away, but all that resulted in was my arms being pinned above my head. My legs weren't an option. Reese had wedged his way between my thighs, preventing me from kicking.

All I could do was lay there feeling heat pool in my belly as his weight pressed down on me. Even then, I retained some resistance.

Until he bit my lip.

Every nerve ending I had suddenly lit up. My entire body wrapped around the sweet taste of his tongue swirling over mine. I felt myself relax into him as a contented sigh left my lips. Then it ended.

Reese pulled away and glared down at me. "The next time you think about Scotty Dalton, I want you to remember this." He bent down, brushing the scruff on his cheek against mine and whispered, "That's what a real kiss feels like."

"O-okay," I whispered back and cleared my throat. "Good to know."

He smiled and walked away to sit back down.

The longer I stayed there, processing what happened, the angrier I got.

Reese had basically just molested me, and now he was sitting there like this was a normal Tuesday afternoon. What the fuck was wrong with him? This shit wasn't normal. People didn't go around kissing other people out of the blue. And certainly not supposed teachers.

I sprang off the table and pointed a finger at him. "Are you crazy?"

And how did Reese respond?

He looked up, arched a brow, and said, "I told you we could do *Romeo and Juliet*."

What the fuck? He knew what I was talking about, and it had nothing to do with that damn book.

"Fuck Shakespeare."

"Hmm." He sat back and folded his arms over his chest. "Your old school said you might be a problem."

What? I wasn't a problem. Sure, I skipped a couple of classes and may have told a teacher or two off…

*Wait a minute…*

"Don't try to distract me with school."

"It's kind of in the job description." Reese tipped his chin and gave me a pointed look. "I am your teacher."

*I was gonna kill him.*

"That's my point." Frustration threw my hands up. "Teachers aren't supposed to kiss students."

"Students shouldn't ask their teachers to kiss them," he shot back.

He had to be kidding. "I didn't ask you to do shit."

I may not remember saying Scotty's name, but I was pretty sure I'd remember asking for something like that.

His next words caught me completely off guard. "You've been staring at me all morning."

"I wasn't… I mean… " I wasn't that obvious, was I? "I wasn't staring."

I was observing. There was a difference.

"Yes, you were," he argued. "You were practically drooling."

*Oh my god. Lord, if you're up there, please kill me now.*

"It's okay." He shot me a wink. "You're not the first girl to get a little chin dribble when I'm around."

It took everything I had to stop myself from reaching up and wiping my chin. I did not have a dribble. Did I? Suddenly, I was very aware of the way Reese was looking at me. More specifically, the playful tug at the corner of his mouth.

"You're cute when you're flustered."

My face dropped. And now I was just mad again.

I held my hand out and marched forward. "Give me that book."

"Why?"

"Cause I'm going to hit you with it."

"So violent." The smirk on the corner of his mouth spread into a smug grin. "Does going commando have you a little on edge?"

*What? How did he…*

"You took my underwear?"

The sparkle in his eye was all the answer I needed.

I literally didn't know what to say. The last person I'd suspect of doing anything like that was Reese. Mind you, I didn't know the guy at all, other than the fact that he was my teacher, that is.

Oh, there was the whole friends with Devlin thing, which automatically added him to the asshole category. But this... I didn't get it.

"Don't look so confused," Reese said when my mouth opened for the hundredth time. "Stealing panties isn't the worst thing I've done."

Pretty sure I didn't want to know the answer to that statement.

"Can I have them back?"

Jeans were not comfortable without some protection, and I only had so many pairs of sweats.

Reese shook his head. "Sorry, no can do."

"Why not?"

"I gave them to Devlin." He shrugged. "But maybe if you ask him real nice, he'll give them back."

Screw Shakespeare, I needed a bigger book to beat him to death with.

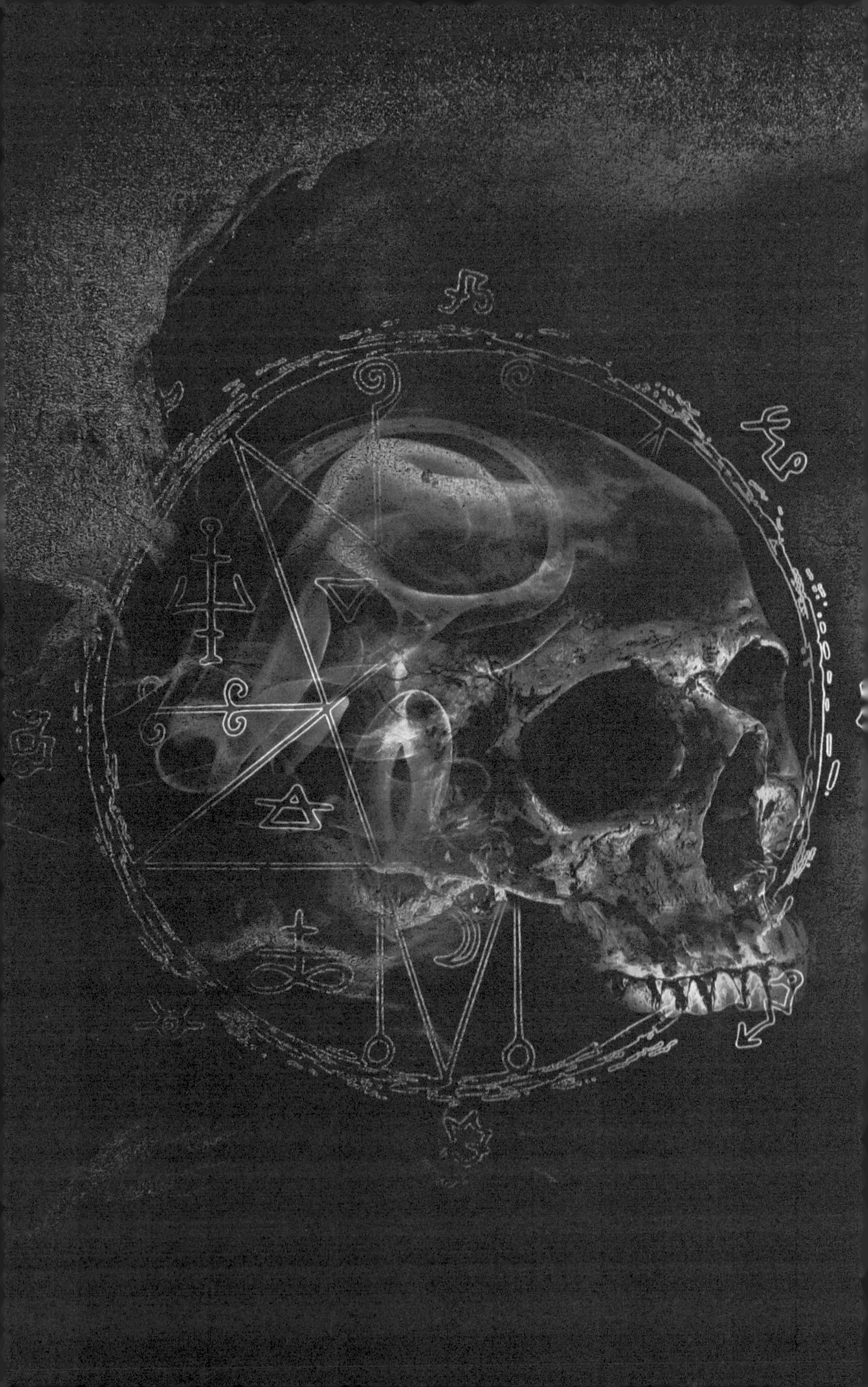

# Chapter 11



Day two of Reese getting hit with a book went well. Minus the part when Angus suddenly decided to check on my studies. To say he was less than impressed with my assault would be an understatement. But in my defense…

"This never would've happened in regular school."

Angus stopped pacing long enough to cock a brow my way. "No, you prefer to send teachers to the hospital in regular school."

Damn. Didn't think he knew about that. "I still maintain that he kicked himself in the balls."

Mr. Jones was a perv who brought it on himself. If he hadn't grabbed my ass, then none of his balls would've had to have been surgically retrieved. So technically, it was his fault. As far as I was concerned, Reese got off lucky.

All he got for kissing me was smack to the face. So what if I was ogling him a bit? I was the teenager in this scenario. Doing dumb shit was kind of in the job description.

"Your other homes may have let you get away with this kind of behavior."

I slumped back in the chair and rolled my eyes as Angus's stern finger waved through the air.

"But I will not tolerate it."

"But you'll tolerate your son dragging me off like a caveman," I grumbled in response.

The stern lines in Angus's forehead deepened. "Pardon me?"

I huffed out a disgruntled, "Nothing."

Every fiber of my being itched to jump up and protest his unfair judgement, but what good would that do? Being the unseen paycheck in the background was one thing. Being grossly outnumbered was another. I was in a house full of misogynistic assholes. Hence why I didn't say anything about Reese kissing me. Angus would probably ask what I did to instigate it.

"You have an opportunity for a high education, Sydney." He gave me a pointed look. "I suggest you start respecting that."

That made me snort. "Yeah, sure."

Higher education for what? Sex ed? How to be an asshole one-oh-one. I think pass.

Angus took a steadying breath and rolled his shoulders back. "All right, have it your way."

The strictness tightening his frown almost made me laugh. So far, I'd been accosted by my so-called stepbrothers, had my face held under water because I was apparently wearing too much make-up, and had all my underwear stolen.

Oh, and let's not forget the being dragged to a dungeon. What could Angus possibly do to make things worse? I was already in the ninth plane of hell. A person couldn't sink any lower than that.

I'd never been more wrong in my life.

"From now on, Devlin will be attending all your classes with you."

"What?" I shrieked. "That's not fair."

The last thing I needed was more time with the king of assholes.

Angus's brows rose as he crossed his arms. "Clearly you can't be trusted alone."

I'd seen the look on his face many times. It was the my-word-is-final stare all parents gave their kids. Though I couldn't help but wonder if he had ulterior motives.

Charmaine had yet to join us for a meal. The only times I did see her, he was there. Keeping us apart would be a lot easier to do if I had an escort following me around.

I wanted to say something. And I might've, if Perry had shown up like he was supposed to. But he wasn't coming for another day or two now. Apparently, an emergency came up. Pretty sure being locked in a dungeon constituted as an emergency, but hey, who was I to argue? It wasn't like I spent ten years of my life in the system or anything.

If there was one thing I learned about CPS, it was that there was no point in arguing once a decision was made. And as Perry had pointed out, technically, I wasn't under their rule anymore. Charmaine, or should I say her dickhead husband, had that power now.

Angus waved his hand past the shelves of books behind him. "Go to your room."

I wasn't happy about his decision, but what could I do? So, I grumbled under my breath and pushed myself out of the chair. For now, I'd play Angus's game. He was just digging himself a deeper hole for when Perry did get here.

"Oh, and, Sydney?" Angus called out as I stormed away. "You will apologize to Reese."

*Like fuck I would.*

I looked over my shoulder and shot Angus a fake smile. "Sure thing."

The only thing Reese would get from me was a big, fat *kiss my ass*. Then again, maybe not. He might actually kiss my ass. Kind of like if I told Wyatt to fuck off. I could see that prick taking it as an invitation for another round of exhibitionistic masturbation.

I blamed CPS for all of this. Family reunification was a bullshit policy created so they could save face. I got it. No one liked the people who split up families. After all, public image was more important than the safety of the child.

Don't get me wrong, I was happy to have Charmaine back, but we didn't need the rest of the Adair household. Especially Angus with his stupid rules.

My fists balled as I rounded the corner to my room. I paused long enough to eye the door next to mine. Was Devlin in there right now? I bet he was gloating over his father's new escort rule.

"Fuck that. Find someone else to follow her around!"

*Or he wasn't.*

Okay, that picked up my mood a little. Judging by the volume of his voice, I'd say Devlin wasn't too happy about his father's new rule. Normally, I'd be all over something that pissed him off—prick deserved a taste of his own medicine. That didn't mean I was pumped to spend time with him.

The next words I heard him growl made me cock a brow.

"I don't give a shit if she's my responsibility."

His responsibility? I must've missed that in the court documents. Last I checked, it was Angus who married my mother, not Devlin. Was Mr. Adair passing the buck off to his son? Interesting. Wonder how Perry would feel about that? Maybe someone should tell him?

My hand froze on the metal knob as I shifted my gaze to the closed door down the hall.

*Or someone could show him.*

There was a reason phones were capable of recording, right? Unfortunately, I had the worst timing in the world. Or Devlin had the best. I stood there for five minutes holding my phone out, but Devlin didn't say another word. Not one that I could hear, anyway. I thought about trying to sneak closer, but did I really want to risk another trek into the pit of snakes?

Sure, none of them were real. That didn't mean I couldn't feel their beady little eyes watching me. I should've grabbed that poor polar bear and taken him to safety. Oh well, Snowball was stuck in there now. There was no way I was stepping foot in that room again. And certainly not for some half-cocked rescue mission for a bearskin rug.

My room was a much better option. I'd be left alone and there was a soft bed, which I happily did a flying belly flop on to. After the day I had, some peace and quiet would be nice. I could pretend I was on my own in a little oasis in the pit of hell. That was easier said than done.

The problem with being alone—oasis or not—was that there was nothing to do. There were only so many times one could count the dots on the ceiling before mind-numbing boredom crept in.

I tried everything to entertain myself. Danced around my room, refolded my clothes, and counted all four hundred and sixty-three tiles in my shower. One of which was slightly off in color from the other sandstone ones around it.

Not exactly something I'd expect to find in the Adair household. At least not without a purpose, that is. Like, say, hiding something? I spent God knows how long trying to pry that sucker off, and all I got was a few scrapes on my finger and a chipped nail. That's when I realized how far I'd sunk.

There I was, looking for secrets hidden in the wall, because why? The man who married my mother sent me to my room? Isn't that the kind of thing parents were supposed to do? I may not agree with Angus's chosen punishment, but I couldn't argue the fact that he was acting like… well… a father.

I didn't know how to feel about that. Most of the adults in my life didn't care enough to ask where I was going, let alone lecture me. I was the burden in the house. That I was used to. I could handle it, but this… I'd almost feel better if Angus bitched about the cost of feeding me or something. That was better than whatever the hell this was.

What was this? A ploy or game? That was the only thing that made sense. I may not have much experience in this kind of thing—on a good day, Charmaine could barely take care of herself—but something was definitely off.

Maybe I was the thing that was off?

My parental relationship with Charmaine wasn't exactly textbook. It wasn't all bad, though. There were days of normalcy between the hiding and paranoia. Like the time she took me to the beach. That was the last time I remember seeing any clarity in her eyes…

. . .

*I couldn't stop staring out at the water lapping up onto the shore. Mom said the ocean was beautiful, but I didn't expect this. I was so bored on the way here—there wasn't much to do in a car—but it was worth it.*

*One thing was for sure: it smelled a lot better than the fish store under our apartment. I hated sleeping there. It was stinky and the kids at school made fun of me, but we didn't want the bad people finding us. According to our neighbor's cat, Oliver, scent was the best way to track something.*

*I didn't know who the bad people were. Mom never told me. Maybe she didn't know? Maybe they could make themselves look like normal people? When I was bigger, I'd figure out a way to find them so she could stop being scared and enjoy the little things. Like squishing her toes in soft, warm sand. That was really fun.*

*Giggling, I looked down at the tiny grains my feet were sinking into. It tickled a little every time I moved.*

*"Sydney," Mom waved at me. "Come here, Darling."*

*"Coming," I sang and skipped over to where she was sitting.*

*It was an okay spot. There was nothing special about it. I didn't complain when she pulled me on her lap, but I didn't know why she picked this place to sit. There were so many other places with pretty things, like flowers, water, and sand. The only thing here was a big, old, ugly tree.*

*My eyes scoured the graying bark on the trunk, then lifted to Mom's bright gaze. "Why's the tree sad?"*

*"Shh." She hushed and kissed the top of my head. "Do you remember when I told you the beach was special?"*

*I nodded. "Yes."*

*"That's because there's buried treasure here."*

*My eyes widened. "Like pirate treasure?"*

*How cool would that be? I bet stupid Clive Tompkins didn't have real treasure in his video game.*

*She leaned in and said, "Better."*

*My nose crinkled as she held up a necklace. How was that thing better than pirate treasure? It was old and rusty. I couldn't tell if it was a flower or something else on the front of the locket.*

*"And now." She held out my hand and dropped the necklace in my palm. "It's your job to protect it."*

*I stared down at the chain in my hand and asked, "Protect it from who?"*

*"The bad people," she whispered. "What's hidden inside is very powerful."*

*My fist immediately tightened around the jewelry. We couldn't let the bad people get it. Not if it had power.*

*"But you must never open it, Sydney."*

*"Why not?" If it was powerful, then maybe I could use it to protect her?*

*Her hands wrapped around my cheeks, cupping my face as she stared deep into my eyes. "Promise me you'll never open it."*

*She was serious about this. I could tell by the way the corner of her mouth jerked in a tight line. It was the same look she gave me when I was in trouble.*

*"Okay." I sighed. "I promise."*

*Guess I'd have to find another way to defeat the bad people…*

Huh? Guess Charmaine wasn't as sane that day as I thought. I think I still had that necklace tucked in the back of my dad's picture. Not sure why I held on to it all this time. Honestly, I forgot about it. Oh well. I had better things to do than worry about some trinket of imaginary power.

I leaned forward and peeked out my open window.

There she was. Miss. Mary Sunshine who woke me up every morning with a creepy ass smile. I watched her move around, watering the flowers below, and smirked. 'When I found a box of condoms in the bottom of one of my bags, I wasn't sure what to do with them, or where they came from.

If I had to guess, I'd say it was one of my foster sister's ideas of a joke. The cherry flavor written across the bottom was a huge tip off for that. My virginity status didn't exactly win me any cool points.

Well, the joke was on them. I was going to use every single one of those expired condoms. And when I heard a familiar voice singing outside, I knew exactly who would get the last two.

The rest I filled up and threw against the wall of my shower. Figured it would be a good way to work off some anger, and it was better than breaking stuff. All I had to do to clean up the mess was turn on the water. But this…

My eyes zeroed in on the head of my moving target.

This was much more fun.

*Come on, happy little sunshine girl, just a few more steps…*

"Let's see how full of smiles you are tomorrow," I whispered and released the water-filled latex balloon in my hand.

My moment of amusement was short-lived. For a small thing, she was fast. I barely had time to enjoy her scream before she darted back under cover.

*Damnit.*

I considered leaning out my window to get a better look, but my phone distracted me. It dinged for a text, pulling my attention away, which was probably a good thing. Something told me Angus would be even less impressed with my water ballooning than he was my book hitting.

Sighing, I reached out to scoop up my phone.

There weren't a ton of people who would contact me. Maybe like three, and two of those were adults like Perry who would message to check in. But I did exchange numbers with Fiona, and for some reason, I was dying to bitch to someone about my current situation.

Not that I was one of those girls who constantly complained about how unfair their parents were, but this shit wasn't right. I was seventeen, not twelve. I didn't need someone telling me what to do. I could take care of myself.

*Huh? Maybe I was one of those girls.*

It didn't matter because the text wasn't from Fiona.

> Unknown number: Bring me your phone.

I rolled my eyes. It didn't take a genius to figure who would send a demanding text like that. And considering I had Angus's number logged in my contacts as Uptight Suit, I highly doubted it was him. Which left one other person.

> Me: Jesus, is that you?

> Unknown number: Do you have a problem listening? Bring me your phone!

The ironic thing was I could actually kind of hear his arrogant tone barking those words out.

> Me: Technically, I'm not listening to anything. Now if you had asked if I had a problem reading…

> Unknown number: Don't play games with me.

> Me: I'm just pointing out facts.

He was the one who decided to call it a game. It was kind of fun poking at him, though. I couldn't help but wonder how many texts it would take to get him to type his name?

> Unknown number: You have five minutes.

Oh, I was being timed, was I? There was a shocker.

> Me: You do know that harassment is illegal in all fifty states.

> Unknown number: What the hell are you talking about?

> Me: Well, what would you call texting threats to some random stranger?

Unknown number: You know damn well who this is.

Me: According to my caller ID, it's unknown number 555-6347.

Unknown number: Stop fucking around!

Me: You should probably know that I'm only seventeen.

Any disappointment I had about missing the look in soaked Mary Sunshine's face disappeared when a muffled curse vibrated through the wall from the room next to mine. This was definitely more fun.

Unknown number: I know how old you are.

Me: Did you know that pedophilia is also illegal in all fifty states?

Technically, it wasn't pedophilia. I was within the age of consent across the entire country for the most part. At least, as far as Devlin was concerned.

Unknown Number: Keep it up, Sydney.

Me: How do you know my name? Have you been stalking me? What kind of perv are you?

Unknown number: The kind that's about to come over there and slap the shit out of you.

Me: Oh, so now you're threatening bodily harm to a minor. Keep talking, buddy. The cops are going to love this conversation.

Unknown number: Jesus Christ, it's fucking Devlin.

That only took me seven texts. Not too bad.

> Me: Oh, hello fucking Devlin. What can I do for you?

A smile tugged at my mouth as I added his number to my contacts list.

*Or should I say Twatwaffle.*

> Twatwaffle: You have five minutes to bring me your phone.

> Me: I had five minutes like 2 minutes ago.

He should really make up his mind. Which was it, five or seven.

> Twatwaffle: Four minutes and twenty-six seconds.

> Me: Did you seriously just spell out the numbers? That's precious seconds shaved off your five minutes.

Seemed like a waste of time to me. Technically, my long message wasn't any better, but I just dropped a water balloon on a maid. Logic left this room a long time ago.

> Twatwaffle: Don't toy with me, Bréagán.

And again, another contradiction.

> Me: How is a toy not supposed to toy?

Thought he was pretty smart giving me an Irish word for a nick-name. It's called Google, asshole.

> Twatwaffle: Three minutes and fifteen seconds.

I glanced down at the band around my wrist.

> Me: Actually, it's seventeen seconds. You might want to get your watch checked.

> Twatwaffle: Are you going to keep being smart, or do what you're told?

> Me: Oh man, that's a hard decision. I'm gonna have to take some time to think about it. Ask me again in 2 minutes and 33 seconds.

That's how you texted time.

> Twatwaffle: Last chance, bring me your fucking phone!

Since he asked so nicely…

> Me: Bite me.

> Twatwaffle: You don't want me coming over there to get it.

My eyes shifted to the last condom sitting next to me, full of water.

> Me: Maybe I do.

No text came. Just a loudly growled "motherfucker!" followed by something smashing against the wall. An angry slam vibrated through the air, signaling me to reach out and grab my ammo.

My eyes followed the footsteps echoing down the hall as I slowly crept closer to the door. I'd never been more focused on a small metal knob in my life. I could feel the light glinting off it, tensing my muscles as it jiggled and twisted before being thrown open

Two steps into my room was all Devlin made before I swung my hand, lobbing the water-filled condom through the air.

Gotta say, I'd never been more satisfied than I was when his eyes widened and the bubble burst on his face. I didn't even care about the backsplash that splashed my shirt. Was my retaliation the best course of action to take?

Probably not.

I was definitely going to pay for it. And that was okay because there was only one thing I could smell in the air as droplets trickled off Devlin's chin. The sweet scent of cherry-flavored victory. This round was mine.

Then his eyes snapped up to mine and fucked didn't seem like a strong enough word for the predicament I was in.

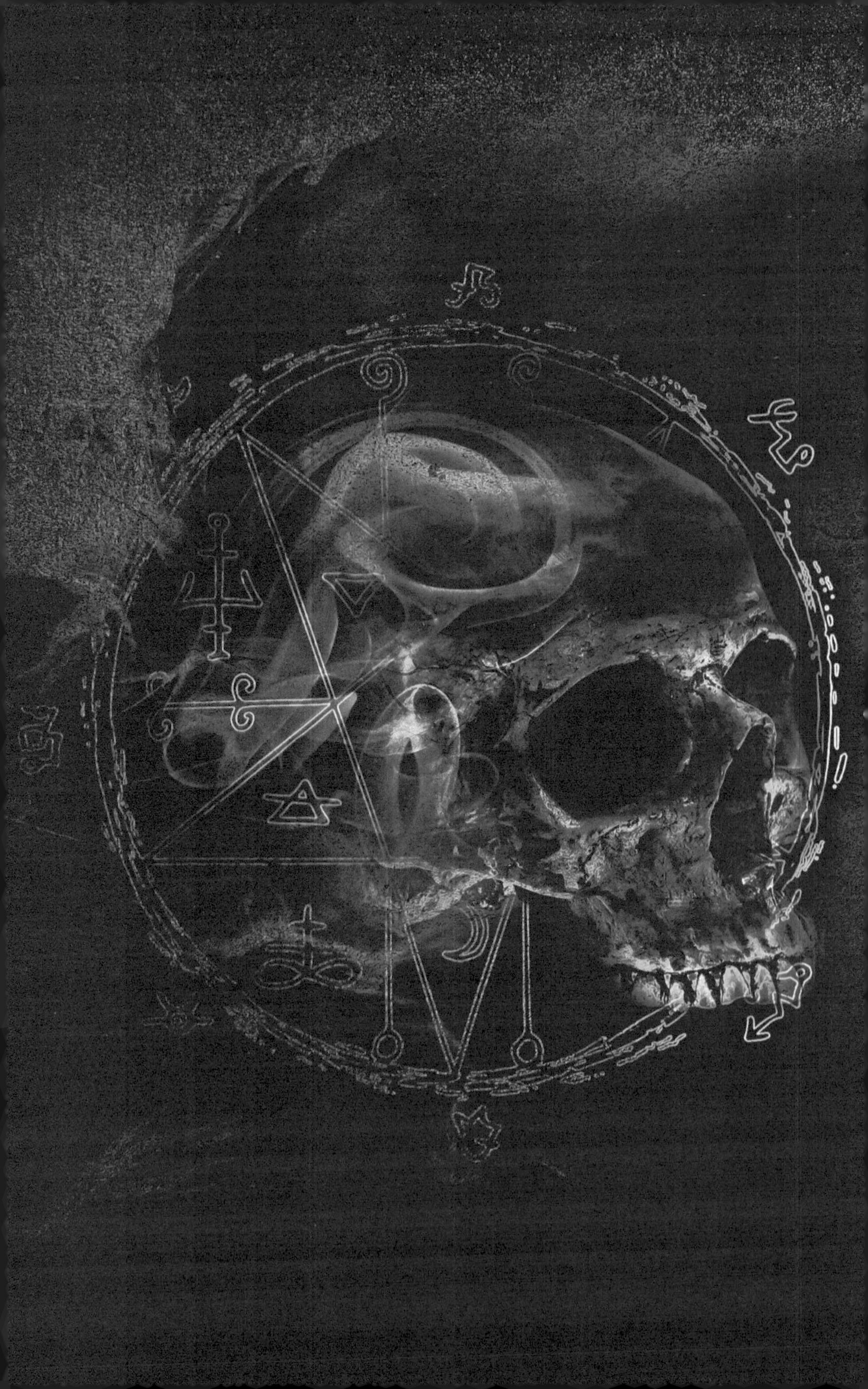

# Chapter 12

Of all the times in my life where the phrase *Oh, shit!* came into play, I never truly understood the full meaning of those two words. But as I stood there watching blackness seep into Devlin's expression, I got it. I knew why girls in movies ran upstairs instead of outside. It wasn't stupidity that led them to make poor choices. It was the mind-numbing effect of terror.

I felt that cloud creep its way through my system. It was a cool, heavy abyss of dread that made me wish the floor would open up and swallow me whole. Regret didn't have shit on that. Hell, I'd take complete and utter mortification over this.

Now would've been a great time for Angus to show up, or Reese. Even Wyatt would have been okay. But I was alone, which wasn't something that bothered me before.

"Did you just hit me with a water balloon?"

Technically, it was a condom. Not that I'd tell him that. I was more worried about getting my legs to move. A calmly spoken phrase shouldn't be that eerie. If there was a tone for impending death, I just heard it in Devlin's voice.

"You want to get wet, do you?" Devlin tipped his chin my way and clenched his jaw. "Fine."

Uh oh, that didn't sound like a good fine. On the upside, when he jerked towards me, my body suddenly remembered how to move. Devlin's arm shot out, reaching for me, and I sprang away, jumping onto the bed with the gracefulness of a cat.

The landing, however… that was another matter.

There was this thing called potential energy return that I hadn't taken into account. Springs—like the ones in this mattress—were designed to bounce back.

So when the full weight of my body slammed down, the springs did what they were meant to and shot me back up, causing me to lose my footing, roll across the bed, and topple off the side.

Gravity pushed down as a whoosh of air blew past me, and yet I still had time to consider the ramifications of my actions. At what point did I cross the line? Was it the text conversation, or the explosion of water that pushed Devlin over the edge? And would I change anything if I could?

I slammed down on the ground with a loud grunt as my lungs concaved and forced out all my oxygen. My brain barely had enough time to register the pain radiating across my chest before Devlin was on me.

He flipped me on my back and growled, "Do you think you're fucking cute?"

That's when I decided that no, I wouldn't change anything if I could. The twitch clenching his jaw was totally worth it.

"I prefer to think of myself as more adorable than cute." Talking wasn't an easy task right now. It felt like every inch of my body hated me, but I still managed to get one more jab in. "You should try it some-time. Brooding asshole isn't really doing it for you."

That was a total lie. I'd just taken a stellar nosedive off a rather high bed and still couldn't stop my eyes from roaming over the muscles flexing in his shoulders.

Devlin was looming over me like the shadow of doom, and I had to squeeze my thighs together when a lock of damp hair flopped over his forehead. Probable death should not be that tempting.

Next thing I knew, his fingers were twisting in my hair, then I was being dragged across the floor.

"Let's see how fucking cute you are after a cold shower."

In hindsight, I should've seen that coming, but I was too focused on clutching at his arm to alleviate the pain tearing its way across my scalp to hear what he said. And if I thought that was bad, having my hands and knees smack down on the tiled ground of my shower was worse. My palms scraped against the floor as a sharp stab shot up my legs, making my thighs convulse.

"What the—"

A sudden shot of water blasted me.

And it wasn't warm water, because that would have been too nice for a prick like Devlin. It was a sharp, piercing, icy chill that sucker-punched me in the gut and stole my breath.

"Not so adorable now, are you?" Devlin growled from behind me.

*I'd show him adorable.*

I'd never shot up so fast in my life. By the way, sudden movements were not a good idea when one was standing on a slippery surface. My feet slid one way as my body prepared to leap away from the wetness raining down on me.

How I managed to stay standing, I had no clue, but it didn't seem that important. Not when my palms smacked against Devlin's chest. Know what did seem important?

The force of my momentum; because the large form I was shoving actually stumbled back a bit. If I could speed going, I could push his broad shoulders out the shower door. There was only one problem with that…

I couldn't pull my hands off his chest. Mainly because the fabric covering it had become translucent. So I could not only feel the hard ridges under my fingers, but I could see them. Wet Devlin suddenly didn't seem so funny anymore.

"You're wearing white," I whispered as my eyes roamed over the black lines of the tattoos under my fingertips.

"So are you."

*I was?*

I glanced down at my own chest and silently cursed myself for putting on a white bra. This was all Reese's fault. If he hadn't stolen my underwear, I could've put on jeans and a black shirt instead of having to find something to go with pink.

I was gonna need a bigger book to hit him with… I would find one right after I got out of here. In order to do that, I had to take my hands off the asshole in my way.

Yet I didn't move. I just stood there, heavily panting, while Devlin tipped his head.

Wow, he was firm. The potential power behind those muscles tingled up my arms and pooled in a needy clench deep in my belly. Did someone turn on the hot water, because it was getting steamy in here?

I could still hear droplets ticking around me, but I couldn't feel its icy sting anymore. I couldn't feel anything beyond the rumble vibrating through Devlin's ribcage.

*Did he just growl, and why the hell was I still touching him?*

A better question was why hadn't I covered myself up yet? I couldn't tell which one of us was shaking more. My arms were visibly trembling, but so were Devlin's. I saw the quake in his shoulders every time his forearms flexed. Fear, uncertainty, and something else was what caused my shivering. But Devlin…

I tipped my gaze down his arm, where his fist was curled up in a tight ball. Almost as if he was getting ready to jump in a fight. My stomach dropped out from under me. Was he going to hit me? Devlin was an asshole, but he wouldn't do that. Would he?

It was when I lifted my chin back up that I realized the only person Devlin was trying to fight was himself.

Lines etched in his brow, while his thick lips screwed up in a tight scowl. "Stop fucking staring at me."

"Stop staring at me," I shot back.

Neither one of us did. We stayed where we were with our eyes locked on the other. I wanted to step back. My calf twitched with the need to get away. But there was something pulling on me.

A tug in my gut that was trying to draw me in closer to him. And the longer I stood there, the stronger that feeling got, until I had to stop myself from involuntarily leaning forward.

"You should leave." One of us needed to, and I didn't know how much longer I could fight this.

"Don't fucking talk." Every inch of Devlin's body tensed as he closed his eyes and sucked in a deep breath. "I can feel your voice."

Normally, a statement like that would make me cock a confused brow, but I got it. I felt the same way. Every deep, rumbling word that came out of his mouth seeped into my bones.

"What is happening?"

"What the fuck did I say about talking?" Devlin barked out. "And stop fucking touching me."

"I can't." Seriously.

I gave up trying to force my arms to drop a while ago. Now I was more focused on not sliding my hands over the solid planes underneath. Because I *really* wanted to. All I could think about was how good his skin would feel on mine. The need for it was so intense that words actually slipped through my lips.

"I want…"

Thankfully, Devlin cut me off. "Don't say it."

The warning in his tone was evident. He was hanging on by a thread, too. If I said one more thing or moved in the slightest, that thread might snap. And that was a truly terrifying thought.

I closed my eyes and concentrated all my energy on remaining perfectly still. If I couldn't see him, then maybe I could gain back some control. It seemed to work too. I listened to the calming sounds of the running shower while reminding myself about how much I hated this prick. I even managed to pull my hands off his chest.

That's when fate handed me a giant-sized fuck you.

When I lifted my leg to step away, the water weighing down my clothes took its toll and yanked my sweats right down my legs.

Devlin's eyes popped open, and I knew I was done.

My hands moved to cover the exposed spot between my thighs while his fingers wrapped around my neck. I was slammed back against the wall before I could suck in another breath.

"Where the fuck are your panties?!"

I wanted to scream *"you have them asshole"* at him, but I couldn't dislodge the words from my throat. I was caught in one of those nature shows. The ones where we followed a lone animal as it struggled to survive the winter.

Except I was at the part where it had snapped, and hunger had taken over. Feral was the only word to describe the glint in Devlin's eyes. Yet somehow, he still managed to maintain a little control.

I, however, was very aware of how my hand felt clamped over my pussy.

Devlin bent down until his mouth was a breath away from mine and hissed, "I should snap your neck."

"So do it!" This was so fucked up and wrong. A death threat should not be the thing that made my core clench.

"I can't." It was disturbing how disappointed he sounded by that statement.

"That doesn't mean I can't break you."

Not sure if I liked the sound of that.

I could feel the heat in his gaze as his eyes slowly roamed over my quaking breasts and down to my cupped mound.

"Are you wet, *Bréagán?*"

"We're in the shower." *Duh.*

"Keep talking, Sydney," Devlin tsked and lifted his arm to push his hand up under my wet shirt. "And I might fuck that smart mouth into silence."

Dear Lord, help me.

That should not have sounded as tempting as it did. Nor should his touch feel that good.

"Move your hands, *Bréagán,*" Devlin growled in my ear. "I want to see that pussy."

Even though I said, "no," my arms still twitched to obey him.

The internal struggle was no longer Devlin's to fight.

It was mine.

Goosebumps raged a hot trail across my skin while his strong fingers slowly made their way up my abdomen to the underside of my breast. My breath hitched as I looked up, silently pleading with Devlin to stop this. I didn't know how. I didn't even know what was happening right now.

He gave me a mocking frown and sang, "You seem confused."

Yes, I was confused. And hot and achy.

"Well, let me clue you in. You belong to me. Meaning…" His fingers clamped around my nipple, giving it a firm yank that ripped a pain-filled screech from me. "I can do whatever the fuck I want to you."

I gritted my teeth against the pain and hissed, "Would Reese agree?"

I'm not sure why I said that. It was just a feeling I had.

"Reese isn't as nice as you think he is." Devlin snickered. "But I think you have other things to worry about right now." He gave my nipple another hard twist and added, "I suggest you start doing what I say. Now move your fucking hands!"

It hurt. His rough touch hurt like hell, but I held back my whimper. I swallowed back my wince and glared with all the hatred I felt right back at him. That only seemed to spur him on.

Devlin's lips curled in a sinister smirk as his finger dug into my flesh.

That did it.

I no longer cared about being discreet and swung my hands up to claw at his arm. Relief was my only concern. That was, until he dropped his arm and pushed his hand between my thighs.

Everything changed then. Devlin's finger pressed down on my clit, and the ache throbbing in my breast turned into something else. A wave coursed through my veins in electric sparks that couldn't be described as simple pain or pleasure.

It was more like a mix of the two. A weird combination that mixed in this perfect, euphoric buzz. I couldn't stop the moan from coming out.

That's when Devlin's mood shifted.

"Fuck me," he breathed out in a growl. "You like this."

"No, I don't," I argued, despite the fact that my hips were begging to grind up against him.

Devlin released his hold on my neck and slid his hand over my chin to give my bottom lip a tug.

"Tell me, *Bréagán*, is it the pain that gets you off? Or knowing that there's not a goddamn thing you can do to stop me?"

Prick. I could stop him if I wanted to. Thought about biting his finger to prove that point when the tip darted in my mouth. But for some reason, I didn't. Maybe it was the desire burning in his eyes that had me stunned. No one had ever looked at me like that before. Like I was the only thing that could satiate the need burning a hole inside them.

He stepped in and bent down to graze his cheek against mine. "You'll still fight me, though, won't you?"

Damn right, I'd fight him.

I swung my arms out to do just that. But then he gave my clit a pinch, and I ended up digging my nails into his shoulders instead.

"Careful now, *Bréagán*, only good girls get what they need."

Fuck him.

"Like you know what I need." I didn't even know what I needed.

Confidence oozed off Devlin's smug grin. That should've been my first clue that I was outmatched. But I was dumb and thought I could beat him. I'd never been more wrong in my life. All it took for Devlin to show me the error of my ways was the one finger he promptly thrust inside me.

My knees threatened to give out as my inner walls clamped down on him. My orgasm was right there, creeping its way up my spine.

"Feel that?" he purred in my ear. "That's your pussy telling me what you need."

I'd never been more terrified in my life. Why was this happening? How could I be so turned on by someone like him? Devlin had never been nice to me. He didn't whisper sweet things in my ear, or tenderly kiss my neck.

He'd never even offered to take me on a date, yet there I was, putty in his masterful hands. What would happen after he was done? Would he walk away, or finally follow through with his threat and kill me?

"Why do you hate me?"

Devlin didn't say anything. He just leaned back and studied my face. But I needed something to help me sleep at night. I needed a reason or excuse. Something to help my mind wrap around the way my body responded to him. Because none of this made any sense.

"Did I do something to you?"

He tipped his head and uttered one word. "No."

"So why do you hate me?"

"Why do you care?"

As far as strange situations went, this was right up at the top of the list. There I was having a conversation about hatred with a guy who had his finger inside me. This definitely was not how I saw my day going.

It wasn't like Devlin's opinion of me would change who I fundamentally was. Nor would it affect the outcome of my life. Unless he really did snap my neck, that is. So, why did I care?

I mulled that question over before finally coming to a conclusion. "I don't want to feel this way about you."

"You think I wanted the responsibility of taking care of a needy fucking brat?"

Yeah, that's it. We were done.

He didn't fight me when I shoved him off me. "I didn't ask you to take care of me, Devlin."

"Yet here I am," he snarled, venom dripping from every word. "Tethered to someone who should've never been born."

"Don't think so highly of yourself." I shook my head and walked over to turn off the shower. "Responsibility like that requires a level of maturity you clearly don't have."

I'd like to see Devlin Adair spend years making sure an insane person ate every day.

"You're treading a thin line, Sydney." His eyes narrowed as his voice lowered an octave. "I'd be careful where that next step lands you."

A part of me wanted to scream in his face. When had Devlin Adair ever sacrificed anything in his perfect little life? When was the last time he put someone else's needs before his? But it wasn't worth playing his game.

He wasn't worth it.

The only amount of my time that Devlin was worth was the second it took me to glance over my shoulder and say, "Get the fuck out of my room."

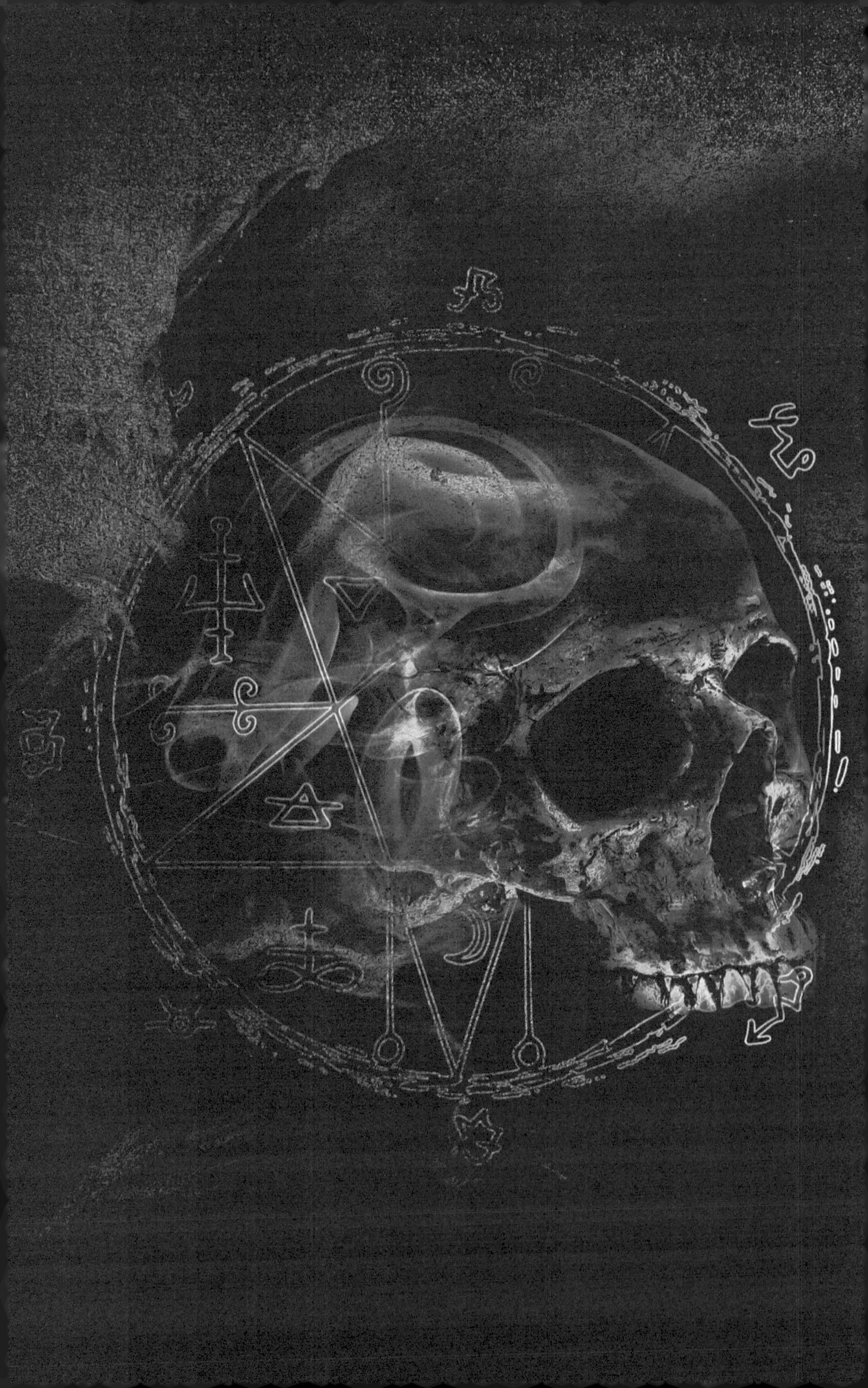

# Chapter 13

 care. Politics didn't have shit on the way girls competed for attention, while boys fought for power. It was a literal jungle where people like me wanted nothing more than to skate by unnoticed.

Being invisible was the only way to survive the chaos. Even then, people still tried to pull me in. There wasn't a dick move I hadn't witnessed, and through it all, I still managed to keep my composure.

Then I came here, where Devlin Adair took all of my calm don't-give-a-fuck-attitude and smashed it under his boot.

Ten years of keeping my cool was gone with seven little words.

*"Get the fuck out of my room."*

I'd never tasted rage like that. Even now, hours later, the bitterness was still there. If Devlin had continued his assault and chased me out of the bathroom, I would understand why anger lingered in my system. But he didn't. Devlin didn't even say a word to me when walked out of my room, and that was somehow worse.

Devlin Adair dismissed me, and now I was planning his murder. I'd been going over and over it in my head, plotting out every last detail, right down to what I'd do with the body. A tap to the head and a dirt nap felt a little too simple.

Don't get me wrong, I'd love to piss on his grave—he'd do the same to mine—but it was all a little mundane. Tossing him into a pit of hungry animals…

Now that seemed more fitting. It wasn't very often that someone got to watch a bunch of pigs tear their enemy apart. I think I saw a couple of farms on the way out here.

Giving the elastic one final twist around my braid, I craned my neck and gazed out the window over the treetops. Not that it did me any good. The town was only visible from the front of the house.

Back here, there was nothing but miles and miles of rocky hillsides and greenery. I'd never seen so many spruce and pine trees in one place.

The difference between them was slight—they were both part of the evergreen family—but pine had a deeper, more vibrant forest color. How I knew that, I had no idea. I must've learned it in school or something. Probably around Christmas time. They were the chosen decoration for that season.

My eyes trickled over the landscape as I tried to imagine what it would look like covered in snow. I bet it would be beautiful. Like one of those holiday movies up in the mountains that Stacy liked to watch. There was even a lake next to a little clearing.

*Hold on…*

I braced my palms on the bench under the window and leaned in while squinting my eyes.

That clearing looked familiar, but it was too far away to be sure. Still, I swear I'd seen that stone slab before. Then again, there were all kinds of rocks around here.

*Oh well.*

I sighed and pulled a royal purple tank top over my head. The color was my favorite. There was something about the rich, deep hue that I liked. The cartoon girl decorating the front, I did not.

She was all big eyes and rosy cheeks with pigtails in her hair in her blond hair. It felt almost mocking the way she smiled back at me.

"What the hell do you have to be so happy about?"

*Stupid cartoon girl with her happy outlook on life. What did she know?*

Know what would make me happy? Some panties. And maybe a touch of poison that I could slip in certain someone's food. But I'd settle for the underwear. All I had in that regard were a pair of black boxers I found stuffed in the bottom of one of my boxes. Yet another joke from an asshole foster sibling.

Isla Holmes wasn't just an asshole, though. She was a spiteful little bitch who wasn't happy when a boy she liked paid attention to someone else. It wasn't my fault the teacher decided to designate James as my lab partner. But she didn't see it that way.

Hence the boxers, because I apparently wasn't feminine enough. In her defense, I didn't have much in the way of curves at the time.

Thankfully, my hips filled out a year later. The boobs, I was still waiting for. I kind of missed that hateful little witch. There's a thought I never thought I'd have. But at least with Isla, I knew what to expect.

Devlin, however…

I slipped out of my room and gave the door down the hall a dirty look.

Did Devlin get off on confusing people, because I have never had anyone make my head swim as much as he did. How could someone be so hot yet cold at the same time? And I didn't mean hot as in looks —which he totally was. It was deeper than that.

I could feel desire coming off him when he looked at me. Mind you, I could also feel rage, hate, anger, and death. Clearly, I was the wrong person to try to untangle that mystery. I could be the one to start the mystery of how he died, though.

*No, Syd.*

Taking a deep breath, I rolled my tongue and let the barbell clacking off my teeth calm my tensing fists. I couldn't let myself stoop to his level. Devlin Nathaniel Adair could hate me if he wanted, but I was better than that.

I paused mid-stride and cocked a brow.

I forgot I knew his middle name, and no one liked that information getting out. I'd die before telling anyone mine.

No, I shook my head. That would be a waste of my time and effort. None of which he deserved. Besides, who was I going to tell? One of his brothers? Pretty sure family was already privy to that knowledge.

"What the fuck do you think you're doing?"

My heart leapt out of my chest as I screeched. "Son of a bitch! Why does everyone in this house have to scare people?"

Seriously. I was getting so tired of this crap. Mind you, if I'd been paying more attention, I might've noticed Devlin throwing his bedroom door open.

Devlin tipped a brow, tempting me to smack that cold expression off his face.

Instead, I sliced a finger through the air and hissed, "A little notice before entering a room would be nice."

*Ring a bell, clap, something to announce an arrival.*

"I'm already in the room."

*Technicality.*

My eyes narrowed. "It's not a room if the door's open."

Yes, I know my statement didn't make sense, but I had to argue something. I'd be damned if he got the last word.

"Got anymore stupid arguments?" Devlin asked while folding his arms over his chest.

I sneered up at him and sang, "No."

He was a stupid argument.

"Good." He leaned over and rested his shoulder on the doorframe. "Then you can tell me why you're lurking in the hall in your goddamn underwear."

"I wasn't lurking." I was distracted. There was a difference. *Besides...* "You have all my underwear."

Asshole didn't even deny it. He just let his eyes fall to the black fabric around my hips and cocked a brow.

Okay, technically boxers were a form of underwear, but that didn't let him off the hook.

"Give me back my panties," I demanded.

"No."

His flat-out refusal stunned me for a second. I kind of expected him to deny it or something.

"You… I mean… How…" I threw my fist down to my sides. "You can't just…"

It was like my brain and mouth had stopped communicating. I couldn't find the right words to throw at him, because there weren't any. If he wanted to hold my panties hostage, that's exactly what he'd do, because Devlin only did what Devlin wanted to. And there wasn't a goddamn thing anyone could do about it.

"They're mine!" I growled.

"They're mine now."

And what did Devlin do when I vented my frustration with a firm foot stomp? Nothing. He didn't do a goddamn thing. He just stood there and calmly watched me. Which only pissed me off more.

I flew forward and jabbed my finger in his chest. "I hope you choke on them."

Devlin didn't say a word. He didn't need to. I could tell I was treading on thin ice from the way he arched his brow down at my finger. Not wanting to tempt the beast I saw darkening his eyes, I cleared my throat and took a step back.

After a few seconds of silence, Devlin asked, "You done?"

"Yes." I'd never been one to back down, but he had this way of making me feel inferior with one look.

"Good, now I suggest you prance your little ass back into your room"—he emphasized that order by walking his fingers through the air—"and put on some fucking clothes."

"I am wearing clothes." It wasn't like my ass was hanging out or anything. All the important parts were covered.

"I'll decide what clothes are."

Was that so? Why was I even having this conversation? Who the hell did he think he was? My dad? Thanks but I already had one of those. "I don't need to justify myself to the likes of you, Devlin Nathaniel."

*That's right bitch, I just middle named you.*

"Is that supposed to annoy me, Sydney Seraphina?"

The gasp of air I sucked in was so loud I wouldn't have been surprised if the twins heard it in their rooms. "How do you know that?"

"I know a lot of things," he shot back.

According to whom? Him? Because I would argue that he didn't know shit about things like, say, tact for one. A fact that I was about to point out when the blond head of a familiar face popped up over his shoulder.

"If it isn't my fiery little pupil," Reese sang while raking his gaze down the length of me. "I'm digging the outfit."

An annoyed sigh brushed past Devlin's lips. "I told her to change."

As much as I hated to admit it, Devlin may have had a point. The way Reese was looking at me made me feel exposed. More clothes didn't seem like such a bad idea.

"Why would you do that?" Reese asked.

"Only whores walk around in underwear."

My face dropped. I changed my mind. Less clothes was a much better idea, because fuck Devlin.

"Since when is that a bad thing?" Reese's light eyes twinkled as he dropped his chin on Devlin's shoulder and added, "I bet she has a wild side."

Oh, I had a wild side, all right. One I'd happily show him just as soon as I found something to hit him with. Where was a book when I needed one?

"I'm not staying long, so get a good look."

Reese frowned. "And here I thought you'd come to play with us."

I snorted.

The only reason I came out here was to get a drink before bed, and I planned on carrying through with that task. Despite what Devlin thought about my outfit. I held my head up and prepared to leave. They could both watch my whore ass walk away.

"Oh, come on," Reese coaxed.

That's when my foot froze mid-stride.

His hand snaked around Devlin's hip into the front of his jeans. It couldn't be what I thought it was. Could it? My eyes widened as Devlin let out a husky grunt.

*Was he?*

Reese must've noticed my confusion because his eyes lit up. "Maybe she does want to play with us."

I literally couldn't move. My foot was still held in the air as my eyes followed Reese's forearm to the bulge moving in Devlin's pants.

What was happening right now? Because it couldn't be what I thought it was.

"Look at that. She already has her mouth open for you."

Oh my God!

Heat flooded into my cheeks. This was really happening right now. Reese was jerking Devlin off. And I couldn't stop staring at the muscle in his forearm. I swear I could feel every flex of his muscle twitch in my core.

When Reese purred, "come here, sweet thing," my foot tried to steer me that way. So I quickly snapped it back on the ground.

"Reese," Devlin hissed in a warning tone.

To which he innocently said, "What?"

"You know what."

I couldn't tell if Devlin said that statement out of annoyance. My eyes were stuck on what was happening under the denim. And the quiet masculine grunts that followed each stroke weren't helping my situation any. I had to actually cough down a whimper.

"She wants to watch me suck your dick; don't you, Sydney?"

*Kind of.*

*Wait... what?*

"No!" I shrieked, finally able to tear my eyes away. "All I want to do is get a drink of water."

It was a simple need. Get a drink before falling into a nice dreamless sleep, where no assholes accosted me or each other. Was that too much to ask?

Reese's brow lifted. "Isn't there a cup in your bathroom?"

*Well, shit, why didn't I think of that?*

"I wanted to stretch my legs." In hindsight, that probably wasn't the best excuse to come up with.

Mischief sparked across Reese's face. "We could stretch your legs."

Devlin's echoing roar boomed out before I could respond.

"Enough!" He grabbed Reese's arm and yanked it out of his jeans. "It's not going to happen."

The look Reese shot him made me take a step back. Normally, he was a pretty upbeat guy. I'd seen my teacher pissed a few times—for some reason he had something against Scotty Dalton—but the darkness that shadowed his face sent a chill up my spine.

"We'll see about that." Reese snarled, then disappeared into Devlin's room.

The next thing I knew, the door was slammed in my face. Not that it mattered any. At this point, I might worry if Devlin left a room without slamming something. The voice that suddenly spoke from behind me, however… That made me jump.

"It won't be long now."

*Fucking Wyatt.*

I slapped my hand against my thundering heart and spun around to glare at him. "Are you spying on me?"

"Not you, per se… more like the situation," he said, twirling his hand through the air.

"What situation?"

"Come on, you're not that dumb." He gave a deadpan look. "You know what I'm talking about."

I honestly had no clue. This was Wyatt. The same man who described a porno like it was a blockbuster action flick. That did take some talent, though. Never thought I'd be pumped to watch a movie called *Arma-get-it-on.*

"You have to see what's happening here."

Sighing, I crossed my arms. "Why don't you enlighten me?"

Wyatt's forehead furrowed as his brows pulled together. "You really don't see it?"

"See what!?" Did everyone in this house major in frustration?

"You and my brother," he explained.

"What about it?"

Unless he was taking bets on which one of us would kill the other first, I didn't see his point.

"Well, Devlin hates you."

*Obviously.*

"And I doubt you think too highly of him."

*Duh.*

Instead of saying anything, Wyatt held up his fists, slowly pushed them together, then made a quiet explosion sound when they met. None of which made any sense to me.

"Are you medicated? Because if you're not, then you should seriously consider asking for some."

He rolled his eyes. "What do you think happens when two fireballs meet head on?"

"They burn."

He looked at me as if I'd just discovered the secret to the universe. "Exactly."

"Uh huh? So about that medication…"

A yell that made my eyes roll came from the other side of Devlin's door.

"Go to bed, *Bréagán!*"

*Bite me, dickhead.*

"See." Wyatt smiled. "That's what I'm talking about."

If he was alluding to the fact that his brother was a grade-A asshole, that wasn't exactly new information. Either way, I was done with this conversation.

"Don't you have some porn to watch?"

"I'm waiting for the live show."

*They did live porn? Eww.*

"You have fun with that." I waved at him and headed back down the hall to my room. "I'm going to bed."

And first thing in the morning, I was tying a bell around everyone's neck.

# Chapter 14



I WASN'T SURE HOW LONG I WAS ASLEEP BEFORE SOMETHING STARTED gnawing at the back of my brain. At first, I thought it was part of my dream.

There was nothing quite as exhilarating as soaring through the air in the body of an owl. But the stronger that sensation got, the more I realized that the disturbing feeling crawling up my spine wasn't adrenaline. Nor was it part of my imagination. Fantasy didn't make the hairs on the back of my neck rise.

The first thing I noticed when my eyes fluttered open was the abundance of shadows dancing around my room. Normally, moonlight cut through and chased some of the darkness away, but it was cloudy out tonight. There wasn't much more than a soft sliver glow bouncing off the floor under my window.

That lack of light made the shuffling sound I heard at the foot of my bed echo in my ear like a drum. My heart picked up pace, pumping sharp slices through my veins. I felt warmth leave my body, cooling my head with fear as it worked its way down to my toes.

As illogical as it was, I thought about hiding under my blanket. It was a tactic I employed as a child when the monster in my closet bared his dripping fangs. But I was in the real word, and the boogeyman didn't exist.

At least that's what I told myself when I tried to muster up the courage to swing my eyes towards the sound. Nothing had ever been more daunting than those few seconds it took to force my neck to turn.

How I managed not to scream when I saw something moving around, I'll never know. The terror was right there, lumping in my throat, but not so much as a breath came out as I lay there staring at the distinct outline of arms and legs.

The something in my room was a someone!

There was nothing creepier than waking up to someone standing at the foot of your bed. If it was possible for a heart to combust from fear, then mine just did. I could literally hear the pop behind my ribs while my lungs struggled to work.

My brain switched into fight mode. I threw the only thing within reach—a pillow—then jumped across the bed to click on a lamp and grab a pen. Light flooded the room, making me squint.

The only thing that saved me from turning my back and running like a coward, was the pen pressing against my palm. Having something solid in my grip made me feel a little better. It wasn't the best weapon, but it was better than nothing.

"You talk in your sleep."

My face dropped.

*Devlin.*

Of course. Who else would creep into my room in the middle of the night? My plans for murder no longer seemed like an overreaction.

"What are you…" I stopped when my eyes swung his way.

Fully clothed Devlin was tempting, but naked except for a pair of gray sweats Devlin…

What was I talking about?

"You also snore."

I followed the black lines inked on his skin and muttered, "Uh huh."

There was a second where my mind actually malfunctioned. There was nothing beyond those hard ridges. Solid and firm bulges of muscle that worked their way down his torso like some kind of erotic painting. He could grate cheese with those abs.

*Get your head out of your vagina, Syd!*

*Right.*

I shook my head and snarled, "What the hell, Devlin!"

If I thought that was going to help me regain my focus, I was dead wrong. One twitch of a solid peck was it took to trap me again.

I was mesmerized by that masculine form. Every breath Devlin took caused his chest to flex as it expanded. And the deep voice that came from behind those ribs poured over me like honey.

"Like what you see, *Bréagán?*"

*Um, yeah. Wait...*

"Get out of my room, Devlin!" I yelled, more pissed at myself than him. "What are you even doing in here?"

It was a valid question. I might've even called him a creep, but given my current drooling status, it seemed a tad hypocritical.

A sigh should not have been as tempting as the one that came out of his mouth. "Reese kicked me out."

"I fail to see how that's my problem."

If I thought Devlin looked great from the neck down, then I'd obviously failed to take into account the five o'clock shadow dusting his sharp jawline. Damnit, why did I have to look up?

His dark hair appeared extra tousled. A couple of strands flopped down over his forehead when he twisted his neck, and I couldn't help but wonder how it would feel to run my fingers through those soft locks.

"But it is your problem, *Bréagán.*"

I apparently had many problems, one of which was the inability to stop gawking. My tongue piercing clacked off my teeth, turning on the little voice of logic in the back of my head. There was an asshole in my room. I needed to focus.

"I'm sorry." I placed my hand on my chest in a fake gesture of sympathy. "You must have me mistaken for someone who gives a shit about your issues."

Devlin's head dropped as he gave a small shake. "I can't believe I'm doing this."

That didn't seem ominous at all.

"Doing what exactly?"

If his goal was to further annoy me, then he was succeeding fabulously. I was thoroughly annoyed by the half-naked wall of muscle and the burning desire to touch it.

"Take your clothes off."

*Exsqueeze me.*

"What?" I must've misheard.

Devlin huffed out a sigh and crossed his arms. "You heard me. I said take off your clothes."

*Or I didn't.*

The laugh bubbled up before I could stop it. I think Devlin had a sense of humor, but that was one hell of a joke.

"Yeah, sure." I chuckled. "Want me to spread my legs too?"

This was great. Okay, maybe Devlin didn't need to die. I could handle this side of him.

"Yes."

Huh? Why wasn't he laughing? In fact, Devlin didn't seem to find this funny at all. Not so much as a snicker passed through his lips.

I choked on my own amusement.

"You're serious?"

His brow arched. "Do you see me laughing?"

*Well, no...*

"Um... Aren't you with Reese?" Given what I'd witnessed earlier, it wasn't a hard conclusion to come to.

"He's why I'm doing this."

What did me getting naked have to do with Reese? *Unless...*

I slipped out from under the blanket and crawled a little closer to the end of the bed, where I could peek at the door. I thought maybe Reese was hiding on the other side of the wall.

He wasn't.

The only thing over there was a closed door.

That's when the floor fell out from under me. Not because I didn't see someone hiding behind the corner, but because there was a tent in Devlin's pants. A rather large one that I hadn't seen before because of the footboard. But there it was, hard, big, and one hundred percent terrifying.

Oh my god. He was serious.

Okay, this wasn't funny anymore.

My head slowly lifted. "You need to leave."

The shower was one thing. We were caught up in the moment, but this…

The scary part was, not a single twitch tugged on his expression.

"This will go a lot easier if you do what I say."

*Yeah, that wasn't happening.* "Go fuck yourself."

What was he going to do? Force me? Even Devlin wasn't that much of an ass.

I started to second guess that assumption when he bent down and slammed his hands around the lip of the footboard.

"Before you decide to run your fucking mouth, I want you to ask yourself something." Devlin leaned in, grazed his cheek off mine, and hissed in my ear, "Would I get off on hurting you?"

My throat bobbed with a thick swallow. Yes, yes, he would.

Suddenly, I was very aware of the fact that I was on my hands and knees.

I shot backwards, pressing my back against the headboard. That's when I remembered the pen clutched in my hand. My eyes dropped down to the tip poking out of my fist. I could stab him. That was why I grabbed it.

"You sure you want to do that?" Devlin challenged.

I cocked a brow right back at him. "You sure you want to do this?"

For a split second, I could've sworn the corner of his mouth curled, but it was gone before I could be sure. The sad part was that, despite everything that was happening, a part of me tingled when his forearms flexed.

I pushed that part down and concentrated on keeping my eye on the predator as he sighed. "All right. Have it your way." He pushed off the footboard and rolled his shoulders back.

A stride had never been more menacing than the one Devlin took around the corner of the bed. Everything about it moved in slow motion. His foot lifting in the air, followed by the long stretch of a leg.

I saw the muscles in his hips guide the movement and felt the firmness of his step landing on the floor in the pit of my stomach. But when his dark eyes locked on mine, I knew the true meaning of helpless.

Devlin was more than a foot taller than me, with a huge, bulking form. I weighed a hundred pounds on a good day. How the hell was I going to fight him off? It wasn't possible. That didn't mean I was about to give up. But I had to at least try.

My grip tightened around the pen as he took another step.

"You better make it count and stick that thing in good." He tipped his chin at my armed hand. "You'll only get one chance."

One chance was all I needed.

"I figure the throat is a good place to go for," I said while shifting down the headboard, away from him.

His dick twitched at my statement. Almost like it was taunting me. That's when I really started to get scared. There was a volume to mass ratio here that, judging by the size of that thing, didn't equate. I was only one tiny person. That thing would not fit inside me.

"Look, Devlin, I'm sorry for what I said earlier, okay? You're totally mature." An apology was worth a shot.

"No, you were right." He took another step, causing my heart to hammer loudly against my chest. "I was acting childish." But it was the final step that caused my heart to stop all together. "It's time for me to man up and take control of my responsibilities."

And by taking control of his responsibilities, he meant taking control of me.

My mouth was so dry that I felt my swallow move down my throat. "I'm not your responsibility."

I'd shuffled so far over on the bed that my ass was teetering on the edge. Not exactly a secure position for me to be, but I wasn't about to move closer to him, either.

Devlin's palms pressed against the mattress, and I could already feel his heaviness weighing me down. "You knew this was coming."

No, I didn't.

I mean, sure, there was the whole thing in the shower, and he was always saying shit about me belonging to him, but I thought that was some bullshit asshole, do-what-I-say crap. I didn't think it meant this. Unless he was trying to scare me?

Skepticism narrowed my eyes. "This isn't funny, you know?"

"Do I seem like the joking type?"

Well, no. But that didn't mean anything. I'd seen some people go pretty far for a prank. Why should he be any different?

Silence fell over the room as we stared each other down. Devlin with his arms braced on the bed, while my body prepared to either attack or run. I was just waiting for him to make the first move.

"You're going to make me chase you, aren't you?"

Not exactly the move I was waiting for. "Maybe?"

I was already set up to dart away. I was even on the side of the bed closest to the door. But something told me that's what he wanted. So I'd stay right where I was. At least that was the plan until Devlin's arms twitched. He lunged across the bed.

When I say I bolted, I meant it. I jumped up and booked it across the room so fast that I should've ended up face first against the door. Not that it would've mattered. I didn't make it that far. I barely made it around the corner before I was grabbed and thrown back on the bed.

Dread seeped through me as my body bounced on the mattress. The only saving grace I had when Devlin quickly crawled over my prone form was the pen still held in my grip.

All my fear and rage went into that swing. But it wasn't enough. Devlin seized my wrist before I could make contact and slammed my arm down, knocking the one weapon I had out of my grasp.

"I told you to make it count." He tsked.

I looked up at him and tried to think of something to say. A witty remark or insult that would make him back off, but it was becoming evidently clear he wasn't going to stop this time. That should scare me more than it did.

Don't get me wrong, I was scared. How could I not be? Devlin was hovering over me with my arm pinned above my head. He was barely touching me, but it felt like he was everywhere. The problem was, I didn't know if my body was shivering out of fear or something else. Something that had my stomach flipping.

For a second, when his eyes lazily roamed down my side, I forgot what was happening. Then he spoke.

"Are you done fighting?"

That snapped me back into action. I swung my free arm and kicked my legs. This time, my strikes did make contact. My palm slapped off the side of Devlin's face while my knee jabbed into his thigh. Did any of that do any good? No.

One grab of my hip was all it took for Devlin to flip me over. He grabbed the back of my neck with one hand, pressing my face into the blanket, then cracked the other palm across my ass.

I think I screamed.

My mind didn't have time to register the pain burning my flesh before the next strike came. And his onslaught didn't end there. Devlin rained down a fury of blows on one cheek and then the other that had me sucking back tears in loud choking gulps.

By the time he finally stopped, my entire body was covered in a fine film of sweat, and my ass felt like it was on fire. I had my face smashed so far into the blanket that I could practically taste fabric every time I choked down a mouthful of air, but I didn't dare move. It was safer if I didn't.

"I'll ask you again," Devlin growled, making me jerk away. "Are you done fighting?"

There was no way I was about to relieve that experience, so I did the only smart thing I could and responded with a small nod.

I whimpered when Devlin's hand smoothed over the back of my head.

"Look at me, *Bréagán.*"

He was testing me. I knew that. Every fiber of my being itched to tell him off, but I was so pathetically grateful that he didn't hit me again that I obeyed and slowly turned my head.

Devlin reached out and swept his thumb over my cheek, wiping away some of the wet streaks staining my face. "Do you have no idea how sexy you are right now?"

Was he crazy? My hair was stuck to my forehead, my eyes felt puffy and were probably red, and my entire body was shaking. Sexy was hardly the word I would use for the look I had going on right now. Full-on ugly-crying would've been an improvement. So why was Devlin staring at me like I was his next meal?

Oh right, he was a sick fuck who got off on hurting others. Almost forgot about that.

"I bet your ass is nice and red." His eyes shifted to follow his hand as he gave my ass a hard squeeze.

My skin screamed from the rough touch, and it took everything in me to stop my hand from swinging out in retaliation. I couldn't stop the whine from bubbling up my throat, though.

"Let's find out, shall we?" It was the only warning I got before my boxers were yanked down my legs.

Instinct made my feet kick out. That action ended the instant I felt his tongue lave a warm, wet trail over my tender flesh.

That was followed by a deeply growled, "Fuck."

All the heat searing my backside morphed into a pool of need that flowed down my thighs. The last thing I wanted Devlin to know was how his touch affected me. So I wriggled and squished my legs together. I should've known that wouldn't work. If anything, it had the opposite effect as what I intended.

Devlin wrapped his fingers around my hips and lifted them off the bed. I thought maybe he was going to flip me over. It would've been better than what happened. Because the second his tongue slid through my folds, my mind checked out.

Even if I wanted to fight, I couldn't. All I could do was ball up the blankets in my fists and moan as Devlin growled and continued to feast. He pulled on me, lifting my torso off the bed so I had to steady myself with my arms.

It was an uncomfortable position, and one that I didn't care about when his mouth clamped down around my clit. I didn't care about anything after that. Not the fingers digging into my hips, or that I hated the man doing it. I just wanted more. I needed it more than I needed my next breath.

"Oh god," I moaned and clawed my fingers into the mattress. "I hate you so much right now."

"The feeling's mutual." Devlin groaned, then sunk his teeth into my thigh.

I screamed, but not because it hurt—which it did. I screamed because that pain shot straight into my core, sending me over the edge. Pleasure tensed my muscles, making my back bow and my legs convulse.

It took a second for me to catch my breath, and when I did, I was no longer lifted off the bed. My back was pressed on it, and I was staring up into the darkest eyes I'd ever seen. Devlin's pupils were so dilated I couldn't tell where they ended and his irises began.

And then I felt it. The brush of something hard against my skin as he pushed his knee between my thighs. The reality of the situation suddenly struck me. Devlin was naked and on top of me. The only clothing separating us was my tank top.

I had to stop this.

Mustering up all of my strength, I looked him straight in the eyes and demanded, "Get off me!"

"No."

Good to see he was still an asshole.

I tried to clamp my legs together and swung my arms when he pawed at my shirt. But it was no use. He had my tank top ripped off my head and legs parted with minimal effort. Actually, it was kind of sad how useless my struggle was.

"I'm serious, Devlin."

"I don't give a fuck, Sydney."

He grabbed my wrists and slammed them down on the bed. My breath hitched as his hips shifted, then I felt something big and very hard press against my opening. My entire body went stiff. This couldn't be happening.

I wanted to fight and wriggle away, but I was too scared to buck. His dick was right there.

"Are you scared, *Bréagán*?"

There was no point in lying. I was sure he could hear my heart thumping.

So, I gazed up at him and said, "Yes."

As crazy as it was, I think a part of me was hoping he'd give me some form of comfort.

He didn't.

"Good." His weight pressed down on me as he leaned in and whispered, "Because this is going to hurt."

Then he thrust his hips and forced himself inside me.

The sound that tore its way up my throat felt like it was ripped from my very soul. God, it hurt. I was blinded from the pain coursing through my body. I couldn't breathe or move. I couldn't even think past it. And what did Devlin do?

"Stop fucking fighting me," he growled and continued forcing his length inside me.

*I* wasn't fighting him, but my pussy sure was. My walls tightened up against the uncompromising hardness stretching them.

Devlin's solution to this was to grab my left thigh and spread my legs farther apart. When that didn't work, he reversed his thrust. Sliding some of his cock out of me before diving back in.

"Jesus Christ, relax. You're too fucking tight."

*Or, or, and hear me out…*

"You're too big," I snarled back at him.

I slapped my free hand against his chest in an effort to get him off me. If my other wrist wasn't trapped in his grip, I'd have used those fingers to claw his eyes out. My leg could only be pushed out so far before it broke off.

Devlin shifted his hips again and gave a grunt of frustration. "This isn't working."

*You think?*

I could see the strain on his face as a bead of sweat rolled down his forehead.

That's when he stopped and let go of my leg. I practically sighed in relief, until he twisted his neck and gazed down into my eyes.

"Do you have any idea how many times I've jerked off to the image of you crawling out from under my bed?"

What?

He released my wrist and leaned down to rest his weight on his elbow. "Do you want to know why I get so angry with you?"

I don't think I did.

"I want to hate you." A tingle trickled down my neck when his fingers traced the line of my jaw. "But the truth is, I've never wanted anyone as much as I want you."

Was this some kind of trick?

I didn't know how to respond to that, or what I should do when his lips grazed mine.

"If you had any idea what I did with your panties…"

The warmth of his breath called to me, drawing my head off the pillow as I whispered, "What did you do?"

"Naughty girl." He tsked and shifted his hips.

The way he said those words did something to me. When his cock slid along my walls, I could feel every hard ridge.

A smirk pulled at the corner of Devlin's mouth.

"That's it, *Bréagán*." He thrust his hips, and my breath hitched. "Let me inside that hot little cunt."

That should not have sounded as dirty as it did. The same sensation I had in the shower washed over me. Everything was suddenly hot and tingly. It felt like Devlin was everywhere.

His heaviness weighed me down, while his scent surrounded me. And it all felt so good. Even the throbbing inside me filled my body with need. I couldn't stop my back from arching to press my breasts against him.

"What is happening?"

The question was meant for me more than it was him, but Devlin still answered.

His fingers threaded through my hair as he yanked my head back. "You're about to get fucked."

He drove into me and let out the sexiest groan I'd ever heard when his pelvis smacked against me. After that, all I could do was grab his shoulders and hold on while Devlin did exactly what he said.

He fucked me. Hard, long, and deep. So deep that I could feel the orgasm cresting in my bones. The intensity of it was terrifying.

I gritted my teeth against the pleasure and shook my head, refusing to let it break loose. If I went over that edge, my heart might burst. But Devlin wasn't going to let me off that easily. I swear it was like he knew what I was thinking.

He wrapped his hand around my neck and hissed, "Don't you dare keep that shit from me. That orgasm is mine, and I fucking want it."

That's when he did some weird voodoo magic sex move, where he swivelled his hips and snapped his cock up against some secret spot inside me. I plunged so hard off that edge that my vision blurred with white dots. And if that ride into ecstasy wasn't enough, he did it again.

I screamed his name, then moaned out pathetic whimpers when my throat got hoarse. And still, he didn't stop. Devlin drove into me with the fury of a man possessed.

"Please," I begged. "No more."

"You'll take what I fucking give you." Devlin grunted and drove his cock so deep inside me that my back lifted off the bed.

Was it possible to die from pleasure? If so, I had one foot in the grave. I couldn't tell if the moisture tricking down my face was tears or sweat.

"I'm sorry." I didn't know what else to say. "I'll be good."

"You'll be my good girl, will you?"

I whimpered and gave a small nod. Those words sounded way too dirty coming out of his mouth.

"We'll see about that." Devlin rotated his hips, making my pussy clenched down around his length. "Open your mouth."

I hadn't realized my eyes were closed until he said that. Opening them was a lot harder than I thought, but I did it. I put all my focus into forcing my lids to flutter. The sight that awaited me wasn't one I was prepared for. Sweat slicked Devlin's hair, and his eyes were completely feral.

"That's not your mouth, *Bréagán*."

The warning in his husky tone was evident, yet I couldn't make my lips part. My mind was completely entrapped by the large, sweaty man on top of me.

I couldn't look away if I wanted to. The way his muscles twitched and lips parted was nothing short of breathtaking. Even the strain pulling on his brow called to me.

"Fuck me." He grunted, slammed into me one more time, then grabbed my chin and pried my jaw apart.

There was barely enough time for my mind to register the feeling of him pulling out of me before the thick head of a cock pulsing with need, splashed something on my tongue. My mouth was suddenly filled with salty fluid as Devlin roared out a long and exaggerated "Fuuuuck!"

My tongue moved around, trying to get rid of the fluid invading my senses, but Devlin clamped his hand tightly around my lips.

"Don't you fucking dare. Swallow that shit."

His eyes stayed locked on mine. I couldn't just see the possessive glint within those dark orbs, I could feel it. And as his release moved down my throat, I knew that what Devlin had been saying was true. I belonged to him.

*Fuck.*

# Chapter 15



It felt as if my limbs were weighed down on the softness of the mattress while the rest of my body lay there, floating on a fluffy cloud of numbness. I was exhausted. My mind, however… that was running a marathon. One thought kept churning over and over again.

*I just had sex with Devlin.*

What the hell was wrong with me?

This was a man who hadn't uttered a single nice thing to me. He didn't welcome me with open arms or even give me warm smile. From the second I met him, it had been nothing but cruelness.

The kindest thing he'd said to me was 'she's wearing too much make-up,' and that was spoken to his brother as if I weren't in the room. He was cold, hateful, and downright mean, and I let him in.

*But did I?*

I looked over at Devlin lying beside me and smacked my lips together as his chest heaved. The salty taste of his orgasm still lingered in my mouth, reminding me of the angry glint in his eyes as he ordered me to swallow it. Come to think of it, everything he did was an order or forceful. I didn't want this.

I didn't want him.

*Did I?*

I was so confused.

"Did you just rape me?"

Devlin's left eye popped open. "You liked it."

Seriously! That's how he was going to answer that question? Then again, maybe he had a point? I could've fought harder. What did a cat or squirrel do when they were cornered by a bigger predator?

They snapped and fought like their life depended on it, because, well, it did. So, if I really didn't want Devlin to touch me, then I should have lost my shit and not stopped until I clawed his eyes out.

But I didn't.

Maybe I didn't want it. Maybe he was right, and I did like it? Why else would I have come? Orgasms didn't just pop up. They had to be worked up to and wanted at least a little.

Sometimes I couldn't get myself there, and I tried. Then along came Devlin with his masterful fingers and magic dick... asshole.

"Is there anything you're bad at?"

"Reese would say I'm emotionally disconnected."

"No," I sang mockingly. "You're such a welcoming guy."

I was with Reese on that one. In fact, I don't think I'd heard a more true statement in my life.

"All right." He sighed and rolled his eyes my way. "I may have taken things a little too far."

I snorted. "Ya think!"

"Too far" happened the first day I got here, when he burst into my room with his brothers.

"Look, I'm trying." Devlin let out a heavy breath that I felt in my chest and lifted himself up onto his elbows. "This shit isn't easy for me."

"Do you think it's easy for me?" I shot back.

That seemed to make him mad. The scowl I'd become used to seeing washed over Devlin's face.

"You don't have to lie next to the daughter of the man who…"

My father? Alertness rolled through my body, causing me to suck in a gasp. "The man who what?"

I'd never wanted someone to finish a statement more than I did at that moment. There was this hole inside me where my father should've been. Was he a good man? A bad man? Did he have any allergies or hobbies? Did he also hate the smell of peppermint?

Did he love my mother? Did he love me? I didn't know anything beyond his name—Rosco Ricci—and that he was from Italy. And even that was information I got from Charmaine.

So who knew how reliable that was? The last place I would've thought to look for answers to those questions was Devlin.

Unfortunately, Devlin didn't finish speaking. Instead, he pressed his lips together in a tight frown.

"Come on, Devlin." I lifted my arm and caressed the side of his face. "Please tell me."

He answered me with a firm, "No."

Frustration caused my hand to smack off his cheek, which probably wasn't the best reaction. Devlin snatched my wrists and was back on top of me before I could blink.

"I suggest you calm down, *Bréagán*."

I lifted my head and hissed, "Fuck you."

Yes, I was angry. I was downright pissed. Given the fact that my father died before I was born, Devlin couldn't have known him that well. But the point was, he did know something. And I deserved to know it too.

His next words made me go still. "Do I need to fuck you again?"

"No," I whispered.

Just the feel of his cock hardening against my leg was enough to make an ache pulse in my pussy.

Devlin let out a huff of air and dropped down onto his left elbow. "If this is going to work, then you need to start doing what I say."

What the hell even was this? Assault? The start of a relationship? Was Devlin my boyfriend now, and if so, where did Reese fit into the equation? Would he be the side piece? Was I the side piece? Were the two of them even in a relationship? And why did I care?

The problem was, I did care. Guilt bloomed behind my ribs as I wondered if I just helped someone cheat? Don't get me wrong, Reese wasn't exactly my favorite person. That didn't mean I wanted him to get hurt.

"Reese is going to hate me."

Devlin snickered, then cleared his throat. "No, he's not."

"Yes, he is." I whined as a tear slid down my cheek. "We're horrible people."

Only a horrible person would do something like this to someone else. A despicable, deplorable human being who had absolutely no regard for other people's feelings. Like the asshole on top of me who dropped his head and started laughing.

Prick.

Glad Devlin found this so amusing. He was the culprit in this situation. I was the innocent bystander who was sleeping until he came along and made me the bad the guy.

I slapped his shoulder and snarled. "Stop laughing. This isn't funny."

"Oh, yes, it is." Devlin chuckled.

Despite everything, I did have to admit that I liked the way his dark eyes lit up when he smiled. A part of me was tempted to kiss him, but I'd already done enough damage. Then again...

My eyes danced over his lips. They were so full, thick, and soft. It was hard not to think about how good his mouth felt.

"Careful, *Bréagán*, looking at me like that is a good way to get fucked."

My body purred at the deep timbre of his voice. Would one kiss really be that bad? We'd already done so much more than that.

Devlin leaned in, bringing his face close to mine, and sucked my bottom lip in between his teeth. "Do you want me to fuck you again?"

The weird part, he didn't seem to be looking at me. But I didn't care, because a second later, he rolled onto his side and threw my leg over his hip. And God, help me, I did want to feel him again.

I was such a bad person.

At least that's what I told myself when my back arched, pressing my breasts up against his solid chest.

I couldn't help it. Everything felt amazing again. The way his palm smoothed down over my hip, and how his fingers tangled in my hair. All of it ignited my nerve endings, sending a trail of hot need across my skin. But this was wrong. I couldn't let it happen again.

I parted my mouth to protest, then quickly forgot what I was going to say when Devlin's lips landed on the side of my neck. He sucked, and I moaned.

Fuck it. I could pay for my actions in the afterlife.

"Fuck, that's hot."

*Was that Devlin's voice?*

"You want a taste?"

*Okay, that was Devlin's voice. Wait a minute…*

My eyes popped open as the mattress dipped, and someone crawled on the other side of the bed. We weren't alone!

I peeked over my shoulder and shrieked. "What the hell, Reese?"

The front of my body tucked into Devlin in an attempt to hide from the mischievous smirk on Reese's face.

What was he doing here? And… "Where the hell are your clothes?"

Was nothing sacred anymore?

I felt a wall of muscle press up against my back as a puff of hot breath wafted over the side of my face. "Why would I need clothes?"

My arm wrapped around Devlin's waist as I nuzzled into his neck and whined, "Go away."

"Not a fucking chance," Reese growled, making me shiver.

When a second set of hands started to roam over my curves, I whimpered and clung to Devlin. Was it weird that I was seeking solace in his arms? A minute ago, I wanted to punch him in the gut, and now he was the only thing grounding me. Because as much as I told myself I didn't want this, my body disagreed.

It liked the way Reese's fingers kneaded my flesh and warmed at the feel of hard muscle surrounding me. I was sandwiched between two men—neither of which I was particularly fond of—and all my hips wanted to do was push back into the hand smoothing over my ass.

"Damn, you really did a number on her." Reese swung his hand and gave my ass a smack that made me wince and jerk closer to Devlin.

Asshole.

"She brought it on herself." Devlin pressed his lips to my temple and growled, "You should've kept your mouth shut."

My bad. Devlin was the asshole.

"Bad girl." Reese tsked, slithering his hand between my thighs.

I tried to clamp them closed, but Devlin slapped his hand down on my knee and held my leg where it was, slung over his hip. There wasn't a thing I could do other than whimper as Reese slid his fingers along the delicate, tender flesh of my pussy.

"Is someone a little sore?" I didn't have to see his face to pick up on the taunt in his words.

That's when I snapped.

"What the hell is wrong with you two!" I slapped Devlin's arm off my leg, then shifted to glare at Reese. "You can't just come in here and do whatever you want."

They could find somebody else to play their sick game. I was not a toy. Why I ever felt bad for Reese was beyond me. They could both take a flying leap off a high rise. I'd even give them a ride.

And did my outburst get me anywhere? No. If anything, it set me back a few paces. The only thing I did get was a playful smirk from Reese before Devlin's arm shot out and grabbed my neck.

"Apparently, you didn't learn your lesson."

Devlin's threat should've scared me, and it did. But not enough to make me hand over my dignity. He could do what he wanted, spank me, beat me, or yell at me. I refused to fold.

"I am not sleeping with Reese."

"You will fuck Reese," Devlin hissed down at me, then looked over at Reese. "But he won't fuck you tonight."

Thank you. *Wait*...

Reese tipped a challenging brow at Devlin. "Like fuck I won't."

"I said no! She needs to rest."

I kind of wanted to kiss Devlin right now.

Reese, however, wasn't giving up. "She can take it."

He cracked his palm off my thigh and moved the hand he had between my legs to shove a finger in my entrance. I tried to wriggle away, but I was outmatched. Between the hold Devlin had on my throat and the grip Reese had on my hip, I had no chance.

Devlin tipped his head and cocked a brow. "Do you want to wait a week to fuck her again?"

Again? What the hell did he mean, again? There would be no again.

"Fine." Reese reluctantly agreed. "But I get to watch her come."

Devlin nodded. "That's fair."

"How is that fair?" I argued.

What the hell was he talking about with this fair shit? Pretty sure I passed my quota when I thought an orgasm was going to kill me. There would be no more coming of anyone. I was done.

That thought went out the window the second Reese pumped his arm and hit some spot inside that made my toes curl.

Reese growled at my reaction and dragged his tongue over the curve of my hip. "Ooo, she liked that."

*Fuck Reese and his sexy growling.*

"No. I d—"

Reese made me eat my words by hitting that spot again. This time with more force. And he didn't stop there. He did it again and again until my fingers were lost in Devlin's hair, pulling on his scalp.

Somewhere hidden in the clouded haze of pleasure that filled my brain, was a series of masculine grunts followed by something warm and wet landing on my skin.

When I came down, I realized I wasn't the only one to orgasm. Evidence of Reese's and Devlin's release was sliding down my thigh and over my breasts. I was too tired to move, let alone say anything.

So I lay there while one of them cleaned me up. I didn't even argue when they tucked me in between them. I just yawned and let myself fall into the peaceful bliss of slumber.

This was the most fucked up step-sibling or teacher/student relationship I'd seen.

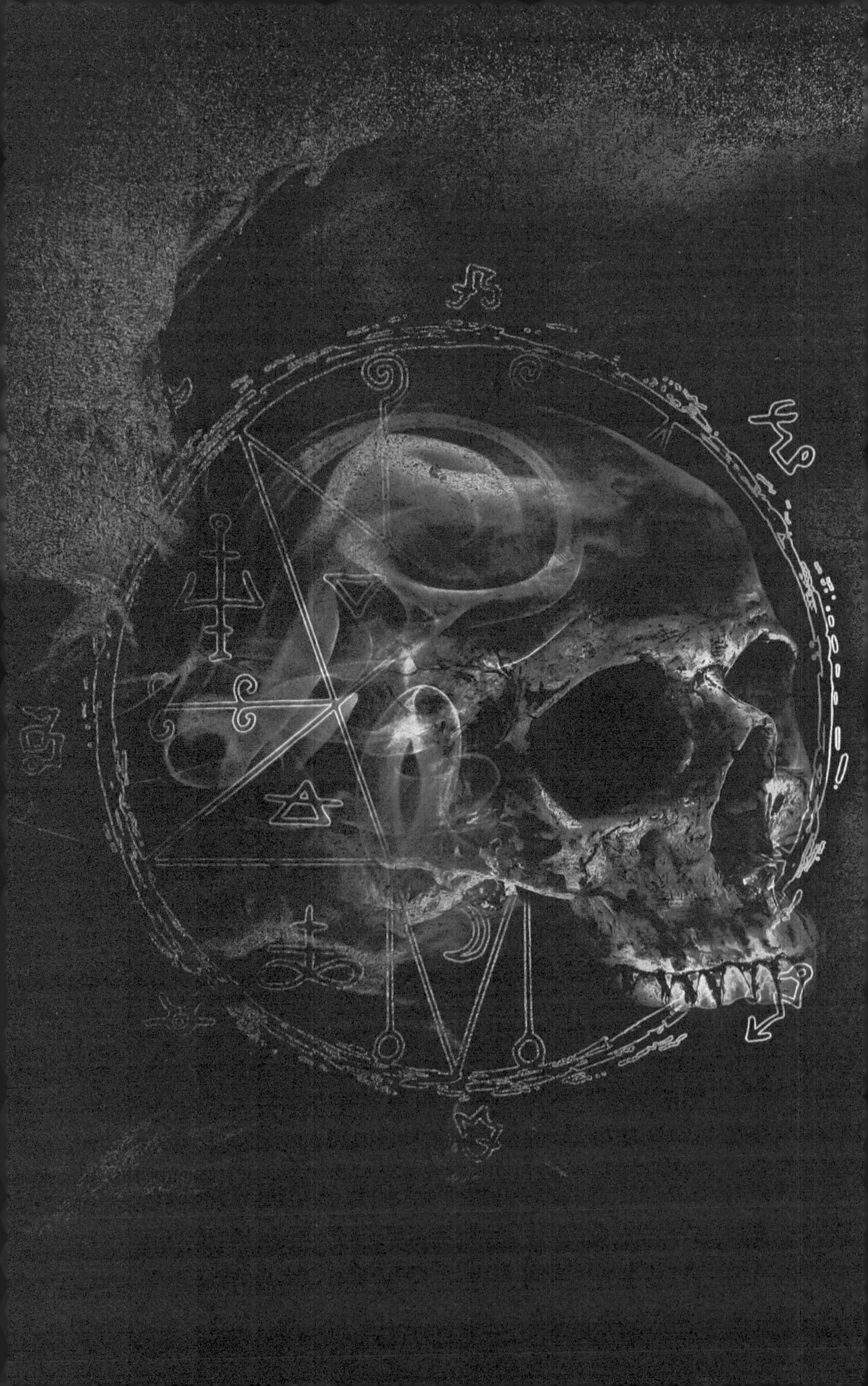

# Chapter 16

Waking up smashed between two men was kind of like sneaking into a sleeping bear's cave. Except the bears were warm, smooth, smelled good, and they were hungry for something other than food. Plus, there was a high probability that if one woke up, I'd wind up finding myself face down and bent over.

So, I stayed as still as I could, and watched their chest rise and fall.

It was kind of like the game I used to play with Charmaine. We'd duck in a dark place and be as quiet as we could. If I won, I got ice cream. Given what I knew now about my mother's mental state it probably wasn't meant to be as fun as I thought it was, but she made it seem that way.

Just because I didn't have the same parental things as other kids didn't mean I wasn't loved.

Maybe I wasn't destined for normalcy. If my current predicament didn't prove that; I didn't know what would. How many other girls would wake up as the filling in a teacher-stepbrother sandwich? Isla would lose her damn mind. Why wasn't I losing my mind?

I should be freaking out right now. Let's face it, I didn't want what happened last night, yet Devlin took it, anyway. Then Reese joined in, and both of them acted as if that was a normal everyday occurrence. Who knows, maybe it was? Maybe the two of them got off on toying with girls. That didn't mean they had to pull me into their bullshit.

"Assholes." I clamped my hand over my mouth.

Damnit! Keep quiet, Sydney.

I sucked in all my oxygen and listened to the steady breaths coming from Reese, while Devlin's chest rose and fell in a similar beat. Neither one of them seemed to be awake. Phew.

Though it was a bit disturbing how in sync they were. Devlin's ribs would expand, while Reese's deflated and vice versa. At one point, I started counting the seconds between their breaths to see if there was a flaw in their pattern.

There wasn't.

It was as even as a mathematical rhythm. There was exactly one point five seconds between the time Devlin inhaled and Reese exhaled. It was strange to notice something like that in two men who were very different.

From what I'd seen, Reese was a pretty happy guy. Everything about him seemed pretty light, including his hair and eyes. Whereas Devlin was just dark. Was Reese the yin to Devlin's yang?

Even the way they slept was opposite. Devlin was on his back, and Reese was a cuddler. His left leg was entwined in my right one, while his arm was threaded around my waist, firmly holding me against him.

Then again, Devlin got agitated when I moved my head off his chest. So maybe he was a cuddler, too. Just in a different way. Kind of like Charmaine's motherly love. Not everyone would see the sweetness in her actions, but I did.

Did I see sweetness in Devlin and Reese's actions?

*Nah, fuck that. They were assholes.*

So why wasn't I moving out of this awkward position?

Almost as if he heard my thoughts, Reese grumbled and tucked my body tighter against him. The feel of a steel rod pressing up against my ass was enough to remind me that waking them up wasn't worth the risk. Add in the twitch under the blanket covering Devlin's hip, and I had a pretty good idea what would happen.

Erections were not part of my ideal morning plan. Especially not with the way my core was aching. I'd flat out ignore the hard-on I was currently having a stare down with, if I could move my head off Devlin's damn chest. Every time I shifted in the slightest, Devlin's arm flexed, which, considering that's where Reese's head was, was not a good thing.

I blew out a defeated sigh.

*Fuck my life.*

My small frame was literally swallowed up by walls of muscles. Both of which radiated heat like a motherfucker. I now knew what a teddy bear felt like. At least it was warm. I guess it wouldn't be so bad if I didn't have to pee.

*Should I stab them? That pen had to still be around here somewhere.*

I rolled my eyes towards the other side of my room and huffed. Why did the bathroom have to be so far away? If it was closer, then I could jump up and run before either one of them knew what was happening. If only I had something else to focus on.

*Like that pen.*

That was my mistake. I moved my shoulder, hoping to be able to peek over, and that caused my hips to wriggle. Reese sleepily grumbled something and pressed himself against the tender flesh of my ass, making me instantly freeze.

*If I don't move, he'll go back to sleep.*

My problem came with the dull burn that radiated from where his dick was digging into me. I couldn't help but wince. Any doubt I had about whether or not I had bruises was gone.

Unfortunately, my small sound was enough to make Reese nuzzle in. "Good morning."

I didn't know who I was more pissed at? Devlin, because this was all his fault—who the hell spanked someone? Or Reese, for having that stupid, sleepy tone in his deep voice. They could both kiss my ass. Metaphorically, of course. I didn't want to give anyone actual options.

"Shh," I hushed back at him. "I'm sleeping."

Reese grazed his fingers over my outer thigh and chuckled. "Sleeping people don't talk."

I begged to differ. One of the first things Devlin pointed out last night was my inadvertent ability for unconscious speech.

Reese's thigh tensed, tightening his hold on my right leg, and he slid his hand over the curve of my hip.

"Stop it," I growled in a whisper. "You'll wake Devlin up."

But Reese didn't stop. He pushed his hand between my thighs and pressed a finger down on my clit, making me smash my face against Devlin's chest to muffle a gasp.

"You don't sound asleep to me."

"Fuck you," I hissed back at him.

In hindsight, that probably wasn't the best thing to say.

"That's a good idea."

Next thing I knew, his dick was no longer pressing up against my ass. It was sliding between my thighs.

"Stop it…"

"Shh," he hushed. "You don't want to wake up Devlin."

*This mother…*

There was nothing else to do but pathetically whimper, "I'm sore," because I didn't want to wake up Devlin. Then I'd have two to deal with.

"I won't stick it in," he purred while dragging his tongue up the side of my face. "I just want to feel you."

Let me just say Reese's fingers didn't have shit on the way his shaft felt sliding between my folds. I had to bite my bottom lip to keep from moaning, and the more he pumped his hips, the harder that task was becoming.

How could someone get fucked without getting fucked? It didn't make sense, yet he was doing it. Every slide of his cock along my pussy wound that coil tighter.

And then the asshole had to clamp his hand around my hip and growl in my ear. "You gonna come on my cock, sweet thing?"

No. Fuck him. Reese wasn't getting shit from me. At least that what I told myself when I muttered, "It's not fair."

This was bullshit. It was my body, damnit!

"You do have a point," Reese agreed. "This isn't really fair."

There was a brief moment when the words *thank you* flew through my mind. Then Reese's hand came down on the erection I'd been having a stare down with. Holy shit was all I could think as he gave the shaft a firm squeeze.

Devlin groaned in response.

Me and my big mouth. They were both going to wake up now, and there was a high possibility that I was about to get literally fucked. Not that I could've voiced my objection if I wanted to. The rumble vibrating through Devlin's chest and into my ear was only adding to the sensation Reese's dick was igniting.

How did I end up here? Being trapped between two men while one got the other off was not a position I ever thought I'd be in. It felt like there was something I needed to do, but for the life of me, I couldn't remember what it was. I looked down at the hand stroking Devlin's cock and felt my hips grind back into Reese.

"That's it, Sydney." Reese dipped his head and nipped at the sensitive spot behind my ear. "Come all over my cock."

Oh, who the fuck cared how I got here? I couldn't change it, so I might as well go with it.

Which is exactly what I did. I moaned and let go, allowing myself to fall over the edge. Reese growled something in my ear, but I was too busy riding waves of ecstasy to hear what he said. Then I came down and saw the desire burning in his eyes.

"I can't wait to feel that piercing on my dick."

When did I agree to that? Did I agree to that? It was possible, but I was pretty sure I didn't say anything.

"Do me a favor." Reese rose his upper body and tipped his chin at his pumping arm. "Slip your hand under the blanket and help me out."

"What?" I whisper-yelled. "I can't do that."

"Sure, you can."

"He's sleeping," I argued.

You shouldn't do things to people when they were asleep. Like accost them into an unwanted orgasm.

"You're too cute," he sang in a tone that caused my breath to hitch.

There was something dark under that playful twinkle in Reese's eyes. A part of me was afraid that he was going to eat me. The words Devlin said yesterday flashed through my mind.

*"Reese isn't as nice as you think he is."*

Was he going to hurt me, too? Because I wasn't sure if my ass could take any more.

*Speaking of my ass…*

Reese's pelvis was digging into my sore flesh. I tried to shuffle away, but he wasn't letting me. He snapped his hips, trapping my lower half between him and Devlin, and tsked his disapproval down at me. "Move again, and I will fuck you."

I didn't know what to do. I'd never seen him so dark and threatening. It was intimidating.

"Are you going to hurt me?"

His answer was to smirk and take my mouth in a kiss that rivaled the one he gave me in the library. It didn't last long, but it was enough to leave me wanting yet again. Our tongues had barely touched, and my head still lifted off Devlin when Reese pulled away.

"How do you do that?" One touch. That was it. It wasn't fair.

Reese smiled, tore the blanket away, and winked. "I'm good with my mouth."

*He could say that… Oh, shit!*

My eyes widened as he bent over me and sucked the thick head of Devlin's dick through his lips.

That woke Devlin up.

"Fuck," he groaned loudly, then pushed Reese's head down his shaft.

My current position put my last thought about being uncomfortable to shame. One man's pec was tensing under my head while the other was folded over me, with his dick still resting between my thighs.

The sad part was that my pelvis started to move. It just felt so good.

My delicate flesh fluttered as it moved along that hot, smooth thickness.

I couldn't help but moan as I watched Rees swallow down Devlin's girth. Which, by the way, was an amazing feat all on its own. I may not have much to reference for size—I'd only seen one other man naked—but Devlin wasn't small.

Honestly, I was surprised that Reese's mouth fit around him at all, let alone that the thing was able to fit inside me. And judging by the hardness I was grinding against; Reese wasn't anything to scoff at either.

One thing was for sure, I needed to get out of here before this went further. Devlin's dick ripped me in half. I wasn't about to test the waters with two. All I had to do to slip out from under them was shift a little to the left.

The mistake I made was glancing up before moving.

The expression Devlin wore stopped me cold. His brows pulled together, while his eyes squeezed shut. His breath stuttered, then he threw his head back with a groan. The blend of rage and pleasure was intoxicating. Was there such a thing as an angry orgasm?

"I should leave," I told myself.

Devlin's hand speared through the tangled braid at the back of my head. "You're not going anywhere."

Not only did I have Devlin's attention, but Reese's light eyes were watching me as he bobbed his head along Devlin's length.

"Get your ass up here." Devlin gave my hair a rough tug. "And sit your ass on my face."

I looked back at Reese, whose eyes were lit up in a way that made me think he agreed with Devlin's order. Asshole even shot me a wink while he slurped down Devlin's length. My no dick day was off to a bad start. I definitely needed to get out of here. I need to get out of here for the sake of my pussy.

"But... I... uh..." *Come on, Syd, think of something.* "I have to pee."

*There we go. I knew I had to do something.*

What did it matter if I didn't really have to go anymore? It was a perfectly plausible excuse, and one they couldn't deny.

Reese popped Devlin's dick out of his mouth and sang, "You're so full of shit."

"I am not," I exclaimed while sucking in a shocked breath that even I didn't believe. "I really have to go."

Devlin cocked a brow. "It's not a good idea to lie when my dick is hard."

*And whose fault was that? Reese.*

"Would I lie to you?" I totally would and judging by the look they gave me in response, both of them knew that. "Are you denying me the right to pee? Because I'm pretty sure that borders on torture."

"Oh, you can pee," Devlin said. "Just as soon as you make us come."

"She already came," Reese pointed out.

I gave him a dirty look in response.

"Oh, did she?" I felt dread seep in the room as Devlin's dark eyes locked on mine. "Without my permission?"

I didn't know what to say, so I blurted, "Reese did it."

"Look at that. She's already playing the blame game." Reese smirked and gave me a little nudge with his fist. "Good for you."

What the hell was wrong with him? *Weirdo.*

"That's it," Devlin growled and sat up. "I'm just gonna fuck you both."

I rolled my eyes. That wasn't possible. "You only have one dick."

A slow smirk spread across Reese's face.

*Damnit.*

"He doesn't own your dick," I sang back.

My mistake was evident in the brow Devlin arched. "You can fuck her now."

"What! No, I just—" I threw my arms up in frustration. "I just want to pee."

Devlin crossed his arms while Reese let out a chuckle.

"Oh, let her go. Maybe she'll play nice tonight."

"Yeah, sure." I snorted, but quickly changed it into clearing my throat when Devlin arched his brow. "I mean… I'll totally play nice."

Devlin shot me a deadpan look. "No, you won't."

*No, I wouldn't.*

"Fine." He tipped his chin at the bathroom door. "Go before I change my mind."

I hopped off the bed and skipped across the room before he had a chance to second guess his decision.

The last thing I heard before I closed the bathroom door was Reese muttering, "Fuck, I know that look."

Once I was safely hidden away from prying eyes, I let out a breath, then took my time. Peed, washed my hands, brushed my teeth, and fluffed my hair out of the braid. My hope was that they'd be gone when I walked out.

My hopes were immediately dashed.

I opened the door to a sight I never thought I'd see. Reese was bent over the bed with Devlin behind him, plowing into his ass.

"God damnit," Reese snarled while throwing his hand back. "Use more lube."

Devlin pushed his face down on the mattress. "Shut the fuck up. You're the one who wanted to let her pee."

I did the only thing I could: tiptoed back into the bathroom and shut the door.

# Chapter 17

My way of avoiding what was happening out in my room was to shower, which was when I noticed that my ass wasn't the only thing bruised. There were deep purple fingerprints on my thighs, and my wrists looked like I'd lost a week-long battle with handcuffs or binds.

Then there were the bite impressions. I gave up trying to count those. Devlin didn't just take me. He marked me. Everywhere I looked, there was another spot proving what he'd done to me.

To say I was pissed was an understatement. He was lucky he wasn't there when I walked out of the bathroom. Pen or not, I would've stabbed him for sure.

There were plenty of other sharp things I could use. Like the letter opener glinting on the dresser. Why else would someone put something like that in a room if not to be used as a weapon?

I did think about giving Devlin a little leeway when I saw the bra and panties lying on my bed. But then I remembered that he was the whole reason I didn't have any underwear in the first place. Besides, what he left was a lace thong. I did not do perma-wedgies, and I definitely didn't do lace.

I still put them on, though. It was better than nothing. Beggars couldn't be choosers. They could, however, put assholes in their place.

Oh, and I was going to put Devlin in his place. If he thought my pyjama choice last night was bad, then he was about to learn how bad my outfit choices could be.

I put on the nicest pair of jeans I had. And by nice, I meant tight, dark, and full of rips. I paired those with a white silk crop-top that had a plunging neckline. Then I took time putting on my make-up, dusting on just enough color to give me the smoldering smoky eye effect. My sex kitten look was topped off with a pair of hoop earrings and a high ponytail.

Was I taking things a little too far? Probably. But what the fuck was Devlin going to do? Nothing.

I had class to attend. And according to Angus, education was important. He made a big stink about the poor quality of public schools. I highly doubted he'd be impressed if I blew off his "perfect" private lessons.

Meaning, Devlin could eat shit and watch me walk around all day with nothing but a white strip covering my bra. I couldn't wait to see the look on his face. Asshole thought he could tell me how to dress. Well, I'd show him.

*Fuck Devlin.*

If I had any doubts about whether the retaliation I might receive would be worth it, those disappeared when I walked past Wyatt in the hall. The second he saw me, he hunched over and started choking on the muffin he was eating.

*Yup, I totally nailed it.*

"Damn, foster care."

"What?" I turned around and bent over, pretending to search the denim fabric of my jeans. "Is there something on my pants?"

"Yeah. Devlin." Wyatt shook his head. "He is going to lose his shit when he sees those pants."

I glanced over my shoulder and sang, "Sounds like a personal problem to me." Then continued down the hall.

Wyatt quickly spun on his heels and followed.

"What are you doing?"

His face lit up with amusement as a smile washed over his lips. "I am not missing this."

"Ugh, whatever." I rolled my eyes.

The whole house could watch if they wanted. All I cared about was making it to the kitchen, where, according to the note Devlin left, he'd be waiting. Couldn't forget the "hurry the fuck up" part of that note. Pfft, asshole. I was surprised he didn't give me a time limit.

I pranced down the hall and marched into the kitchen with my head held high.

That's where I was met with the loudest, "What the fuck!" I'd ever heard.

They burst through the air and rang in my ears with the sweet sound of victory. Devlin wasn't just pissed. He was downright murderous.

"*Bréagán*," he growled through his teeth. "Are you trying to push my buttons?"

*Yes, yes, I was.*

I internally smiled while innocently singing, "Is something wrong?"

"Yes, something's wrong." Devlin sprang out of his chair and waved his hand through the air. "What the fuck do think you're wearing?"

"Um, they're called clothes," I shot back.

"Those are not clothes."

"I think the store I bought them at would disagree." Not that I actually bought them. All my clothes were hand-me-downs. Side effect of growing up in the system.

About that time, Wyatt sniggered and slipped past me to lean against the island. I think he was getting more enjoyment out of this than I was. His brother, however, wasn't appreciative of the audience.

He threw his finger up at Wyatt. "What the fuck were you thinking, letting her walk around like this?"

"I just went with it." Wyatt shrugged and popped the last bite of muffin into his mouth.

Couldn't help but snicker at his calm demeanor. Here was his brother, getting ready to explode, and Wyatt was cool as a cucumber. I kind of felt bad for Magnus. It had to be hard to have a twin who only cared about pranks and porn. God forbid, a naked humor store ever opened. Wyatt would be their best customer.

Devlin sucked in a deep breath. "I'll deal with you later, and you…"

His glare snapped back to mine, and the only words that flew through my head were *uh oh*. He was across room, seizing my elbow, before I could do or say anything.

"Do you think you're smart?"

Not right now, I didn't. Actually, the longer I stood under his oppressive glare, the stupider I felt.

Not that I'd tell him that. I had to maintain my pride somehow. At this point, it was all I had. Devlin had pretty much taken everything else, including my virginity.

"You're the one who treated me like a whore," I hissed up at him. "So I figured, why not dress the part?"

"Oh, now it's getting interesting," Wyatt said, making us both shoot him a dirty look.

My hand twitched, ready to slap him, when Devlin leaned in.

"If you think your ass is sore now," he softly growled in my ear. "Just wait."

I'd had just about enough of this misogynistic bullshit. "It's not my fault you have mommy issues."

The second the words left my mouth, I knew I'd crossed a line. Devlin's fingers dug painfully into my arm, and I couldn't blame him. The pain of losing a parent was serious. Not something to throw in someone's face. Even Wyatt shook his head. I really was a horrible person.

I hung my head in shame and whispered, "I'm sorry. I didn't mean it."

And I didn't. It was just something spat out in a moment of anger. I was prepared to accept whatever punishment Devlin decided to dole out. I held my breath and waited for the inevitable. But it never came. He didn't even yell.

Instead, Devlin let out a sigh, wrapped his arms around me, and pulled me into his embrace.

*What the hell?*

I stood there with my face smashed against his chest, waiting for the other shoe to drop. There had to be a point to this. Some twisted agenda that would make me plea for mercy or run away crying. But he didn't do anything other than hold me.

Was this a trick? Some way to lull me into a false sense of security? It had to be. Devlin Adair wasn't the caring and hugging type. Right?

When he didn't utter some threat or let me go, I carefully lifted my arms and tentatively tapped his back.

That's when it happened. A wave of anger and sadness washed over me, bringing tears to my eyes. I had no idea where the feelings came from, but I couldn't stop them from dripping down my face.

All the emotions I'd pent up over the years got poured into his chest. The countless times Charmaine said *they* were coming. The years I watched her mind deteriorate, and the nights I went to bed, scared and alone in a strange house.

Everything came out in those tears. Everything except for what happened last night. For some reason, that didn't feel like a mistake or bad memory. It felt right, like it was supposed to happen.

*What the fuck?*

When I finally stopped crying and just stood there, tucked into Devlin's large frame, I whispered, "I hate you."

"No, you don't," he said, smoothing a hand down my back.

*No, I didn't.*

"But you will if you keep acting out."

* * *

Devlin escorted me back to my room, where I changed into something more suitable before heading off for my daily lesson, which was being held in the atrium. Apparently, that's what the indoor greenhouse was called. Devlin said we'd be able to concentrate in there. Whatever that meant.

As far as rooms built for concentration, I think a library won that award, but whatever. I wasn't about to argue. I liked it in there. All the plants and birds were peaceful. So much better than boring shelves and books.

"Now, some plants need a higher temperature. Like an orchid, for example." Reese fingered a purple flower nearby. "They need at least fifty degrees."

"That's a Bearded Iris," I pointed out. "And the ideal temperature for an orchid is seventy-three degrees."

Reese arched a brow. "Anything else you'd like to share with the class?"

I looked up from the notebook I was doodling in.

"Yeah. That shrub"—I pointed the end of my pencil at some leaves that were a little brown on the end—"shouldn't be that close to other plants. Its roots need room to breathe."

Reese looked over at Devlin, who cocked a brow my way. Not sure what they were so amazed about. Anyone could find basic gardening knowledge like that online.

"What about this one?" Reese tipped his head at an orange flower.

I shrugged and went back to my horrible drawing of a stick man getting kicked in the nuts. That plant was fine. Actually, it was doing pretty well compared to some of the others. It even reached up and grew a bit.

*Wait...*

That wasn't normal? Flowers didn't grow that fast.

I shifted my gaze back to the colorful petals. Did they always have a touch of purple in them? And where did that vine come from? The ivy was all the way over on the other side of the bridge.

"Did one of you move that vine?"

Rather than answer me, Reese and Devlin exchanged a look.

I rolled my eyes and muttered, "Whatever."

Thanks to Devlin, I was sitting in a hot room with a hoodie and jeans on, and there was a string riding up my ass from the only pair of underwear I had. I wasn't in the mood to play their games. Bet they were comfortable in their t-shirts.

*Pricks.*

My next outfit was going to be a burlap sack. Let's see him complain about that. At least I wasn't ogling them. There was a bonus. Well, not openly ogling them. They were still nice to look at. It was kind of annoying how good they looked in a pair of jeans.

"That shouldn't work in here."

"I know," Devlin said to Reese while looking at me.

My lip curled back at them. "Have you guys been drinking?"

They were acting weird. Which was saying a lot.

"Tell me something, Sydney." Devlin leaned forward to rest his arms on his thighs. "How do you feel right now?"

"Well, someone made me wear a sweater to the heat center of this stupid house, so I'm a bit irritated."

When was the last time he had to sweat his ass off?

"I mean, what do you feel when you look at us?" he clarified.

I took a second to study the curious look on Devlin's face, then turned my attention to the intrigue sparkling in Reese's eyes.

"Yeah, I'm still gonna go with irritated."

Reese once again shot Devlin a look. "Are you hot?"

Seriously. I responded with a *duh* glare. If he couldn't see the sweat trickling down my brow, then he was blind.

I wasn't sure what I said, but they were pulling me out of my chair before I could blink.

"What the hell is wrong with you?" I snarled and tore my arms out of their grasp.

The ground beneath me suddenly lurched. I stumbled back from the heat wave crashing through the air. Reese reached out and said something. I couldn't hear what he said, though. His lips were moving, but nothing came out. Either that, or it was blocked out by the insane crunching filling my mind.

I winced and covered my ears. "What the hell is that?"

Couldn't they hear it? It was getting louder by the second. I looked around, trying to find the source. It seemed to be coming from everywhere. I tried to shut it out, but I couldn't chase it away. Not even my fingers in my ears could dampen the screeching sound. It was starting to hurt.

I'm not sure where Reese came from. I felt his hands cup my face before I saw him. He whispered one word.

*Sleep.*

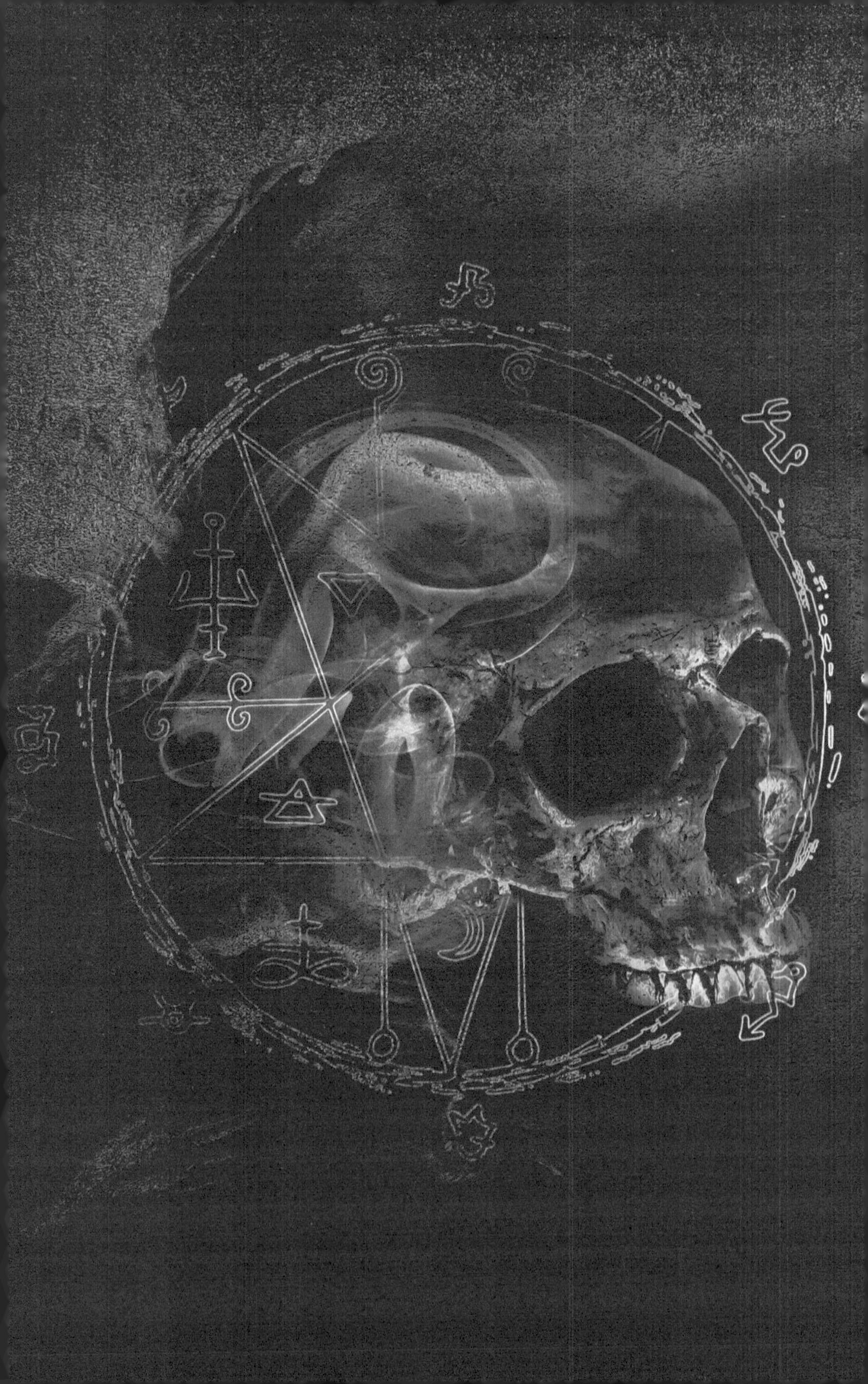

# Chapter 13



THERE WERE SO MANY PLANTS. I TUGGED AND PULLED, TRYING TO GET away, but they were everywhere. On my arms and legs, wrapping around my neck and torso. They were pulling me into a slithering pile of snake-like vines. I could feel them all over my skin.

I tried to fight them off and call out, but no one was there, or if they were, they couldn't hear me. The only audible sound was horrible crunching. It echoed through my ears every time a leaf bloomed, or a vine thickened.

They were growing at such an exponential rate that I could hear it. The plants wanted me. They called to me, and I couldn't fight them off.

Somebody, help!

"We need to finish this."

Oh my god, was that Reese? I searched the thickening greenery for his light eyes, but it was so dark. The light I did have was dwindling by the second.

"I know."

*Devlin! He was big and strong. He could pull me free. But which way did I go?*

"I'm not fucking around, Devlin. The ritual needs to be completed. Now!"

*Ritual? What ritual. It didn't matter. Reese's voice was louder when I turned to the left. I dove and parted the vines with my hands, swimming through the river engulfing me. I had to get to them.*

"I know." Devlin sighed, and I swear I felt his breath on my forehead.

"She can't control it. We need to complete the second part of the bond so we can help her."

*My heart skipped as I kicked my feet and swam faster. Reese definitely sounded closer.*

Devlin's deep tone echoed down from above. "I said, I know."

*I needed to go up.*

"She could've died, Devlin! While you may not care about that, I do."

*Don't worry, Reese., I'm coming. I'm not going to die.*

"I get it, Reese." I felt a hand brush over my forehead as a whisper wafted across my ear. "I like her, too, okay?"

*A whoosh of air brushed down around me and sucked me up into a whirling vortex. Then everything was gone. The plants reaching out and horrible sound were gone. It was quiet, and still, and warm? I was lying back against something hard. No, not something... someone.*

My head was swaying with the steady breathing of a chest. Devlin's chest. I recognized the subtle citrus scent. Never thought I'd be happy to be in his arms, but I was.

He felt so good. I wanted to stay tucked in the strength of his arms forever. A smile crested my lips as I murmured and snuggled in closer to his warmth.

"She's awake." Reese's words were followed by the softness under me dipping.

Was I on a bed? Yes, yes, I was. Not only that, but I was in my room. My lids fluttered open in time to see Reese crawl over a pair of long legs. Devlin's legs. He was sitting behind me, holding me up against his chest. How did we get here?

I remember being in the plant room, Reese was talking about orchids or something. And then… "What happened?"

Devlin's arms tightened around me while Reese barked out, "You scared us. That's what happened."

What the hell was his problem? I didn't get a chance to ask. Reese sprang forward before I could open my mouth. He cupped my face and started peppering me with kisses.

"Don't," *kiss*, "ever," *kiss*, "do," *kiss*, "that," *kiss*, "again," *kiss, kiss*.

"Get away from me." I swung my arms out, swatting at the lips invading my space. "Weirdo."

Reese snatched me out of Devlin's arms and smashed my face up against his chest. "I'll never let you go again."

"What the hell is wrong with you?"

When I tried to wiggle away, Reese flattened his giant hand on the back of my head and held me tightly in place. My cheek was pressed so far into his hard pec that my lips were squished out in a duck face. It was uncomfortable, to say the least.

I rolled my eyes over at Devlin and huffed out a sigh. "Is he on drugs?"

"Probably," Devlin grumbled back.

"Shut up." Reese reached his arm over and pulled Devlin in. "You can both take my love."

I was wrong. Being squished between two walls of muscle was way more uncomfortable.

"Not that I'm complaining about the sudden need for affection"—I totally was—"but breathing would be nice."

And still Reese didn't let go. "Don't you worry about breathing. I'll make sure you get all the oxygen you need while I ride you hard."

All right, that was it.

I elbowed Devlin in the ribs and shoved Reese away. Part of me thought that Devlin might have an issue with my rough treatment, but he just crossed his arms and muttered, "Thank you." Which made me cock a brow.

If anyone should've been annoyed in this situation, it was the person who was forced to be the sandwich filling. Was that my life now? The filling in an asshole sandwich? Apparently, Reese thought so. The second I'd broken free of his hold, he started pawing at my shorts.

*Wait… shorts? When did I put those on?*

*Pay attention, Syd. You have bigger problems.*

I jumped back into Devlin and kicked my foot out. "Stop it."

"You saw what happened." Reese looked up at me, his green eyes round and glimmering. "We are going to do this."

"Yes, we are." Devlin cut him off. "But after she gets some food in her."

I was so confused. What happened? Devlin was oddly calm, and Reese was acting like someone threatened to take away his favorite toy.

*Vines… trapped… can't breathe….*

Intrigue tipped my head. Did we have class today? We must have. Otherwise, Angus would be giving me a lecture. "Were we by a lake or waterfall?"

I distinctly remember the sound of trickling.

Reese cocked a brow at Devlin. "No."

"Are you sure?" I could smell water and hear… birds?

"Nope." Reese shook his head. "No lake or waterfall."

He was lying. There was something. I could almost see it, but it was buried in the back of my mind behind something else.

"You were mad," I said, looking at Devlin.

He folded his arms over his chest and sighed. "I'm always mad."

That was a fair point. But still…

I reached down and scoured my brain for the image eluding me. That was a mistake. I was suddenly smacked in the face with a long, thick dick and the sounds of Reese grunting in pleasure. The vacating of my thoughts was swift.

I sat up and cleared my throat. "Isn't it time for dinner?"

The weird part: Reese's lip was curled in a smirk.

If I thought they were going to leave me alone to get ready, I was wrong. According to King Asshole Devlin, I was ready. Funny, considering all I was wearing were pyjama shorts and a t-shirt.

Pretty sure that constituted as 'whore attire' in Devlin's world. But whatever. I wasn't about to delve into the fucked-up reality he deemed logic.

So I went with it and followed them down the hall to the dining room. Not that they gave me much of a choice. Reese practically pulled me out the door, like he was in a rush to get this over with, while Devlin pushed me.

I had a new respect for yo yos. And a thoroughly plotted out murder plan that involved a fork, sharp knife, and a couple garbage bags.

The sight of Angus perched at the head table wasn't doing anything to improve my mood.

He nodded at us. "Good evening."

I had to hold back a snicker. Good evening. Who spoke like that? What was he, a vampire? Some lord that time-traveled? On the upside, Angus seemed extra perturbed today, so there was a plus.

That's when I noticed the guest sitting next to him. He was straight-laced and wearing a black suit with his hair slicked back. Making me think he was a business associate of Angus's. But if that were the case, why weren't Wyatt and Magnus here?

I let Devlin and Reese guide into the chair between them and eyed the stranger's dark hair. He looked kind of familiar. I swear I'd see that dimple in his chin somewhere else.

"Who's this?" Devlin said, asking what we were all thinking.

Angus leaned forward to fold his hands under his chin. "This is Pascello Ricci."

My eyes widened. "Ricci?"

"Yes, Sydney." Angus nodded. "He's your uncle."

*I had an uncle?*

Pascello tipped his head at me. "Ciao, Sydney. It's a pleasure to meet you."

His accent was thick and obviously Italian, but I couldn't stop staring at his eyes. They were the same color as mine. I barely noticed Devlin's hand clamp down around my thigh.

So many questions floated through my head, yet I didn't know what to say. Where did he come from? Did he know what happened to my father? Did he know about Charmaine? Why didn't he come earlier? That's when I started to get mad.

All this time, I had family out there, and they let me rot in the system. He didn't come to pull me out of foster care or help Charmaine and me out when we struggled to pay rent. I didn't even get a letter. There was nothing. No attempt at contact whatsoever.

"Why are you here?"

Pascello tipped his head, "I understand this must be confusing for you."

I snorted. There was the understatement of the year.

"We only recently discovered where you were."

*We? I had more family who ignored me?*

"Your mother… she… what's the word?" He pressed his fingers together and looked up as if searching for something. "Hid you."

He couldn't blame this on Charmaine. If he really wanted to find me, then he would've. I couldn't help but wonder if one of the bad people who drove her insane was currently sitting across the table.

"You can't have her," Reese suddenly blurted out. "She's ours."

The look that Pascello gave him rivaled some of the expressions I'd seen Devlin wear. "Is she?"

"You know the rules," Devlin piped in. "The bond has already started."

Pascello lifted his finger to point at Devlin. "But it's not complete."

"That doesn't matter," Angus argued. "She was chosen."

Pascello shot back. "Last I heard, your sect had her chosen for a different role."

What the hell were they talking about? Chosen and bonds. Was everyone in this house crazy?

"I don't belong to anyone!" I snarled at them all.

I was not a commodity to be traded.

"Si, Sydney." Pascello sat back and tipped his brow my way. "Brava ragazza."

I don't know what he said. I didn't care. Why should I? He didn't care about me.

Placing my palms on the table, I slid my chair out and stood up. "I'm not hungry."

My intent was to leave and go hide in my room, but Pascello chased me out.

"Sydney, wait."

I rolled my eyes and huffed out an exasperated breath. "What?"

Pascello grabbed my hand and held it with both of his. "I know you have no reason to trust me."

He could say that again. A part of me wanted to trust him. This man was the only connection to my father that I had. But I didn't know him, and most importantly, he didn't know me. I was starting to think nobody did.

"I need you to hear me when I say, you have even less reason to trust them."

That got my attention.

I looked up into his silver eyes just as Devlin came barging out into the hall. "Time to go, Ricci."

Pascello gave me a small smile and patted the top of my hand. "Call me."

Devlin didn't waste any time escorting my uncle out. I stood there watching them go, then looked down at the note in my hand.

*You are but a sheep in the wolves' den.*

Underneath was a phone number.

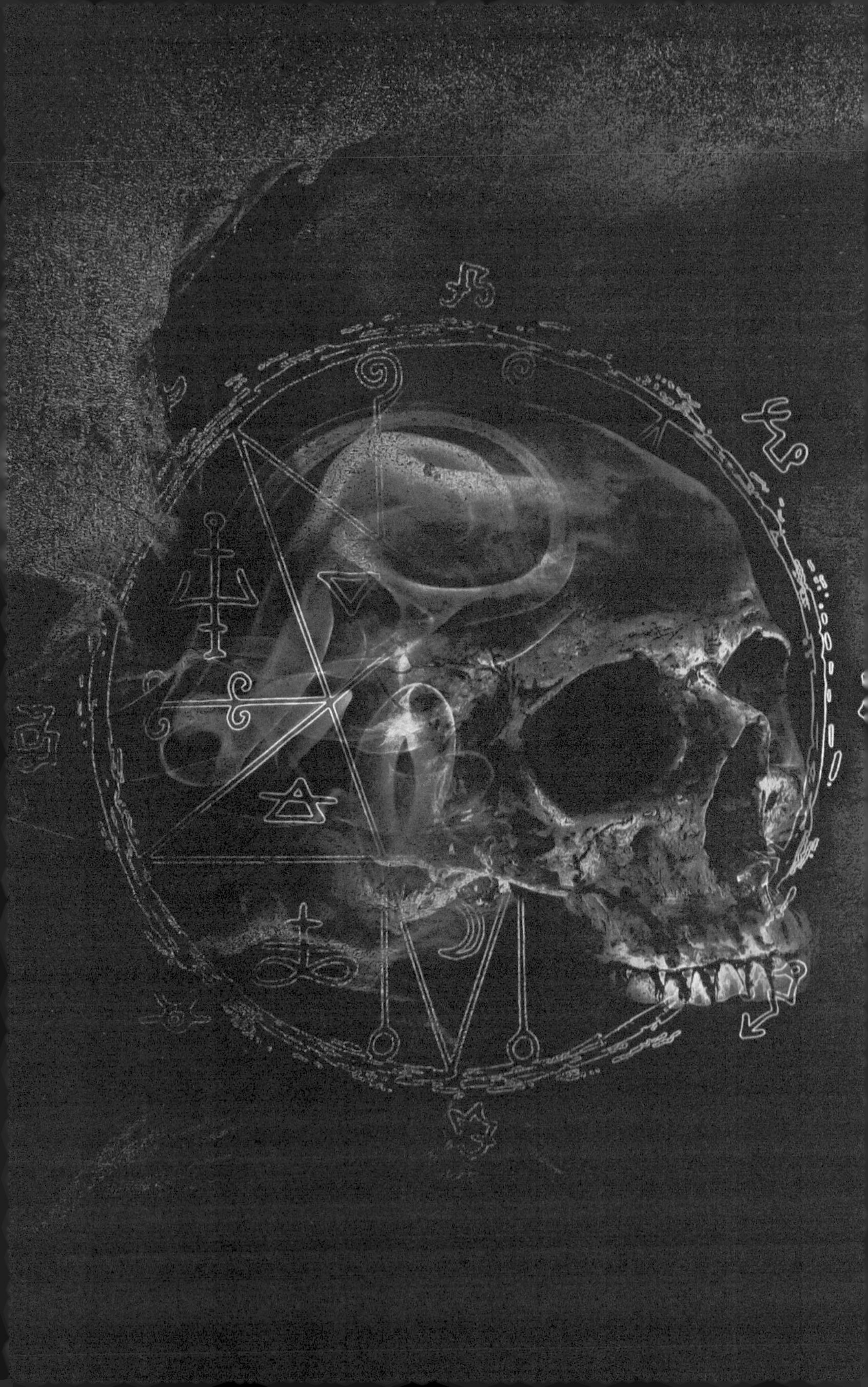

# Chapter 19

I managed to tuck the piece of paper in my pocket before Devlin stormed up and snatched my arm. "What did he say to you?"

"None of your business." I sneered up at him and attempted to tear my arm out of his strong grip.

He tightened his hold and dug his fingers into my flesh. "Every-thing you do is my business."

*Like hell it was.*

My arm swung through the air, cracking my palm loudly off the side of his face. Nothing was quite as satisfying as the way his head snapped to the side. Fuck him, fuck the Adairs, and fuck my so-called uncle. Charmaine and I didn't need them.

When Devlin's darkening glare slowly rolled back, I lifted on my tiptoes and hissed in his face, "You don't own me."

All my bravado and the world fell away as Devlin's lips curled in a slow smile.

"We'll see about that."

He scooped me up and threw me over his shoulder so quickly that all I could do was cling onto the back of his shirt in hopes that I wouldn't go careening headfirst over the other side. It was terrifying how strong he was.

A smart person would've taken that as their cue to stop fighting. Unfortunately, I was not that person. Once upon a time, I was the one who made the smart choice.

Then I came here, and asshole stepbrothers turned into horny teachers and stepfathers who thought they could act like fathers. The sudden pop up of an uncle was the straw that broke the camel's back.

I was done.

Devlin could fill the hole in his chest by tormenting someone else.

Refusing to give into anymore demands, I bucked my hips and kicked my feet. Was I worried about falling down and kissing the ground? Hell no. My lips were puckered in readiness. Bring the floor on.

My knee jabbed into Devlin's gut. "Put me down."

Based on the grunt I heard him huff out, I'd say I got him good. Not that it did me any good. Devlin simply smacked his hand down on my ass.

"Keep it up."

Then he strutted away as if he weren't carrying around the wiggling form of a girl. Which only pissed me off more.

"I hope you brought your A-game," I growled while raking my claws up his back. "Because I'm not stopping."

If it was the last thing I did, I was going to draw blood.

Devlin laughed. The asshole actually laughed. Rage teemed through me as his shoulder shook with a chuckle.

"Three days ago, I wanted to kill you," Devlin said while turning down the hall toward the bedrooms. "And now you want to kill me."

"I fail to see how that's funny."

"The irony is"—he stopped in front of my door and looked over his shoulder—"I'd have done it. Would you?"

No, I wouldn't. I thought about it, but I wouldn't actually do it. As much as I hated Devlin, there was a part of me that would miss that grumpy face if he wasn't around.

My chest puffed out with a heavy sigh. "What do you want from me?"

"Everything." Devlin walked into my room, dumped me on the bed, then tipped his head down at me. "I want everything, *Bréagán*, and in return, I'll give you everything I am."

I wanted to call him out on his bullshit, but there was nothing in his face that said it was bullshit. No twitch in his expression or glint in his eye that would give me a reason to call him a liar. The only thing looking back at me was stone-cold truth.

Then the reality of his words struck me. He didn't say everything he has, he said everything he *was*. Devlin was going to give himself to me. That was too much for me to handle.

"But... Reese..."

"Already has him."

I was the only one who turned to see the man strutting through the door.

Reese walked over and stood next to Devlin. "It's you we need."

"And it's you we'll have," Devlin added.

*Bloody* was the only word that came to mind. Because that was the only possible outcome when one dove headfirst into a tank of sharks. So why was I considering this?

My eyes shifted from one to other and back again. "Give me one good reason why I would even consider this?"

When Devlin's knee pressed down on the mattress, I fell back in an attempt to keep some distance. It didn't work. He crawled over me before I could right myself and back away.

I looked up at him.

He looked down at me.

Next thing I knew, his lips were on mine. Reese kissed like he was riding a wave of desire, but the way Devlin's mouth moved was nothing short of domineering. I couldn't just taste him. I could feel his need in every inch of my body. And God help me, I gave in and kissed him back.

My tongue touched his, and that was it. I didn't know if seconds, minutes, or hours went by. It was all a blur of tangled limbs and heavy breaths.

Reese joined in at one point, and one mouth became two. One took my lips while the other stripped my clothes off, after which they dropped their own clothing on the floor.

By the time I was able to take a breath, it was too late to argue. We were all naked. Devlin was sitting back against the headboard with me on top of him while his legs spread mine open, and Reese crawled in between my thighs. One hard cock was under my ass, and the other was being stroked as it inched closer to the aching spot between my legs.

I wriggled, trying to pull my arms free from Devlin's hold. "Wait…"

That was all I got out before Reese ducked his head and laved his tongue over my clit. The moan that came out of me caused Devlin to groan and drag his mouth along the side of my face.

"That's it, *Bréagán*, let go."

"I don't—" My argument was cut off by a sharp inhale as a finger was thrust into my opening.

All speech capability was gone after that. Reese knew exactly how to pump his fingers so he'd hit that spot deep inside with just enough force to drive me close, but not push me over the edge. I begged him to let me come, but he just smiled and continued his torture.

My pussy cried when he pulled his fingers out of me. I was so close that I couldn't do anything beyond mewling like a cat in heat when he lined his cock up. All I needed was one little flick. Hell, a strong puff of air might do it.

"Look at me, Sydney."

I whimpered and rolled my head to the feral glint in Reese's light eyes.

"You know your friend Scotty Dalton?" He folded over me, pressed his palms into the mattress, then whispered, "I burned his house down."

His hips snapped, forcing his entire length inside me. My back bowed off Devlin as a wave of pleasurable pain crashed over me.

I couldn't breathe past the pain of being stretched so quickly, but I couldn't think past the orgasm clouding my mind. That strange concoction of sensations got more intense with each thrust of Reese's hips.

I felt Devlin's hand wrap around my neck, and I heard him growl, "You're so fucking hot when you come." But I couldn't do anything other than hang on while Reese fucked me.

Just when I thought I couldn't take any more, he stopped.

I opened my eyes to thank him but stopped when I saw where Reese had his attention fixated.

"Fuck me," he growled. "Look at that shit."

Even Devlin was leaning over to watch, and I gotta say, I couldn't blame them. The sight of Reese's thickness disappearing into my body was awe-striking.

I followed each slow stroke, mesmerized by the way my delicate pink flesh wrapped around him. It was astonishing how my pussy had to stretch to accommodate his girth. It shouldn't have been possible, but it was.

"Would it take two?" I wondered aloud.

Both Reese and Devlin's eyes snapped to me.

"Oh, it'll take two," Reese said, giving his hips a swivel that made my breath hitch.

"But you're nowhere near ready for that," Devlin finished.

I'd never been more thankful for Devlin's refusal than I was in that moment. I wasn't even sure why I asked that question. The cock under my ass made me feel bad. Shouldn't he get attention too?

"What about you?" I asked, looking back at Devlin.

A smirk tugged at the corner of his mouth. "You close?"

At first, I thought he was talking to me. Then Reese lifted my hips and drove his cock in so deep that white dotted my vision. "Almost."

I held onto Devlin while Reese did exactly what he said he would. He rode me hard. And my pussy loved it. The sounds that came out of my mouth weren't human.

I screamed until my throat was hoarse, then when my voice ran out, I used my hands to claw at the muscle engulfing me. Reese pounded into me then slowed down, dragging out every orgasm until I thought need would kill me.

When Reese slammed his hips in and groaned out his release, I was ready to cry. Then Devlin grabbed my hips and slid me down his length, taking over while Reese fell back and caught his breath. They continued to pass me back and forth until I passed out from exhaustion.

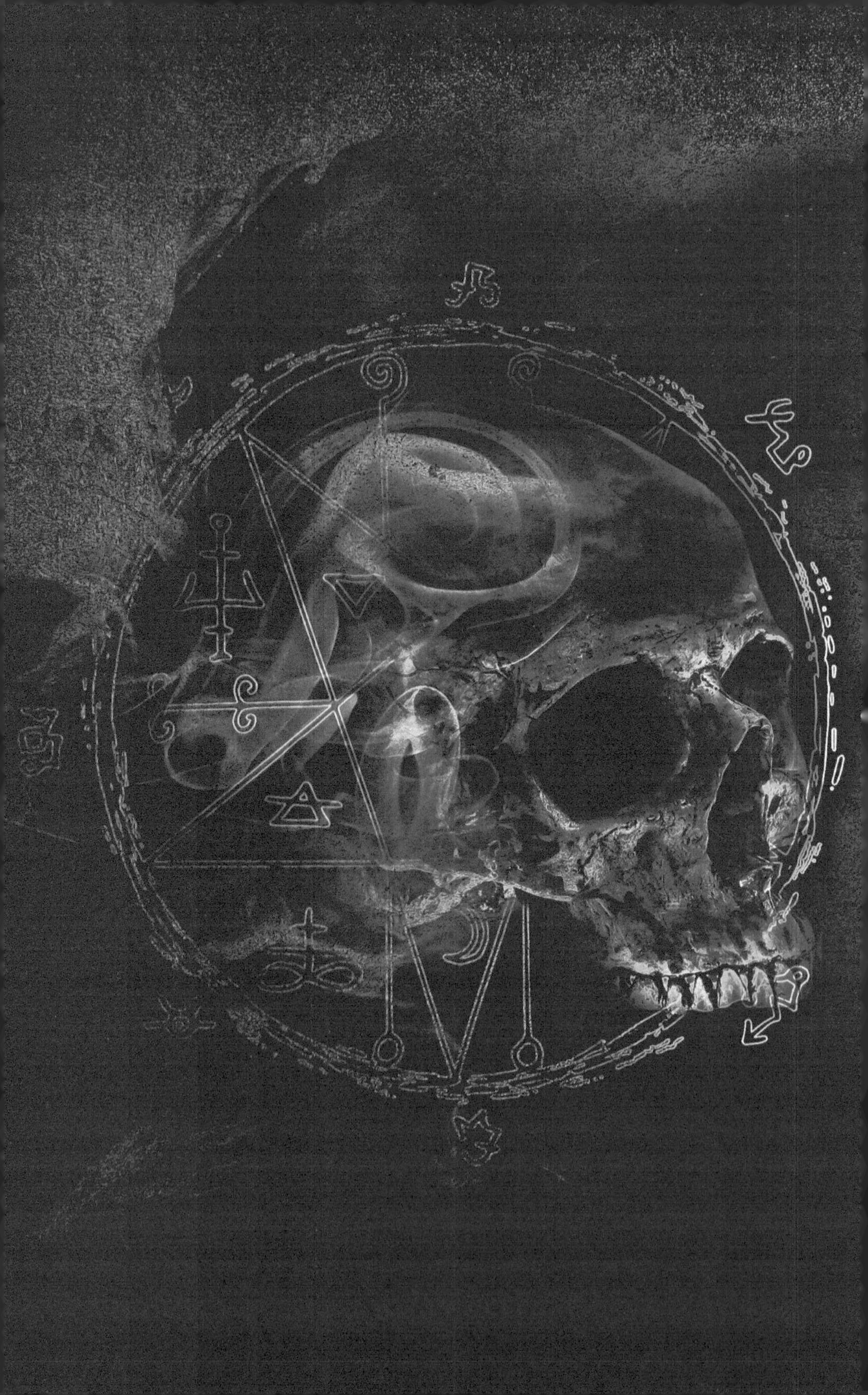

# Chapter 20

Every minute of the next two days was spent with Devlin and Reese. They not only wouldn't let me out of their sight, but they kept catering to me. More so Reese than Devlin.

If I was hungry, I got food. If I was tired, someone carried me to bed, and if I looked at either one of them in a certain way… Well, let's just say I spent a lot of time trapped on my bed.

Don't get me wrong, it was kind of nice to have someone make me feel special for once, but it was a bit suffocating. Again, more so Reese than Devlin, who stuck to his demanding asshole attitude.

He decided what I'd wear, when I'd sleep, and what I would eat. If Angus hadn't sent them on an errand, I might've spent the third day cleaning up murder scenes.

Thankfully, I finally got some breathing room, which I took full advantage of. I spent the afternoon walking around outside with Charmaine. It was nice. I hadn't seen her smile like that in years. It, of course, didn't last.

Two hours into our time, and she was talking about the infamous *they* again. I managed to get her back to her room before she had a full-blown panic attack, then went in search of Angus.

I was starting to be okay with Devlin and Reese. And the okay part was teetering on the edge. They had their good qualities. I hadn't found more than a few, but I was sure there was more in there. Angus, however…

If anyone should be worried about her state, then it should be her so-called husband. I could count the times I'd seen them together on one hand. Angus had never really shown interest in her, which was bothersome all on its own. Add in his serious demeanor, and there was definitely something wrong. And I wasn't going to ignore it anymore.

I marched down the hall to Angus's office—which, by some miracle, I remembered the way to—and lifted my fist to knock on the door. The voice inside stopped me.

"Yes, she's the daughter of the traitor, Rosco."

Did he just call my father a traitor? A traitor to what? Pretty sure I'd know if he was executed by the government for something. It was kind of hard to hide that information.

"Pascello is petitioning the council for custody."

One didn't petition for custody, they sued. In a court. Unless counsel was a fancy word for court, he was talking crazy. Still…

My brows knit as I leaned in and pressed my ear up against the door. I was curious as to why my uncle would want custody. He didn't know me or Charmaine. I wasn't even sure how well he knew my father. Might help if he'd told me something beyond *don't trust them.* Know who said shit like that, people who shouldn't be trusted.

"Of course I'm sure she has the mark."

Whoever Angus was talking to, he didn't seem pleased. I could hear him pacing around in there.

"No, Gregory, I didn't see it. The boys did."

My mind went back to the first night when my stepbrothers held me down in my room. What was it with these people and strange marks? I glanced down at my pant leg where my birthmark lay underneath.

"If he wasn't sure, Devlin would've spilled her blood on the altar already."

What!?

My eyes snapped back up to the door as Angus shuffled past the other side.

"I should thank her mother. If she hadn't run off, we'd have sacrificed the baby without knowing."

My hand flew up over my mouth to muffle a gasp. Babies and sacrifices? Was he talking about me? Who the hell were these people? Some kind of satanic cult? I heard about this stuff on the news, but I didn't think it was real. Who would? It was crazy.

"I can only thank the spirits that Devlin saw the mark before it was too late. She was set to the die the next night."

*Oh my god.*

The floor started to spin as I slowly backed away, then turned and ran down the hall. Angus didn't marry Charmaine because he loved her. He brought me here to kill me in some twisted ritual.

I froze.

Ritual. How many times had I heard someone say that word? I thought they were dreams, but maybe they weren't. What had they been doing to Charmaine? What had they been doing to me? Were we drugged? Is that how Devlin and Reese pulled me into their web?

Charmaine and I had to get out of here. But how? We didn't know anyone and there were people everywhere. We were trapped.

That's when I remembered the note I'd tucked away in my room. It was time to find out just how much my uncle cared.

# Epilogue

DEVLIN

My eyes trickled over the red pool laying under a set of open, dead eyes. Everything in here was in order. All the books were neatly tucked into their shelves. There wasn't a single ruffle in the carpet or paper on the floor. Even the waste basket was clean.

Whatever happened, he didn't see it coming. Based on the empty mug and trail of blood staining the corner of his mouth, I'd say it was poison. Fast acting stuff, too. He still had his pen held in his hand, like he was getting ready to sign something.

My phone dinged with a text, drawing my attention to the screen. The words I read caused my fists to ball.

Reese: Sydney's gone.

I tried to tell Reese we couldn't trust her. Never trust a Ricci. Her father killed my mother seventeen years ago. Sydney should've died back then on the day she was born. But no. Fate decided to fuck with me and make her the third in my triad. And now…

I looked back down at the body slumped over the desk.

She killed my father.

I was going to hunt that little bitch down, and this time when I found her, I was going to slit her fucking throat.

Who said you couldn't fight fate?


Book one in the same world by Brooklyn Cross: Anywhere

# AFTERWORD

Thank you for reading Backfire
If you enjoyed this book please consider leaving a review. Reviews are always appreciated by authors.

If you'd like to be among the first to know about new releases and get an inside look into my world join my Facebook group T.L. Hodel's Murder Of Ravens.

# Also by T.L. Hodel

**The Order Of Ravens And Wolves:**
Aftereffect
Scartissue
Happenstance
Accident-Prone
Relapse
Panic-Button (coming soon)

**Deviant House:**
Innocence
Innocence corrupted (coming soon)

**The Lost Souls:**
Adversaries
Frenemies

**Brothers Of Shadow And Death:**
Backfire
Backstab (coming soon)

**The Seven Sins Series:**
Pride

**The Buchanan Brothers**
Twisted Abel
Twisting Tallon (Coming soon)

# ABOUT THE AUTHOR

T.L Hodel is a Canadian author, poet and artist. Though coming from a difficult childhood she excelled at writing, having her first poetry published in junior high school. When she's not writing she occupies her self with numerous crafts, hobbies and is an avid gamer. She lives in Calgary with her kids and cat, and may have a slight weakness for horror movies. (Okay, that's a lie, she's probably seen them all)